# IN THE DARK . . . ALONE?

She moved in the way she'd always despised and struggled to avoid: shuffling, hand extended protectively in front of her, shoulders stiff, head unnaturally angled. Like a blind person.

She had no idea which way to go, or how she'd know which way she was going, could think only: *Away. Get away.* She wasn't even certain which way was "away"; she wouldn't have thought it possible to get turned around in an alley.

Something scurried. She froze. Had she really heard it, was it really rats, or was this just another part of the cliché—after dark in an alley reeking of urine and garbage, there must of course be rats? She didn't hear it again. There were other noises.

Terror was only barely tamped down by almost unbearable frustration. She moved again in the direction that felt like forward.

A figure materialized out of the gloom more or less ahead of her, distant and then, in a split second, close enough to touch. . . .

OTHER *LEISURE* BOOKS BY MELANIE TEM:
**THE TIDES**

# SLAIN IN THE SPIRIT

# MELANIE TEM

LEISURE BOOKS     NEW YORK CITY

*For George:*
*Everything's grist for the mill.*
*And for Steve,*
*who understands how I see the world.*

A LEISURE BOOK®

April 2002

Published by

Dorchester Publishing Co., Inc.
276 Fifth Avenue
New York, NY 10001

ISBN 0-8439-4989-9

The name "Leisure Books" and the stylized "L" with design are trademarks of Dorchester Publishing Co., Inc.

Printed in the United States of America.

Visit us on the web at www.dorchesterpub.com.

# ACKNOWLEDGMENTS

My thanks to Dr. Dale Lervick for sharing his ophthalmological expertise, and to Janice Madsen for teaching me that there are Christians and then there are Christians.

# SLAIN IN THE SPIRIT

# *Chapter One*

"Don't be afraid. I won't hurt you."

Leila froze.

In the mirror above the sinks, she could just make out the man's form, glare from the fluorescent light bars all but washing out her own features, let alone his. Struggling for visual detail, hating that she had to struggle, she thought he was Anglo, thin, dark-haired, wearing a white shirt and a dark tie.

"This is the women's rest room," she pointed out, as if he might have made a mistake. She hoped it *was* the women's rest room. After a two-hour movie and a large Coke, her need had been too pressing to wait for somebody indisputably female she could follow in. The sign had seemed straightforward, no symbols to decipher or cutesy labels in fancy illegible print; just a blessedly simple LADIES, at eye level on the door, though she hadn't wanted to stand staring

1

at it until it came into complete focus. No urinals, unless they were behind some wall she wasn't aware of, and on the end wall was mounted a dispenser she'd assumed was for tampons, though admittedly it could just as well be for condoms.

For all her recognizance, it wouldn't be the first time she'd gone into the men's by accident. And there were other arguments for always having an escort. She might get lost, or fall down steps she didn't see, or mistake some other green light for the WALK signal and step out into traffic. Cathy complained—sometimes fondly, sometimes with admiration, but sometimes with bitterness verging on disgust—that she was stubborn.

On the other hand, Cathy didn't much like her self-pitying moods, either, what the two of them had, in an uneasily ironic alliance, come to call her "bitch-to-be-blind" days. Leila was all but certain, though they'd never talked about it, that the disability—the difference, the dependence—had been part of Cathy's initial attraction to her. But sometimes it oppressed them both. In Boston this week on business, Cathy called every night at six, and Leila waited for her call, even though Leila was fine by herself in familiar surroundings and Cathy knew she was fine. Tonight she'd casually mention having gone to the movies by herself. Or maybe she'd wait until Cathy got home, protecting her from undue worry, savoring the secret.

The array of things she really couldn't do was insufferable, and there was often no way around her infuriating dependence on other people, especially Cathy. So when it was even remotely possible to do things alone, sometimes it seemed worth doing them. Nobody she knew had been interested in seeing this movie, and she was damned if she was going to restrict her life any more than she had to.

Resenting, as usual, how *difficult* every damn thing was for her, she nonetheless did take precautions: She'd come to the early show so she'd be home before dark. In her bag she carried the cell phone with battery fully charged, her ID in case someone needed to contact Cathy in an emergency, her wallet bloated with singles so she wouldn't hand over a ten by mistake. It was true that there were accommodations she refused to make. The few times she'd submitted to using a white cane, it had made her so self-conscious and angry that her mobility had actually decreased; sometimes she thought about getting a guide dog, but Cathy was mildly allergic and getting trained would be a major hassle and, anyway, she was a cat person.

She'd chafed at the more subtle visual nuances she'd surely missed with nobody in the next seat to provide whispered commentary, but it had still been a great film. She'd been feeling triumphant, although she thought it somewhat pitiable that an act as ordinary as going to a movie should seem courageous. There'd been a few awkward moments at the ticket counter and the refreshment stand, and a few seconds of mild panic in the dark little anteroom between the last row of seats and the hall door, but no disasters. Until, maybe, now.

As far as she could tell, from sounds and the ambient feel of the echoey space, she and this guy were the only ones in here. Where were the infamous slow-moving ladies' room lines when you needed them? She didn't want to embarrass him—and it would be secretly gratifying to be magnanimous in the face of somebody else's blunder—but he was making no move to leave. "Uh," she ventured, "can I help you with something?" which taken literally was silly but might shift the power balance between them in her favor and, if he answered, give her clues.

"Christina," he said fondly. The voice seemed vaguely familiar, but her name wasn't Christina.

"Well, you've got the wrong woman and you're in the wrong place." Not wanting to appear frightened—*not* frightened, really, but even more hypervigilant than usual—Leila shut off the faucet, tore off a paper towel, turned to face him as she dried her hands. "You better get out of here." Then, softening it, "The men's room is on the other side of the snack bar." It pleased her to be *giving* directions for a change.

"I only wish to help you."

Indignation welled. She took a step toward him. "What makes you think I need help?"

People were forever trying unhelpfully to "help" her. Acquaintances and total strangers alike, and

4

even friends who ought to know better, would grab her arm to steer her, call out "Be careful!" without specifying what to be careful of, intervene when she was taking longer to do something or fumbling more than they could tolerate, speak for her when they thought she wasn't responding to nonverbal cues.

Was that all this was, a particularly brazen and misguided attempt to be helpful? Had he seen her making her way out of the theater and concluded she couldn't manage on her own? Leila was not always gracious, nor did she think she needed to be. "I'm fine. I don't need your help," she told him. Even more infuriating than un-requested and un-required assistance was the frequent refusal of would-be assistants to believe that she knew what she needed and would ask for it; she spoke firmly and started toward the dim gap where she'd placed the doorway in her mind.

He was in her way. "I won't hurt you," he repeated, in an excessively gentle tone.

"You're damn right you won't." She shouldered past him, wishing she didn't have to come into contact with him but feeling it urgent to get out of this room and into the hallway. She was aware of the crisp cottony odor of his white shirt, the heat of his body through it, a light aftershave. He put his hands on her upper arms. She flung them off. "Don't touch me," she warned, glaring toward the upper half of his face, although she couldn't look anyone straight in the eye.

He smiled and took her shoulders again. Now she felt a pang of actual alarm. "Don't be afraid. You know me. Russell Gavin, remember?"

"Jesus Christ," she breathed. "I didn't recognize you."

"Sshh," he admonished. Leila couldn't guess why. "We haven't seen each other in—what? Twenty-five years? Twenty-eight?"

"The last I knew you were in Florida."

"Yes."

"What are you doing here?"

"I've come to be with you."

"But you have a family, three kids under, what, ten? Are you still married?"

"Oh, yes. Quite happily. And we had a new baby last year." He paused expectantly.

"Congratulations."

"Thank you." Annoyingly, he'd missed her wryness. "My wife can manage on her own. She supports my mission."

Deliberately, sure it would offend him now that she knew who he was, she expanded, "Jesus H. Christ."

He shook her a little. "Stop it, Christina. No need to invoke the Lord. It's the Lord who's sent me."

Leila grasped both his sinewy wrists and dug in her nails. He flinched but didn't let go. "Get your hands off me," she hissed. "I thought I'd made myself clear when you wrote me that wacko letter."

6

"That was Satan speaking."

"In your letter or in mine?" It was a taunt; she knew what his answer would be.

"Satan has closed your heart to the message God is sending through me."

You're crazy, Russell. Leave me *alone.*"

He removed his right hand from her left shoulder, and for a moment she imagined she'd been so assertive he was simply obeying her command. She made a small lunge toward what she hoped was the exit, though she couldn't tell exactly where the opening was or whether the curved corridor leading to it was clear. Out of old habit, she cringed at the prospect of bumping into people, as if that was more important now than the danger Russell Gavin might pose to them if they interrupted his plans, or the possibility they could help her. From years of trying not to be conspicuous by reason of her vision, and on the chance she was somehow misreading this situation, she doubted she'd even say anything in the event of a collision, beyond, "Oh, sorry."

It was Russell she collided with. "I can't let you go," he told her reasonably.

"This is outrageous! Who do you think you are—"

"I am the servant of Christ Jesus. I am your friend."

"We are not friends. We were never friends in the first place. And I told you I wanted nothing more to do with you."

She might as well not have spoken, then or now. "You and I are going to walk together out through the lobby to my car."

Leila snorted incredulously. "I don't think so."

"Come with me, Christina." He held out both hands.

It was the name that brought her to fury. "Why are you still on this kick about my name? My *name* is Leila Blackwell."

"And that name is at the root of your troubles," he answered eagerly. "Both symptom and cause."

"Troubles? You mean, like being accosted by a religious fanatic in the women's rest room?"

He didn't take the bait, and he also didn't move out of her way. If she didn't leave soon, she'd miss her bus, and the next one didn't come for forty minutes. " 'Leila,' " he went on. "means 'black, dark.' "

He'd gone through this insulting dissection of her name in his letter, nearly three years ago, and she didn't want to hear it again. But if she could keep him talking, maybe somebody would come in and interrupt this scene. "Yeah, so? What's wrong with that?"

"It isn't wise to call oneself by a name that means darkness."

"Are you saying that there's something wrong with blackness or darkness? Isn't that just a tad racist?"

"Satan is the Lord of Darkness."

"It's *my* name, Russell. I like my name. How dare you—"

"And 'Blackwell,' a surname you actually chose for yourself"—he shook his head and tsked—"clearly refers to the well of blackness toward which Satan is shepherding you. I explained all this to you, but you have apparently made no changes. Satan's power is too strong for you to resist alone."

If he only knew, Leila thought almost giddily. *Blackwell* was an amalgam of her original surname, Orblach, and Cathy's, Wells. Fifteen years ago, delighted by this external sign of their melded lives, they'd both changed their names legally, ordered new checks, changed credit cards, sent out announcements. Russell Gavin had not, however, been among those with whom they'd shared their bliss. In her annual Christmas letter to him that year, Leila had said only that she'd never liked her last name, and now that her parents were gone she'd decided to use something more euphonious. Correctly, she'd counted on him not being interested enough to ask about it; she'd felt a little guilty not coming out to him but had wanted to avoid that particular debate with a man she hardly knew who had always been decidedly conservative.

"You don't know the first thing about the meaning of my name," she spat at him now but went no further.

"I have chosen for you the name Christina Luce."

"But it's not my name."

"It's the Lord's name. 'Christina'—'pledged to Christ.' 'Luce'—"

" 'Light,' " she finished with him. "As in Lucifer. Which is another name for Satan, right?"

"When he was named Lucifer, he *was* of the light. As you shall be."

"Go fuck yourself." She heard how feeble it sounded.

"From this moment on, you are Christina Luce."

"Get out of my life, *Russell.*" Wishing she could think fast enough to come up with an equally presumptuous moniker for him, she settled for a snide twist on *Russell,* of which he took no notice.

"Christina, Christina, you don't understand. I'm kidnapping you."

She stared at him. She *willed* someone to come into the rest room—another patron here too long after the twilight show, a cleaning crew, the beginning of crowds for the evening features. She barked a laugh. "I beg your pardon?"

He smiled indulgently and nodded confirmation.

She laughed again. This was a joke, surely, or he had some idiosyncratic definition of kidnapping. Not daring to take him seriously, she was amazed by the strength of her need not to be played for a fool. "Give me a break," she said, but her voice quavered.

"It's for your own good, Christina my dear. You'll see. You'll thank me."

Now her mind raced through possibilities for escape. None seemed plausible, but the possibility of *not* escaping was even more farfetched.

He continued softly. "I have a small handgun in my pocket, trained on your heart."

Was this a legitimate threat, or was he taking advantage of her limited vision by pretending to have a gun? Again, the abhorrence of being tricked competed almost equally with her self-protective instinct. She looked down at the pocket in which his hand was concealed, but, predictably, couldn't tell whether there was a gun-shaped bulge in it or not.

"Let's go."

She hesitated. "I—I don't see well." He knew that; in a newsy note with a Christmas card a few years ago, she'd told him about the detached retina which had abruptly decreased her congenitally poor vision, and that had precipitated this whole thing. But people seldom knew how her vision translated into everyday function; there was no simple or useful answer to "How well can you see?" and even when she tried she was often second-guessed by people who apparently didn't think she knew what she was talking about.

He was waiting. "Go on, Christina. I'll be right behind you."

It was easiest to follow someone, especially if she could keep her gaze on white shoes; she'd noted Russell's white sneakers, stylistically dissonant with his tie. Men of old-fashioned gallantry, of which she would bet he was one, could hardly bring themselves to precede her. "You lead," she instructed him, realizing how ludicrous that was under the circumstances but hoping he'd do it out of deference to her disability and she could somehow lose him in the crowd.

"No, I'll be behind you. With my gun."

Anxiety flooded her, but she recognized that it was about the wrong thing, and in a peculiar disjointed way she marveled at the tenacity of established thought patterns. Here she was, apparently in the midst of being kidnapped at gunpoint, and what had her in a panic was being forced to lead the way across the crowded lobby and parking lot when she couldn't reliably see where she was going. If she'd been alone, on her way to the bus stop as planned, she could have taken her time to locate predetermined landmarks like planters and benches and water fountains, made her way slowly enough that unexpected obstacles wouldn't have been catastrophic. As it was, she was almost sure to stumble into people or objects, trip over steps and protuberances masked as patterns in carpet and pavement, take wrong turns.

Which, she told herself, could be an advantage. Could call attention to her and this madman, attention she ought to welcome. Might activate a passerby's helping impulse which, for once, would be helpful. She took a deep breath and walked ahead of him out of the rest room, sliding her fingers along the curved, tiled wall.

Navigating required such concentration that Leila couldn't watch for an opportunity to signal someone, duck behind a counter or an EMPLOYEES ONLY door, scream "Help!" or otherwise create a disturbance. The rest rooms and the twelve-plex theaters opened onto a dim hallway with squares and rectangles of white running lights here and there—around movie posters, she presumed—and at each end a bluer-white glare, a window or a bank of fluorescent lights, that created haloes and obliterated details. On her way in, Leila had made a mental note that, although the delineation between the shiny light-colored rest-room floor and the darker busy pattern of the hall-way carpet looked like a difference in depth, in fact there was no step. She headed across the hall to the opposite wall, through crowds swarming in both directions, noting bitterly that now streams of women were turning into the rest room.

Right behind her, Russell said helpfully, "The lobby's to the left."

"I *know*," she snapped. She didn't always need actually to trail a hand along a wall for guidance; often just the way it dulled and contained sounds was enough to keep her from veering off course. She still proceeded slowly, though, so that bumping into a protrusion from the wall or tripping over a depression in the floor wouldn't damage anything, herself included. Now, turning left, she went even more slowly than usual, hoping someone would notice, hoping Russell would get impatient and blow his cover.

Ordinarily, in the interests of maintaining a relatively normal pace, she used the sighted guide technique, lightly grasping a companion's arm just above the elbow and walking half a step behind. If she'd been doing that with Russell, she could have felt the tiny muscle contractions heralding his movements, which might have increased her chances of getting away. But relinquishing that much control required trust, which at the moment was in short supply.

And touching somebody like that implied and elicited intimacy. More than once an erotic charge had buzzed between her and her guide; more than once, in fact, one or both had openly observed as much, and either something had come of it—a kiss, a proposition, an "I'm flattered, I'm very attracted to you, but I'm spoken for"—or Leila, preferring physical to emotional clumsiness, had dropped her hand. The very thought of touching Russell Gavin made her skin crawl.

Then she was thinking of Cathy, how it pleased them both to imagine onlookers' assumption that Cathy was merely guiding Leila when in fact they were lovers and would have held hands or linked arms anyway. Always uneasy when Leila went somewhere alone, although she understood why it was important and didn't always hide her impatience with her roles as taxi driver and escort, Cathy would be frantic when she couldn't reach her at six o'clock tonight. The sudden awful thought struck Leila that they might never see each other again.

Over her shoulder Russell was out of her narrow field of vision, but she snarled in his direction, "People will be looking for me, you know." Too bad it was still summer vacation; during the school year, which began in less than two weeks, the principal would consider her unaccounted for by 7:45 in the morning, when a roomful of first-graders was without a teacher. "You won't get away with this," she finished lamely. If he answered, she didn't hear it over the din.

In some places the floor was striped, in others speckled or solid-hued. Leila suspected these designs were random, or at most merely decorative, but she hesitated nonetheless at every transition, sliding a foot forward cautiously before committing to a step, straining her eyes and squinting. People cut in front of her with alarming regularity, and she was forever muttering, "Excuse me. Ex-*cuse* me," though it seemed to her that any rudeness was at least evenly divided between her and them. She considered adding quietly, "The man behind me has a gun," but no one stayed long enough within range.

Whenever she went unescorted to a complicated physical environment like this, she meant to use techniques her voc rehab counselor had taught her. Some of the strategies he'd suggested, such as watching for movement by the car one position clockwise around an intersection when she couldn't see the signal light, had turned out to be useful. Others, like counting the steps from one point to another so she'd know how far it was on the way back, more often than not ended up producing more data bits than she could keep straight. Today, for instance, although she had dutifully counted from the lobby to the rest room before the show, she'd forgotten by now how many steps there'd been and, in any case, the counselor hadn't had any tips about keeping your bearings while a gun was held on you.

This, she chided herself, was serious. She'd known Russell long enough, though never very well, to believe him perfectly capable of what he claimed to be doing.

Daylight through tinted glass made confusing hatch marks on the floor and walls, and she couldn't tell whether the outside doors were open or not. Closed: Now she saw the push bar across the middle. Though she had no direct experience with this sort of thing, she supposed that once outside in the parking lot with Russell she'd have even fewer options. He was close behind her now, making sure they'd go through the door on the same swing. She stopped. He stumbled into her. People were streaming in the other doors, not an arm's length away. "Help!" she tried to shout, but for some reason she couldn't raise her voice much above a normal conversational level. "Help!"

She thought a few people glanced at her, but no one took any action. Quickly Russell shifted his weight against her and pressed a small hard object between her shoulder blades. In the split second before she recoiled, from him as much as from the weapon, he twisted what she had to assume was the barrel, as if boring it into her flesh, or threatening to. He didn't say anything.

As she'd learned to do when she couldn't determine which side of a door was hinged, Leila leaned on the center of the bar. This shortened the fulcrum and made the door harder but not impossible to swing open. She and Russell emerged into the lot. The late-afternoon sun was still high, so there was considerable glare, but she saw a bus pulling into the stop on the corner, separated from her by one row of parking spaces, an embankment that looked no more than knee-high and who knew what else.

She hadn't run since her retina had detached; she doubted she'd ever in her life run full-out. If there was ever a time to dash, dart, sprint, lope, race, this was it, and maybe she'd even be able to keep a parked car between herself and Russell's alleged gun long enough to leap onto the bus just before its doors closed and it pulled away. The mental scene was exciting. She couldn't see the route number from here, but it didn't matter. For just a moment she worried about whom else she might be endangering, then made her break.

The side of her ankle slammed into the end of a yellow concrete parking barrier that in no way had been distinguished from the yellow painted lines.

She cried out, forced herself to keep going and ran smack into the rearview mirror of a van she'd been sure she was clearing. The mirror broke off and clanged, then smashed onto the pavement. The bridge of Leila's nose throbbed, and her vision blurred even more than usual, *Nice move. Let's just detach the retina the rest of the way,* she railed at herself.

Russell caught her arm. "Here we are," he announced cheerfully, as though she'd done nothing at all. He steered her to the car in the next space. Frantically Leila tried to discern the vehicle's identifying characteristics, but its color might have been any of a half-dozen shades of blue or green, and she had no inkling of its make. Never having driven, she paid scant attention to cars other than for their utilitarian value, so she wasn't even sure which end the license plate would be on if she could manage to glimpse any of its numbers or letters.

Russell kept a firm hold of her elbow with one hand while he unlocked the passenger door with the other. It occurred to Leila that this must mean he'd let go of the gun, but she didn't have time to figure out how to use this fact before he'd handed her chivalrously into the front seat. He tucked her skirt inside; she slapped his hand away from her thigh. Obliviously, he tugged her shoulder harness out and leaned across her for the buckle end.

This was more than she could stand. Sometimes, when she used accessible public transportation, drivers would lean close over her to fasten her seat belt, and in addition to the fact that it was quite unnecessary, Leila loathed this invasion of her personal space even when they were pretty young women or grandfatherly men. They often acted affronted when she insisted on doing it herself. The thought of Russell Gavin's fingers at her hip, breath in her face, arm across her chest repulsed her. "Give me that." She yanked the belt out of Russell's hand and fumbled to find the receiving buckle to insert it. He stood watching until it clicked into place, then locked her door, shut it and went around the front of the car to the driver's side, head pivoting to keep her in sight through the windshield.

Leila had a recurring dream in which she was driving a car. The driver had had a heart attack, or she'd just wanted to go out for a spin, and there she was, behind the wheel, speeding down steep hills with no clear idea where the brake pedal was and making turns without signaling because she didn't know how. Always the feeling was of exhilaration and terror, and of being about to be stopped by the police; always she woke up before she got wherever she thought she was going. In the four or five seconds it took Russell to trot around the car and get his door unlocked, she had the fully developed fantasy of sliding over behind the wheel, starting the car, screeching tires as she backed out of the lot with Russell standing openmouthed in her dust or clinging to the hood or, best, smashed and bleeding where she'd run straight over him.

He had the ignition key, of course. He settled himself almost primly before he inserted it, then smiled sideways at her as he started the engine. "So far so good," he observed with a satisfied sigh. They might have been partners in this enterprise.

She turned her head to stare out her window. Her throat was tight and her eyes burned; the tears would have been mostly from rage, but still she detested how weak they'd make her seem. The last time she'd wept out of sheer fury had been in a confrontation with another teacher over the new reading program the district had imposed, and any chance she'd had of making her point had been lost. She bit her lip, wondering why that was effective in stopping tears.

Russell backed the car out of the space and turned onto the street. Leila noted they were traveling west. "We'll be spending a good deal of time together while the Lord's work is being accomplished. We might as well catch up on each other's lives. So tell me, Christina, what have you been doing since I heard from you last?"

Leila bit back a sarcastic reply, swallowed hard and countered, "You first."

# *Chapter Two*

For Leila, the voice was a window to the soul. At least a peephole. Or a one-way mirror, to observe without being observed, since, to her continual amazement and frustration, other people seemed only minimally aware of what could be gleaned from speech patterns and tics, voice tone and timbre, the various uses of breath.

Often without fully realizing it, she relied on the voice more than any other characteristic to identify people, especially those she didn't know well. Someone's head cold or dental work could make her worry, despite all other evidence to the contrary, that she was talking to the wrong person. Now, she couldn't shake the sinking feeling that if she'd recognized Russell's voice sooner she might somehow have avoided this situation.

To Cathy's vast annoyance, Leila would stay on

the line with a telephone solicitor long enough to fashion a demographic profile—educational level, race, place of birth, use of alcohol or tobacco, sexual orientation—all from the intrusive voice on the line. That was a game, half-playful vengeance against telemarketers, with no way of verifying conclusions and no need to do so.

Now, closing her eyes in the twilit car and concentrating on Russell's voice, the stakes were so much higher that she might be getting it all wrong. Middle-aged, male, Caucasian, college-educated and well-read; she'd already known all that. No smoker's huskiness or drinker's liquidity. Not obviously gay.

She enjoyed teasing out accents—the Minnesota or Pittsburgh *o,* the Boston *ar*—embedded in a more-or-less standard American way of speaking, and had made something of a study, by region and ethnicity, of the various ways English speakers compensated for the lack of a second-person plural; "y'all" and "you'uns" and "you guys" and the most sensible, "yous." The Midwestern cadences of their hometown still in Russell's speech had been overlaid with a slight Southern patina. Nothing unexpected there.

Even to Cathy, and certainly to the world at large, Leila didn't disclose everything she picked up, often nearly unconsciously, from voices. Emotional states ("Is something wrong? I can hear it in your voice"), physical conditions ("You sound exhausted"), imperfectly concealed lapses of attention, unacknow-

ledged condescension, flirtatiousness, annoyance—
comments or inquiries about such things were likely
to be denied, or resented, as if she'd been spying.
And, besides, keeping her own counsel also helped
to maintain what she'd come to regard as a strategic
advantage. Listening to this man—her kidnapper, of
all things—she was, quite literally, reconnoitering
the enemy.

What did he want, exactly? Where were the
chinks in his self-contained world view? Was he
tired, cocky, distracted, homesick, worried? What
could she use to free herself? She was practically
blind; was there any point in trying?

He hadn't needed to be asked twice to talk about
himself. With a mixture of enthusiasm and frustration, he was describing his job in insurance
administration. Whether because of the present circumstances or the nature of the work itself, she
couldn't quite get a picture of what he did every day.
The firm wasn't one she'd heard of, but she made a
mental note of it, and of the way his tone hardened
slightly when he mentioned his supervisor, Marla or
Marta or Marna—she couldn't verify the name without being obvious about it.

He moved on to his family. Leila stored the names
in her memory for future reference; she'd known all
of them except that of the newest child. Something
in his speech cadence when he mentioned his wife
made her guess, hopefully, at marital discord. His
pride in his children was audible, especially his eld-

est daughter Stephanie, a high school freshman with, to hear her father tell it, remarkable talent in everything from astrophysics to dance, and a religious zeal like his own.

Then he launched into an animated monologue about what was clearly his passion: for the better part of a decade he'd been developing scientific proof of the divinity of Jesus Christ and of the corollary that Christ was the most important figure in the history of mankind. *Humanity,* Leila corrected silently; biting her tongue about such things was uncharacteristic of her, but a confrontation over sexist language did not seem in her best interest at the moment.

He had about a hundred finished manuscript pages, he told her, and another fifty or so of notes. He anticipated wrapping it up in the next year. "And then what?" she ventured to ask, hating the necessity of playing along but hoping her skepticism and profound disinterest in the topic did not show.

"What do you mean?" He was obviously taken aback, perhaps not having thought of that, or more likely surprised that his plan wasn't self-evident.

"Once you have this great treatise done, what's the next step? What will you do with it?"

After a dramatic pause his reply was as quiet and resonant as an oration in a sacred space. "Then I will release it to the public and save the world."

An adequate response was hard to come up with. Sorely tempted to mock, Leila was at the same time beginning to fathom the extent of the obsession she'd fallen prey to.

And she couldn't deny the tiniest niggle of doubt: Surely there had been people throughout human history, Jesus among them, who in fact had changed, if not saved, the world. People who knew things others didn't. People with truth, or Truth, to tell, who'd seemed nuts in their time and place. If she ran into one of those—in, for instance, the person of Russell Gavin—would she be able to distinguish among garden-variety insanity, sociopathy, simple self-aggrandizement and divine madness?

Under the circumstances, this was a dangerous train of thought. She was a hostage. This man had designs on her life, her values, her very name. Not only that, he had a gun. This was a clue, she told herself snidely; she couldn't imagine the Savior resorting to firearms to prove a point. She didn't know where the weapon was right now; it wasn't visible to her anywhere on or near Russell, but that didn't mean much. Being threatened with a gun was such an astonishing event that she knew she'd have to keep forcibly reminding herself of its existence.

She spoke truculently. "So, I'm practice, is that it? Saving me as rehearsal for saving the world?"

"Oh, Christina, I'm sorry if I gave that impression. No, no, you're important in your own right. Every human heart is as the whole world in the eyes of God." When she didn't say anything, he prompted, "Forgive me."

"Oh, please, don't mention it! No problem!" She caught his nod and smile, as if he'd missed her sarcasm entirely.

They were on an interstate. Leila had a working knowledge of the street rotation in most parts of the city; when she'd first moved here she'd purposely walked a lot and studied those street signs low enough to be readable, gathered blue-and-white bus schedules in a shoebox and traveled one after another until she had a kinesthetic understanding of the pattern. But the highways were harder. They looped and changed direction, crossed over and under each other, cut across the basic street grid in ways she couldn't quite get a handle on. She never had been good with maps and, since the laser surgery to stop the retinal detachment had narrowed her field of vision, following a line for more than an inch or two was all but impossible. Her experience with highways was entirely passive and once removed, with no sense of three-dimensionality, and until this moment that had seemed fine, since when she used them somebody else was always necessarily in charge.

Now, straining for details, she thought she recognized a business park just off the highway, the glass and concrete of the flagship building veneered to create coppery reflections—traffic, dimming sky, other buildings, reflections in the windows of other buildings of the coppery building itself; when she was merely a passenger, relaxed and willingly in the hands of someone else, the architectural effect was pleasing, but now it obfuscated and, for a long angle as they passed, blinded her. She rubbed her eyes carefully, so as not to dislodge her contact. The downtown skyline was to her right. Green highway signs sped past, but except for the configurations of unreadable information on them they were indistinguishable from each other.

It was the end of rush hour, traffic moving smoothly though still heavy, the sun setting. Factoring in the time she'd intended to catch her bus home, she figured it must be about seven-thirty by now. Knowing she couldn't read her watch visually in this light, she flipped open the hinged crystal and touched the hands surreptitiously, although she didn't know why it should matter if Russell knew she was doing this. She could read only a very little Braille and her fingertips didn't quite have the sensitivity to feel the number dots reliably, but the position of the hands indicated approximately 7:20, or maybe 6:20; the later hour seemed likelier. She snapped the crystal shut and wound the watch. In the interest of geographic orientation—if, say, she was giving telephone directions to a rescuer or, better, fleeing on her own and then leading the police back to bring this bozo to justice—keeping track of how long they'd driven before they got to wherever they were going could be important.

It might have been thirty minutes. The sky darkened. Headlights and taillights brightened. Leila indulged in a rather detailed fantasy about how she'd soon demonstrate bravery and quick-wittedness, an unwise diversion with enormous appeal.

Russell interrupted his discourse to repeat his earlier query, which patently had an ulterior purpose. "But what have *you* been doing, Christina? Enough about me! Tell me about your life."

*Cathy,* she thought at once, and her heart seized. "There's nothing about my life I want you to know." Glimpsing sharp movement, she supposed he'd glanced at her and then back to the road, and she wondered if she'd gone too far, or not far enough.

"Well, of course, I already do know a fair amount about you," he allowed convivially. "After all, we've been friends for a long time."

Leila set her jaw, bent her left knee up onto the seat to turn and lean toward him, gesticulated heatedly and even—a risk, given that he was the driver and an armed lunatic—lightly smacked his forearm. "Now you listen to me: We are not friends. We never were friends. You were always weird, Russell, *weird,* but I thought you were harmless and didn't deserve to be treated the way you were in high school. I thought you were *interesting,* God help me!" Instantly wishing she'd chosen a different figure of speech for emphasis, she rushed on before he said anything. "We have nothing in common. We don't see things the same—" A thought struck her and she stammered as the direction of her tirade shifted mid-phrase. "Is that—is *that* what this is about? Are you trying to make me your *friend?* Because trust me, Russell, kidnapping is not the way to a woman's heart."

Weaving in and out of traffic with an aplomb that for some reason surprised her, Russell spoke patiently. "You were born with seriously damaged vision, blind in one eye and extremely nearsighted in the other, for reasons the doctors could never determine. Your parents divorced when you were in junior high. You didn't get along with either of your stepparents." He'd laid all this out in the closely reasoned, insulting and fundamentally loony epistle of three years ago that had caused her to terminate their correspondence. She hated hearing it again and opened her mouth to cut him off. "Your mother drank."

Leila winced; had her mother's alcoholism been common knowledge, then? She and Russell had certainly never discussed it, and his letter hadn't mentioned it. So he'd been thinking about her, gathering more ammunition, *researching.* She shuddered.

"Eight years ago you wrote that your sister had been injured in a skiing accident."

"She broke her leg," Leila protested, drawn into this ridiculous debate despite herself. "She's fine."

He was not to be deterred. "Three years ago you wrote that your vision had suddenly gotten much worse. Don't you see the pattern of your life, Christina? Don't you see what God is trying to tell you?"

Familiar turmoil rose in her, familiar disappointment in her life. Sometimes she affected a bitter flippancy about it: "Don't mind me, I'm just having a bitch-to-be-blind day." But it was more than that. She felt star-crossed. The disability had made things extraordinarily difficult to begin with, and difficulties just kept piling up. The best thing in her life was her relationship with Cathy, and it was strained and constrained because it was lesbian in a straight world and because Leila could never trust that Cathy stayed with her out of love and not pity.

Russell was on a roll. She could tell he'd been waiting for the chance to make his case to her in person, and he was barely able to contain his enthusiasm, cloaked as it was in friendly concern. "You said there'd been no trauma to your eye, no head injury, no disease. No cause."

She shook her head. "It's common for the eyes to change shape as we get older. That's why people with twenty-twenty vision get reading glasses in their mid-forties. Because my eye was already so myopic, the retina couldn't stretch any more to accommodate age-related changes, so it tore. This isn't a mystery, Russell."

All that was factual, but Leila didn't entirely believe that her afflictions weren't personal. Russell echoed her thoughts. "The real cause is much more personal, as personal as you can get. There was, and is, a Plan." She could hear the capital *P*.

Though the better part of valor would be to keep her mouth shut, she felt compelled to counter his neat, reductionist summary of her life. It was the same argument she regularly mounted against herself; hopefully it would have more effect against him.

There had been happinesses and high points. She'd made lists. The Saturday mornings gardening with her father as a small child, never mind that she was likely to mistake intentional plants for weeds. Her mother's sculpting, and her mother's hands over hers in the clay. Teaching, still, after all these years and despite all the administrative dumbness. A cat, latest of a succession, purring on her shoulder. Wynton Marsalis's trumpet. The smell of lilacs and marigolds, the feel of new terry cloth, the taste of grapefruit, the sight of geese in a low-flying *V* even though she couldn't see any of the individual birds. Cathy. *Cathy.*

But her practiced judgment of these good things as individually and cumulatively paltry kept her from laying them out for Russell. They couldn't hold a candle to her list of adversities.

"And," he continued with a certain hint of triumph in his voice, as though this was his ace, "you've never married, never had children."

"Yeah? So?" She wished she were more flabbergasted than she was. He wasn't the only one who'd consider this a misfortune. She herself yearned now and then for something more recognizable as family, though whatever that was didn't have anything to do with a man, and she wasn't sure it had to do with children, either.

She glanced at him as if she could see his expression, which of course she couldn't. Since he went no further along this track she decided he must not know she was lesbian; surely he'd regard that as irrefutable proof of her alliance with the Devil. "I never wanted marriage and children," she insisted. "That's a choice."

"Satan's handiwork."

"You are awfully damn sure of yourself, aren't you?"

"Yes, Christina, I am. But it isn't me. It's God." Leila sank back in her seat. But Russell wasn't finished. *"And."* The unattached conjunction served to hold his place in the conversation while he paused to switch lanes. His turn signal clicked, stopped, started clicking again, and Leila felt a pang of trepidation; they must be nearing the place he was taking her. "And now your career is in jeopardy."

"What?"

He nodded. "Because of your resistance to this new reading program, both your enthusiasm for teaching and your credibility in the school system are suffering."

"But—but I wouldn't say my career is in *jeopardy.*" She hated that she was sputtering.

"Don't you see, Christina? One after another, trials are visited upon you."

"And if I change my—my spiritual allegiance, the district will see the light and stop pushing this rigid system down our throats? Is that what you're saying?"

"I'm promising you that if you change your spiritual allegiance and ally yourself with the forces of goodness and light, things will go easier for you all the way around."

"How do you even know about the reading program? That's happened since I broke off communication with you."

"I've been watching you."

*"What?"*

Again, smugly, he nodded. "Collecting data. Preparing myself for this mission."

"You're kidding."

"That's how I knew where to find you today. I've been waiting for just the right opportunity."

So, going alone to this movie, instead of proving and expanding her independence, had made her vulnerable in ways she could not have imagined. She felt the start of self-berating and tried with limited success to quell it.

He took his hand off the wheel to pat and stroke her wrist. Not having seen this coming, she didn't pull away soon enough, and the touch of him set off a strong visceral revulsion. "The way out of this slough is to learn to love the Lord with all your heart and all your soul, with everything you are or wish to be. And I will help you to do that."

Leila's head was spinning. She could not find

words. She clasped her hands and pressed them between her knees.

"I love you, Christina," he said, clearly and simply.

She leaned her head back against the seat. "Oh, shit."

"You are my sister in the family of the Lord. Jesus loves you. I love you."

At least he wasn't confessing romantic interest after all. But her relief was short-lived.

"I will stay with you as long as it takes," he pledged.

"As long as *what* takes?"

"As long as it takes to free you from Satan's power and deliver you into the love of God."

"Are we talking"—she could hardly bring herself to say something so frightening and so ludicrous—"are we talking *exorcism* here?"

"In a manner of speaking," he answered easily, "yes."

Through panic, Leila did her best to stay focused as they followed the curve of the exit ramp, but by the time Russell'd turned onto a street—left; at a traffic light; on the opposite corner a gas station or some other small squarish building with high tubular fluorescent lights out front—she had only the vaguest notion where they were. Streetlights, trees, houses immediately reassembled; she was always surprised and gratified by how an area could become thoroughly residential so close to businesses and interstates. She was almost sure she didn't know this part of town. At least she wasn't seeing any familiar landmarks, and pressing her face against the window was making her feel even more vulnerable: a 7-Eleven and a McDonald's like every other, a relatively open half-block that might be a park.

She was lost, and in danger. Real fear washed over her. "Where are we going, Russell?" He wasn't likely to tell her and she couldn't keep her voice steady, so asking was probably a tactical error, but it seemed even more foolish not to try.

He answered readily. "My brother owns rental property over here. It's been vacant for some time. Problems with the health department and zoning." He tsked again. Fussy disapproval appeared to be a personality trait. "My brother has never been what you'd call careful about details. You remember my brother Carl."

Russell had numerous brothers and she didn't know which one was Carl. She didn't ask. She waited. Her palms were clammy.

"When I told him I was coming here on business he gave me the house key and asked me to check on the place. I said I'd be happy to." He gave a pleased chuckle but did not say, "The Lord works in mysterious ways."

"The Lord works in mysterious ways," she supplied recklessly.

If he caught her sarcasm this time, he ignored it. "Not as mysterious as people think. It's just a matter of becoming familiar with Him."

"So you're planning to hold me hostage in a condemned house?"

"I don't think it's that bad."

Her mental images of rats and cockroaches had an extra dimension of horror because she wouldn't be able to see the vermin until they were inches away from her, would hear and smell them for a long time first, might well touch them before she knew they were there. Then came the sudden awful realization of how vulnerable she would be visually, and how quickly: In a few hours she would have to take out her contact lens, and without the nighttime ointment and the solution for soaking the lens overnight, both at home in her dresser, she wouldn't be able to put it in again; by her ophthalmologist's estimate her vision unaided was "essentially unmeasurable," so she would be effectively blind.

She found herself considering telling Russell all this and throwing herself on his mercy. "Take me home," she'd beg. The tears burning behind her eyes would fall. She might even clutch his hand. "I'll do what you want. I'll change my name to Christina Luce. I'll follow Christ. I promise I'll—" The internal plea bordered on hysteria. She managed not to say it aloud, but the voice in her mind persisted: "I'm scared, Russell. I want to go home."

He slowed and turned onto what was probably a side street. Peering out the window, Leila saw a high, scalloped, white latticework structure lit against the indigo sky, then with a little thrill knew what it was:

the old wooden roller coaster at the tiny amusement park on the west side of town, closed now for the season but unmistakable even silent.

Without any of the backing and filling and swearing many other drivers indulged in, most notably Cathy, he parallel-parked at the curb, evidently getting it right the first time.

Killing the engine and unbuckling his seat belt, he reached between the seats for a sack on the floor behind him. Leila could tell by the stiff rustling that it was a brown paper grocery bag, and by its heft as he swung it past her that it was full of fairly heavy objects, but couldn't guess what was in it.

Russell rested the bag on his knee and took her hand in both of his. She didn't bother to pull back. As though he'd read her mind, which was a scary and not entirely incredible thought, he squeezed her hand and said to her again, intently this time, as if insinuating more layers of meaning, "Don't be afraid, Christina. I won't hurt you." Terror all but closed her throat.

# Chapter Three

She stumbled going up the front steps, four of them and no two with the same rise. The unpleasant tingling in her extremities set off by a near fall was more intense than usual this time; for a few seconds her hands and feet actually hurt, and her ears rang. This response—adrenaline, she supposed—always seemed to her a bit extreme, melodramatic, not to mention useless, since it occurred too late to be a warning, and she didn't know whether it was commonplace or some sort of neurotic overreaction.

Determined to stay out of Russell's grasp, she righted herself before he reached for her arm. But he grabbed her anyway and pressed the bare inside of her elbow just below her sleeve. She recoiled, and he allowed her to fling off his hand.

There was no porch light, and the house was in the middle of the block, far from the streetlight at either intersection. For future reference she noted the absence of railings; a six-inch miscalculation at the top would likely result in an ankle-twisting fall. With nothing solid to hold on to, she was off balance, unmoored in space, and had to make a conscious effort not to flail. The porch floor was concrete, uneven under her feet.

When Russell pulled open the screen door, it sounded rickety. In her own house, for which she was already pining as if she might never be home again, she identified door sounds almost subliminally: the solid front door, the hollow-core kitchen door, the one to the basement echoing very slightly in the enclosed stairway, the bedroom door muted by carpet.

Cathy sometimes tried to make this ability to distinguish the sound of one door from another seem fun and admirable. "Wow!" she'd exclaim, shaking her head in phony wonderment. "I don't know how you do that!" Leila took no pleasure in her auditory discrimination abilities. She wasn't convinced they were any better than anyone else's, and the necessity for her to pay attention to such things was further proof—as if any was needed—of her abnormality.

Now, however, she tried to make a deliberate mental imprint of this particular creaking and rattling, as a future aid to keeping track of Russell. But it was too brief, she'd heard it only once, and it would sound different from inside the house, where she apparently was going to be for a while.

Waiting for him to get the key into the lock of the inside door, she leaned against the porch wall, then made a clandestine examination of it with her hand concealed by her hip: stucco, she thought, or cement block; probably too smooth for plain brick and definitely not wood. She was reasonably sure there'd been no house number painted on the steps, and none was affixed to the metal mailbox by her shoulder; if there was one above the door, she wouldn't be able to decipher it anyway.

Behind her left shoulder, though, was something hard-edged protruding from the porch wall. Raising her hand as though only to steady herself, she traced the outlines of metal numbers and was able to decipher all four: 2564. Piece of cake, she congratulated herself.

Russell was having trouble with the key and had to put down the grocery bag he was carrying in order to use both hands on the knob. She tried to assess escape possibilities, but her disgust at the tableau they were making, quite as though returning to his place after a date, contaminated every other perception.

She did slide her right foot sideways enough to find the edge of the porch, with no railing, and wondered if she could jump off into what felt like an overgrown hedge. Fear of falling was great, and familiar; fear of Russell was too huge and too amorphous to grasp. She took an actual step sideways,

40

her right foot off the solid concrete and onto a nest of branches that cracked and swayed.

"Oh, no, you don't," Russell said, almost playfully, and yanked her back next to him.

Her right eye was starting to sting and itch from wearing the contact all day. From the bottle in her pocket she squirted in a soothing eyedrop, turning away from Russell with the intention of disguising a strategic vulnerability from the enemy.

The key turned. She'd been hoping it wouldn't, as if, that segment of his plan thwarted, Russell might just give it up and let her go. Retrieving the bag and pushing open the door, which made a sort of muttering sound, he started to go in first, thought better of it, stepped aside for her.

"I can't see." Fear of the immediate, smaller, familiar dangers—falling, crashing into something, appearing helpless and dependent—was, foolishly, keener than fear of the more abstract and much more threatening situation as a whole. She did her best not to whimper, to make it a simple statement of fact.

"You don't have to see, Christina. I'm right here with you. I'll be your eyes. Go on in."

Though it shouldn't have, his reassurance—backed up by her knowledge that he had and would use a gun—emboldened her just enough to lead the way. With great caution, she slid a foot forward until it came into contact with the threshold, braced a hand on either side of the door frame and went in.

41

Russell's proximity behind her forced her to take several steps.

Her first impression was of a strong unpleasant odor, then of liquid dripping onto a hard surface. Russell shut the door, altering the tactile and auditory qualities of the enclosed space, and she heard the click of a dead bolt. The dripping was a leaky faucet. The smell was of rodent droppings, cat pee, rust. Russell flipped a wall switch and the light in the ceiling came on.

They were in a kitchen. Leila saw sink, refrigerator, tiny table and one chair. Patches of dark and light on the floor, which might be designs in the linoleum or might be holes, warned her to move cautiously through here. A short counter on either side of the sink was piled high with mostly unidentifiable objects and substances; she could pick out a milk carton, a shoe. The lightbulb must not be more than 25 watts, and its globe was doubtless filthy and cobwebby, rendering the room more shadowed than lit by what could barely be called illumination. She could make out no other doorway; there must be one unless this was a single-room house, which didn't seem likely.

Russell shoved some of the mess aside to set down the grocery sack. "Please excuse the disarray. I wasn't expecting company." He chuckled, then paused, actually looking expectantly at her as if she ought to appreciate his little joke.

In fact, acute anxiety almost did cause her to strike

a Bette Davis pose and sneer, "What a dump!" She bit her lip and, guessing he'd persist until she made some sort of response, shrugged. "Hey, I'm practically blind, remember? I don't see messes." This wasn't true, but it had a nice sardonic ring.

"Let's look around the place," he said brightly, as if it was a companionable suggestion, and to her horror took her hand, tightening his grip when she tried to twist away.

Falsely together, they made their way across the kitchen and into the next room, which turned out to be a living room with a sprung sofa pulled out crookedly from the near wall and some other piece of furniture in the opposite corner, both grayish. Leila supposed the splotches on the gray walls to be stains from water or something worse; they could be holes.

"Oh, good, here's the bathroom." In order to find the string he pulled, she'd have to circle a hand in midair, probably for some minutes. She tried to pay attention to its general coordinates, but they were lost in gray space.

Dim dirty light showed toilet, stained sink, shower with a garish and bizarrely new-feeling plastic curtain. No toilet paper, she noted miserably; no toothpaste. Maybe that's what was in the grocery bag—supplies for setting up housekeeping. The possibility wasn't cheering.

Russell gestured toward a toilet that was obviously filthy even though she didn't see the filth. "Do you have to go?"

"Yes, Daddy," she whined extravagantly before she could stop herself. "Gotta go potty!"

He laughed indulgently. "Okay." When she didn't move, he tugged her by the hand toward the toilet. "Go ahead."

"You can't be serious."

"I'll turn my back." Playfully, he demonstrated.

"Stand sentry outside the door if you're worried. I mean, I can't exactly get out of here. There aren't any windows. Are there?" It seemed reckless to be talking so openly about escape.

"No windows," he concurred, "but I can't take any chances."

She gritted her teeth and tightened her muscles. "I'll wait."

"Well, I can't."

He dropped her hand, and she did think instantly, desperately—pointlessly—of trying to run. He lifted the toilet seat and unzipped his fly. She saw nothing there but his hand but turned her back anyway, wondering disgustedly what they'd do when one of them had to defecate.

When his stream started, he gave a soft little moan of relief, to which her own bladder responded plaintively. He finished with a trickle, and Leila waited for him to zip up and flush before she turned around.

He washed his hands without soap—maybe he hadn't thought of that; maybe they'd have to go to the store and she could get away there—and flapped them to dry. No towels, she noted. What about washing themselves? She wasn't going to shower with this guy; sponge baths would be bad enough, but even for sponge baths you needed washcloths and towels and soap.

On the way out of the bathroom he said thoughtfully, "We'll need to go out for provisions. I can already see I've overlooked a few things. My wife takes care of the shopping at home."

Her heart leaped, but she kept her voice steady. "Good. I'll need eye stuff."

"What do you mean?"

Reluctantly, she explained. "When I go to bed I take my contact out and clean it and soak it in saline solution overnight. I put an ointment in my eye while I sleep, and specially viscous eyedrops in the morning before I put the lens back in. All that stuff is at home. All I carry with me is the daytime eyedrops and a case." What, she wondered suddenly, had happened to her purse?

He'd started shaking his head about halfway through. "You won't need any of that."

When he said no more, she supplied, "Let me guess: God will restore my sight."

"That's right. That will be the sign."

"The sign of what?" she demanded, although it wasn't hard to figure out.

"The sign that you've been saved," he told her reverently. "Won't that be wonderful, Christina? You'll see normally for the first time in your life. And you'll be with the Lord." Hugging her, he sounded like a happy child, which struck her as both sad and sinister.

Longing, never far beneath the surface, swelled in her at the hope he offered, vain though she knew it to be, that her eyes could be magically healed. This was dangerous. Realizing, too, that he'd set up a success criterion that might well mean he'd never let her go, she swallowed. "But in the meantime, I need—"

"In the meantime, there's no reason for you to see. You're not seeing the truth anyway. In fact, I want you to take your contact out now."

"Russell—"

"Take it out, Christina. Just take it out and give it to me." He was imperiously holding out his hand.

"I don't think so."

There was a pause. He'd expected her to acquiesce. Although she couldn't see him clearly, she fixed him with a steady stare, triumphant, challenging.

Then he lunged, grabbed the back of her head with one hand and stuck the other forefinger into her eye. She yelled, and reflexively her eyelid clamped shut, but his attack knocked the contact out of position. It lodged like a rock under her lower lid. Instantly her surroundings filmed over. Russell's white shirt blurred and hurt her unprotected eye. The unlit living room slipped into dim fuzz.

He got her into a headlock in the crook of his elbow so he could use both hands on her eye, and though she flailed and spat and scratched, he was quicker and more precise than she was and managed to pop the contact out of her eye. "Don't test me, Christina," he warned her a little breathlessly. "Don't test the Lord."

She could still see enough that in a familiar environment many things would have been identifiable; indeed, for the sake of comfort the first hour or two of most days she didn't wear the contact and could easily cook breakfast, retrieve the paper from the porch, feed the cat, get dressed if she remembered where she'd left her shoes and if Cathy had helped her match her socks in the drawer.

In this place, though, the shapes and light/dark patterns she could see were almost all obscure. Edging sideways to find a wall, she tripped over something she'd had no inkling was there. Without the protection of the tint on the lens, the diffuse glare from the kitchen ceiling light and bathroom bulb, though not exactly painful, was intensely aversive.

The contact must have adhered to the tip of his finger, as it often did to hers. He was holding it up, peering at it. "It's huge," he marveled. "And thick. How do you stand wearing it?"

"You get used to it," she snarled. An attempt at reclaiming it would risk losing it altogether. Such a dominant presence when it was in her eye, its actual bulk was so minuscule and its smooth surface so skinlike that he might not even realize it had fallen off his fingertip.

A few months after the detached retina and laser surgery, when she'd been utterly convinced she'd never be able to function in the world again, the ophthalmologist had slipped her first contact into her eye. Remembering her surprise and delight when things had slid into new focus, in some ways better than before the retina had detached, Leila thought she'd weep now at the loss. Every now and then the lens would vanish in the process of putting it into her eye, and Cathy always had a hard time finding it, sometimes couldn't; at home, she always kept a spare. If she made Russell drop it, it would likely be gone for good. Helpless rage made her head swim.

Russell was intrigued. "Looks like one of those things you put around the holes in notebook paper so they won't tear, only black."

"My eye is so light sensitive now they call it photophobia. That's because the pupil is permanently fully dilated, like when you have an eye exam? And I don't have a natural lens anymore, since the laser surgery, so the eye doesn't focus on its own. Plus the contact is highly magnified—that's why it's so thick—" She knew she was blathering, but she had some sort of notion that if she explained to him all the reasons she needed that contact, he'd let her wear it.

"Interesting. All the efforts man makes to alter the work of the Lord."

"Why isn't that contact the work of the Lord, too?" Never having thought in these terms, she was on shaky theological ground here.

Poking at the lens in his palm, he didn't reply.

Leila was about to caution him that it could tear when he stepped back into the bathroom and flushed it down the toilet.

"Oh, you asshole," she gasped. Then, roaring, "You stupid fucking weirdo, who do you think you are?"

Now she was in tears and couldn't hide them from him. He came to her quickly and held her, though she made a puny effort to push him away. He patted her back and crooned, "I know it's hard, Christina, I know it's hard. But you're not alone," and for just a moment she collapsed against his thin, slightly sweaty chest.

Then she stopped crying and pulled back. "I still need ointment and drops," she told him firmly. "That has nothing to do with vision. My eye is stinging already."

"I'll pray on it," he promised. "I'll let you know God's answer."

For a moment she was speechless. "Ooh," she sneered, "I'd really appreciate that."

"No problem," he said, without a trace of irony. "Would you like to see the bedroom?"

"No. But gee, thanks."

"It's nothing fancy, but it's where we'll sleep, so I thought you'd want to familiarize yourself with it."

"We?"

"One bedroom, one bed."

"If it's all the same to you, I'll sleep on the floor."

"No," he said. "You'll sleep with me. Tied to me,

as a matter of fact, so in case the Enemy gives you thoughts of running away I'll be sure to wake up to intercede on behalf of the Lord."

"Jesus Christ!" she breathed, and Russell slapped her.

Leila had never in her life been slapped in the face, and her first reaction was incredulity, even as the recoil sent her stumbling sideways. Still, she didn't hit a wall or any other solid object, and she righted herself on her own, hand to her stinging cheek. Rage took over then, fueled by a stubborn refusal to believe she was at serious risk, and she shouted at him, "Jesus H. Christ! Jesus *fucking* Christ! How do you like that, Russell? Jesus fucking Christ!"

He advanced on her and, although she couldn't tell exactly where he was, she drew herself up to meet him. She intercepted his hand as it swung toward her again, twisted his wrist, with her other fist punched him in the belly hard enough that the air rushed out of him in a satisfying grunt.

But then a blow knocked her to the floor. Her left ear rang and throbbed. She was dizzy, nauseated.

While she was scrabbling to get up, the toe of his tennis shoe connected hard with her stomach, her breast, the side of her neck. He was *kicking* her. This was even more infuriating than being slapped.

She caught his ankle and wrenched him off balance. He came down on one knee, exclaimed in pain, reached for her and, when she met his hand with her elbow, got a handful of her short sleeve and bent her arm back.

She tipped against him and his other arm came around her neck. All but growling, she lowered her chin as far as she could and sank her teeth into the fleshy pad under his thumb. The taste of him was sharp, salty. He rammed the side of his hand into her mouth, dug his fingers into the hollow under her jaw until her bite loosened. In her mouth was blood, hers or his.

He rose onto his knees, and for a split second his hands were nowhere on her. She got one foot under her and started to push herself up, but he shoved her off balance.

Crouching over her gargoylelike, he began slapping first one cheek and then the other, snapping her head back and forth, and proclaiming in rhythm with the blows, "You—will *not*—take the Lord's name—in vain. You—will *not*. Satan, get thee *gone.*" Spittle sprayed her. His breath was sickeningly sweet.

"Okay! All right! I'm sorry! Stop it! I won't!" Leila was screaming now, trying to shield her ears and eyes, cowering. "Stop it, Russell, please stop!"

He stopped, finally, not because she'd begged him to but, apparently, because he and the Lord had decided it was enough. There came a time when she scooted backward and he didn't come after her. He knelt and she lay on the thin smelly carpet. A thick quiet took shape with them in it, Russell panting a little as if after a good workout and Leila breathing

51

raggedly while pain blossomed all over her body.

*I've been beaten,* she marveled silently. *This man beat me up.*

Sounds from outside grew audible, allowing Leila to hope someone might have heard their battle. Children shrieked in play or in fear. A horn honked and was answered by another, greeting or road rage. Heavy bass from a passing car vibrated the floorboards under her, and not far away someone was squeakily practicing a woodwind. A siren shrilled, coming closer, and both Leila and Russell stiffened, but it went on past.

Russell patted her hand. His gentle touch nearly brought back tears. "Really, Christina, you mustn't speak the Lord's name in vain. You mustn't."

Leila said nothing. Her head was pounding, and she was afraid her vision was darker than usual, though under these conditions it would be hard to tell.

"Let us pray." Russell spoke conversationally, as if suggesting they have a bite to eat. Already kneeling, the stance from which he'd been hitting her, he leaned toward her now and extended his hands, palms up and fingers bent, to within inches of her face. She flinched. All the fingers were wriggling, but he didn't touch her. It took her a long moment to understand that he was beckoning, and another before she comprehended what he wanted. Then she struggled to her knees, bracing one fist on the floor until the dizziness subsided.

Russell had now clasped his hands at his chest in what she'd have taken for a parody of supplication if she hadn't begun to grasp the depths of his sincerity. She didn't think he closed his eyes, however; he seemed to be regarding her watchfully, sternly, and she folded her hands, too, hoping she was doing it right.

During the preparatory silence, Leila had an unsettling sensation of swaying. Her knees began to ache, amid the aches and throbs and occasional sharp pain from her injuries. Her eye stung. She thought she might throw up. Russell began.

"Lord, there is someone here who needs you. Christina, Your daughter, is lost and afraid. I have spoken to You of her before, and now, by Your grace, she is here. Her body is in danger. Her mind is in danger. Her soul is in danger. Lord, I pray, allow her no rest until she opens her heart to You. Lord, I pray, give me the strength to be Thy sword and Thy balm."

# Chapter Four

Balm. That was not a word she'd heard very often, and she doubted she'd ever used it herself. But it stuck with her, along with "sword" and "no rest," as she was falling asleep, wrist bound to Russell's wrist by strong, slick, pre-measured twine.

She thought "balm," too, when she was awakened by Russell smearing some kind of gooey substance over her eyes. At first, not being able to open her eyelids brought on claustrophobia, odd for someone who even with her eyes open saw so little. Almost immediately, a breathless, crazy kind of logic took over: He was trying to treat the injuries he'd caused her; he hadn't meant to hurt her; he was dismayed by what he'd done; she could use his contrition as a lever to free herself. It must be a favorable sign that they were no longer tied together, except that she was horrified not to have been aware of him doing something to her, even untying the already hated cord.

As her mind cleared from fitful sleep, she realized her eyes hadn't been hurt and didn't need care, and when she tried to sit up he pushed her firmly back down with strong fingertip and knuckle pressure around both sockets. This wasn't balm. This was another assault of some kind. Could those bones break, crumble into the cavity of her skull?

Singsong, he was reciting something that sounded biblical. She seemed to have come in in the middle of a story, but that might be another deceptive impression; she remembered being mildly annoyed by how the Bible ignored common grammatical rules, mixing verb tenses, randomly scattering capital letters, using commas and semicolons interchangeably, for no good reason starting all sorts of sentences with "and."

"And as Jesus passed by, he saw a man which was blind from his birth."

*"Who," not "which,"* Leila thought automatically but had neither the energy nor the courage to say it aloud; copyediting Russell's Holy Scripture was probably not the better part of valor.

"I must work the works of Him that sent me, while it is day; the night cometh, when no man can work."

*Maybe men can't work at night, but a woman's work is never done.*

"As long as I am in the world, I am the light of the world."

Utterly against her will, Leila was curious to know what was going on. She was also exhausted. The massaging of Russell's fingers and palms lulled her, and she found herself relaxing just a little into this situation from which there was no imminent release. It wouldn't hurt to hear the rest of this story, and might, in fact, provide useful clues.

"When He had thus spoken, He spat on the ground, and made clay of the spittle, and He anointed the eyes of the blind man with the clay."

"Wait. Wait a minute." Leila's ignorance of the Bible, in her youth a sort of badge of honor and for most of her life something she hadn't thought about at all, was suddenly a decided disadvantage. Unfamiliar with this or any passage, she didn't know whether she was interrupting him; his vocal tone had dropped, which might indicate at least a pause, but she supposed he could go on like that for a long time, practically chanting. "What *is* this stuff?"

"Mud."

The mud, if that was really what it was, had already begun to stiffen, making whatever he was doing to her feel slightly muted though no less insistent. His fingertips and, she thought, knuckles, were circling carefully, leveling, pressing. Leila observed that this didn't hurt. In fact, it was soothing, but in a superficial way, since it didn't do anything for the dryness of her eyes, which had worsened with sleep and was by far her biggest discomfort.

She lay still under his ministrations, not fighting.

56

Did that mean she was already capitulating? Was this the Patty Hearst phenomenon, the Stockholm syndrome?

Leila made a point of imagining herself sinking into the lumpy mattress, but the visualization wasn't nearly strong enough to get her away from Russell, even in her mind. He wouldn't allow her to turn her head.

"Where," Leila demanded, "did you get mud?"

"I brought a Kool-Whip container of dirt from home." He was proud of himself. He had been prepared, she had to give him that.

"And you *spat* into it?" She wished she didn't have to ask.

"Holy mud. The Lord's facial."

Leila barked an incredulous laugh. Surely he was being at least a bit self-mocking. Surely he couldn't take seriously such patent nonsense. But she detected no hint of irony. Her stomach roiled. Could she catch some disease from his saliva through her eyelids?

His voice had risen in pitch, volume and cadence. Practically burbling with satisfaction, he was rubbing the mud harder and faster into her face. "And said unto him, 'Go, wash in the pool of Siloem.' He went his way therefore, and washed, and came seeing."

*And came seeing.* The phrase pierced her. Under her forcibly closed eyelids tears welled, and she imagined the mud being moistened and smoothed from underneath, her own longing co-opting her into some sort of partnership with Russell.

Like a horse shuddering off flies, she wrinkled her face, hoping to loosen the mud mask around the edges. Already it was itching, pulling at the flesh. "But that was *Jesus's* spit," she tried. "Why would yours work a miracle?"

"I am invested by God with certain powers." She started to shake her head, but his hands tight on each temple stopped the motion and intensified her claustrophobia. "Lie still," he commanded.

She took a breath. "I don't get it. I thought we were waiting for my sight to be restored as a sign that I'd started walking the path of righteousness."

The sarcasm was plain, but Russell seemed to take what she said at face value. "The Lord helps those who help themselves," he told her patiently. "We aren't to just wait passively. We have free will."

"Easy for you to say," she snapped, then chided herself. Smart-ass rejoinders had caused more than one tiff with Cathy and were likely to get her into real trouble here of all places.

"Oh, Christina," Russell said sadly. His hands slid down onto the exposed skin of her neck, and she could feel the scratch of a thumbnail half-ringing the nub of pain where he pressed under each ear. "You have free will. You are free to choose between the Devil or the Lord."

She couldn't stop herself from retorting stubbornly, "I wouldn't call this *free.*"

His hands were around her throat now, thumbs pushing just hard enough to elicit a cough. The warning was clear. She managed to pry loose the pinky boring into the right side of her neck and bend it back, but probably not enough to hurt him.

He took his hands away, and she despised the intensity of her relief. A bit breathless from such physical and spiritual exertion, he patted her head and all but crooned, "You just stay still for a while now, Christina. I have something wonderful for you to listen to."

Hard plastic clicked, and then Leila jumped at the exhortation of a shrill, stern woman's voice to "Praise the Lord!"

The thudding of her heart and the adrenaline geysering through her system made breathing hard. She tried to calm herself: This was a tape, nothing but words, with no power to harm her, no power of any kind that she herself didn't grant it. By the time she was breathing more or less normally again and had stopped shaking, the voice was loud enough to hurt her ears. She fumbled for the tape player to at least turn the volume down, and when she couldn't find it nearly plunged into full despair; the bungee cord of rationality held and snapped her back, but just barely, and she allowed herself a moment of astonishment at how quickly she'd come to this point.

"Jesus loves you! Amen! Jesus wants you! Amen! Jesus died for your sins! The least you can do is give Him your soul! Amen!"

The preacher's exaggerated speech patterns would have rendered her words ridiculous even if they hadn't been in themselves. But they were, Leila reminded herself, patently ridiculous. They were also dangerous, because of a sort of primal allure. She struggled to sit up. The emphatic voice filled the dark room, further entrapping her.

"God and the Devil are in battle for your soul! The Fiend lurks behind every corner, under every rock, inside every dark place. Beware! Beware! Beware!"

Russell had left her alone. Perhaps he imagined this formidable preacher would keep her in line with nothing more than her voice from the tape; indeed, that didn't seem entirely implausible to Leila, for the feeling of exposure was intense as she eased herself over the bare, sprung mattress to the edge of the bed. The mask hung heavy on her face. She'd slitted her eyes open, but that made only a thin lighter line at the bottom of the brownish miasma inside her right eyelid. The left eye—which had never functioned beyond the barest light perception, sensing light energy rather than seeing it—now perceived nothing.

She couldn't bear the mask against her face another minute. For some reason, the task of getting it off seemed to require an enormous amount of courage, and not only because it risked Russell's ire. She took a steadying breath and placed both hands over the dried mud, which had become an object in its own right. The feel of it reminded her of papier-màche, and she had the eerie sensation of witnessing the formation and, soon, destruction of a sculpture from the inside out.

"You cannot enter the Kingdom of Heaven by your own will. God has to invite you. God has to choose you because you have chosen Him. No matter what good deeds you do on this earthly plane, no matter what kind of person you are, no matter anything, *anything*, it's all meaningless when it comes to your eternal soul. Turn away from darkness! Turn toward the light!"

Finding the edges of the thing, she got her nails under it and tugged. The mask cracked. Pieces of it fell away, and the sudden air on her skin, stuffy as it was inside this closed-up room in this closed-up house, felt wonderful. But she was also aware of an inexplicable sense of loss.

"Give yourself to the Lord! Praise the Lord! Praise the Lord! Amen!"

Rapidly, listening for sounds of Russell coming back though she didn't know yet exactly what those sounds would be—did the floorboards creak? were there interior doors in this house?—she peeled and clawed most of the rest of the mud off her eyes, in the interest of expediency resisting the urge to scratch away every last particle of it. Russell had left a light on in the room, so dim she hadn't been aware of it through the mask. "Praise the Lord!" cried the voice on the tape. Resisting also the strong impulse to search until she found the damned machine and turn it off or unplug it or slam it into a wall, Leila stood up.

The floorboards did creak when she put all her weight on them. She froze, listening. She heard nothing that sounded like him, and she couldn't wait long, so she found different positions for her feet and took a step. Nothing else creaked, but the swishing of her bare soles across the wooden floor seemed thunderous. Trying to slide her feet along rather than stepping, she bit her lip as a splinter went into her heel. She wished she could find her shoes—and her purse—but that wasn't likely to happen except by sheer luck.

A fuzzy opening in the dark expanse of the room might be the doorway. She'd left the bed now and was maneuvering in gauzy space without landmarks or boundaries and, although she held her hands out from her body and made small patting motions in the air so that if she ran into something it would be a gentle collision, every step was vertiginous.

Her eyes felt crackly-dry by now, and there were regular slashes of actual pain. Suppose she came out of this not fully sighted but completely blind? *That'd serve him right,* she thought with an attempt at flippancy, but the possibility, which at the moment seemed quite real, terrified her, had always terrified her. She moistened the tip of her little finger with her tongue and touched it to both corners of both eyes, providing only fleeting relief.

She stumbled into something that hit the floor

dully and rolled. "Praise the Lord!" shrieked the tape again, and Leila, hating it, hoped its camouflaging noise was sufficient.

To avoid the object she'd knocked over, she swung her feet out sideways, first one and then the other in a clumsy dance that made her feel so silly she almost couldn't do it even though no one was likely observing her. When her left ankle brushed something she veered slightly to the right. Nearly to the lighter rectangle now, which in fact was the door, she held one hand straight out in front of her until she found the door frame she would have to walk through without any real knowledge of what or who was just beyond it.

Holding her breath, she inched her way out into a space that sounded and felt longer and narrower than the bedroom. She didn't remember a hall, but there was a wall close ahead of her, and none on either side as far as she could see or reach. Acute kinesthetic confusion dizzied her for a moment, then settled into simple disorientation: Which way was the door?

Very cautiously she pivoted to press her back against the wall and turn her head to the right so she could use the vision she had to its best advantage. Going right would be easier, and was as good a choice as left. She listened, heard nothing from Russell, reminded herself how imprecise even the most well-developed auditory faculty was, reminded herself that it was the best she had and began to move rightward along the corridor wall.

The preacher behind her sang, "Praise the Lord!" one more time and the tape snapped off. In the sudden quiet, Leila heard something, felt the approach of something, a split second before Russell grabbed her from her blind left side in a furious hug.

Grunting, she braced herself for another physical attack. Instead, Russell breathed like a lover into her ear, "Christina, Christina, can you see?"

"Yes!" She lifted her face to his in what she meant to be an attitude of exultation, hoping he couldn't tell that her eyes were no more focused than ever. "Yes, Russell, I see!"

His embrace tightened, and she could feel him gently sobbing, which, astonishingly, caused her a little stab of guilt. He was stroking her hair now and rocking, crooning, "Oh my God, oh my great God."

She pulled back, hoping to extricate herself entirely, but he kept his arms around her, as if determined to absorb some of the miracle himself. From her reservoir of unshed tears of rage and pain and fear, Leila let herself weep now as she cried, "It's a miracle, Russell! It really is a miracle! I can see clearly! Thank you! Thank you, you were right!" Laughing was harder, but she did that, too, and even forced herself to proclaim, "Praise the Lord!"

One hand still pressed into her back, he laid the other against her face, heel on her chin, thumb and little finger on her cheekbones, a finger on each eye and the middle one on the bridge of her nose. She knew to stay very still. His fingertips pressed too hard on her eyeballs. What could he be feeling?

After a long moment, he stepped back, clasped her hands between his and regarded her in what she took to be a suspicious manner. She did her best to give the appearance of meeting his gaze. He pulled something out of his back pocket and pressed it into her hand. A flyer, folded in half lengthwise, thick slick paper, white with red and black or blue. "Show me," he demanded. "Read this to me."

She couldn't, of course. Without glasses or contact lens, she wouldn't have known there was any print on the paper at all unless she'd been told. She made a show of looking at it, frantically trying to come up with something to say or do that would masquerade as reading.

He tsked. "Really, Christina, did you think I would just take your word for it?"

"This is crazy!" Balling up the flyer and throwing it into his chest with as much force as she could muster, Leila shouted, "Russell, this is nuts! My eyes are not going to be healed no matter what you do! And anyway, what's wrong with my eyes the way they are? Who are you to say they should be healed? Why isn't *this* the work of the Lord?"

Hearing herself, she stopped in surprise. She'd never before thought of her disability in that way. Russell didn't say anything for a moment or two, and

Leila waited almost eagerly; arguing on his own terms, maybe she'd made a point.

But then he pulled her roughly behind him into the kitchen, where he rummaged one-handed through the sack he'd brought, twisting her wrist in the process. "You're hurting me," she protested, not expecting it to make any difference, which it didn't.

At last he found what he'd been looking for, a roundish and not very heavy mass bigger than his hand with something dangling from it. Too quickly for her to keep her footing, squeezing her wrist painfully, he half-dragged her into the living room, pushed her into a straight-backed chair that tipped backward under her sudden weight and braced himself against her to hold her there, bony shins boring into her knees. When he slammed her arm onto the arm of the chair and began trussing it, she realized that it was rope he'd brought in the bag, no doubt in case of just this eventuality.

Roaring, she pulled her other hand free and shoved it up under his chin. His head flew back and he gave a shout, but it wasn't enough to loosen his grip or shift his weight off her. She pinched the skin of his forearm; he yelped and wrenched the rope tighter. "Stop it, Christina. I have the power of the Lord on my side. You and your Master are no match."

Unable to get sufficient distance or angle to kick, she wrapped her legs around his and twisted her body. For an instant he did seem to lose his balance, but both her hands were tied down now and she couldn't do anything with the brief advantage. Stumbling backward half a step, he righted himself, squatted and rapidly bound her legs to the legs of the chair. The knee she managed to bring up bounced harmlessly off his abdomen, and he gave it a swipe with his fist that sent a numbing nerve pain through her entire leg. "Fuck," she groaned, then waited for his punishing blow, but apparently that wasn't the sort of obscenity he objected to because he took no perceptible notice of it as he ran the remaining length of rope several times around her torso and the back of the chair, knotting it at the level of her shoulder blades, where she wouldn't be able to get at it even if she freed her hands.

Task accomplished, he sat back on his heels and regarded her. Leila imagined how she must look, legs splayed, skirt pulled in at the crotch, bared flesh of thighs and calves ugly where it was flattened against the chair and indented by the snug rope, hair unkempt, face mottled by remnants of the mud mask. Since her retina had detached, her physical self-image had been uneasy and wavering at best; in most mirrors she could make out only a minimal reflection, and photographs were almost entirely beyond her. It would have helped if she could have relied on Cathy for cues and clues about what she looked like, but Cathy seemed hardly to notice her appearance; the best Leila could hope for was a "Fine" in response to her anxious "How do I look?" Suddenly, foolishly, she was furious with Cathy about that.

Russell was praying again. He'd rocked forward onto his knees and laid his head on his folded hands on her thigh. Pointlessly, she cringed. "Lord, be with us in this time of trouble," he intoned. "Thy daughter Christina is here before Thee now. She needs Thee. Holy Father, I beseech Thee, bring her into Thy grace. May she neither rest nor eat nor move nor think of anything else until she has come to Thee with all her heart and all her soul."

Leila's blood ran cold. She raised her voice over his. "I have to go to the bathroom."

"And grant us, Lord, as a sign of Thy daughter Christina's release from the Forces of Darkness, her full sight, that she may glory in the beauty of Thy creation."

"Russell. I'm serious. I have to go to the bathroom and my back hurts and the rope is cutting into my ankle."

He was silent for a long time. His steady warm breath on the skin of her thigh repulsed her. Outside someone called, but Leila heard no answer. Her right eye itched fiercely.

At last Russell murmured, "Amen," and straightened. Bracing his hands on her knees in a wholly unnecessary skin-to-skin contact, he pushed himself to his feet, bent and kissed her cheek, and left her alone.

# *Chapter Five*

Within the first ten minutes, she'd wet herself. All through the trickle and then the flow and then the gush, she tightened her sphincter muscles, but they were no match for her body's determination to expel what would turn into poison if it accumulated inside. Warm at first, the urine quickly turned cold and clammy. Her attempts to decrease the discomfort by shifting position in the chair were fruitless; she just squirmed.

Her eye hurt steadily now, with occasional jabs of sharper pain. She swore she could feel the actual abrading of the cornea. If she could get eyedrops and ointment soon, the damage might be slight and reparable. If not, which was more likely, she might well lose what little remained of her sight. Dread clammy as urine pooled dangerously in her mind.

When her retina had detached and her vision suddenly worsened, Leila had been amazed by how traumatized she'd been. Never having had much usable vision, she'd have thought losing more wouldn't be such a big adjustment, since a good many coping strategies had already been second nature.

But, for what had turned out to be seven weeks after the laser surgery, she'd been required to wear a patch and keep her face as nearly as possible parallel to the floor. Her sense of where she was in space, badly distorted, had never fully recovered, and the visual changes—not all of them even actual losses—had sent her reeling.

For months she'd been subject to bouts of inconsolable weeping, mini-hallucinations in which she'd glimpse unattributable but sinister movement in something as innocent as a shaft of sunlight across the floor and, more than once, a long waking daylight dream of huge black wings unfolding to engulf her. She'd huddled in the house, afraid to go even onto the patio. With maddening regularity she'd misplaced objects—items of clothing, money, audio tapes, the bottle of dish soap, her toothbrush, eye medicine; there was little point in searching, since the likelihood of her happening upon them was minuscule, and some of those things were still lost, three years later.

Stairs had been terrifying. When Cathy had persuaded or coerced her outdoors, streets had been terrifying. Escalators had been terrifying, and the moving walkways at the airport had induced outright panic.

Falling over a chair not two inches out of its usual alignment, she'd badly bruised her hip. Bending down to pick up a dropped carrot, she'd slammed into an unseen open cupboard door hard enough to gash the bridge of her nose. The blood and the bruise became emblems of her estrangement from the physical world.

Over time, she'd settled down. There'd been no hallucinations or black-wing dreams for a long time. She'd learned to move slowly—she hoped not tentatively—so that collisions were less damaging. Systems had developed for keeping track of the relative position of herself and her possessions, noting and remembering environmental configurations, cataloguing nonvisual characteristics of people, objects, places. This necessary hypervigilance had steadily spread until now it was her way of being in the world and she could never really relax.

Leila wouldn't say she'd adjusted to the changes in her vision. But then, she wouldn't say she'd accepted the vision she'd been born with. Despite the fact that she'd never known anything else, it was an acute and bitter loss. She'd been cheated, and calling it anything else would be capitulation.

Now, tied up, cold and wet and bewildered, she could feel her eye being harmed and her sight further compromised moment by moment. The simple things that would stop or heal the damage were utterly unavailable to her. Profound helplessness bore down, a physical weight. No longer did she make any attempt to stave off tears, but she had energy only for a childlike, even animallike whimpering.

Any light that might have been within her field of vision had been turned off; she could see nothing but a gauzy, featureless darkness, and now there were no sounds except a faint white noise as from a distant appliance. She might have been hurtling weightless and with no sense of motion through space, or on a platform suspended over a rising void, or in a flotation tank.

Urgently needing to touch something other than the floor and the chair she was tied to, she flung her head back. But there was no wall or anything else to connect with, and her head bobbed loosely, sickeningly.

She missed Cathy. "Missing," though, was far too mild a term for the firewall of grief sweeping through her. She'd never see Cathy again, in all the senses of the phrase. If she ever got away from Russell, she'd surely be totally blind, and everything about Cathy she loved to gaze on—the graceful hands, the swell of breasts under a particular powder-blue shirt, the strong silhouette backlit by morning light through the kitchen window—would be lost.

But she wouldn't get away. She'd die here. She'd never again hear Cathy's sweet alto voice, scolding or cajoling, telling the events of her day and asking about Leila's, singing in the shower, moaning in ready sexual abandon to Leila's finger and tongue, declaring devotion. They'd never walk again in that practical and loving posture, Leila's hand grasping Cathy's crooked arm just above the elbow, the exquisite attunement to each other's every movement, a functional necessity, having become an expression, too, of how much, after all these years, they were in love.

Weeping aloud, Leila slumped sideways against the rope, and the chair tipped over. Instinctively her hands tried to come up and break the fall, but her forehead hit the floor, then her shoulder, then her hip and the corner of the chair. The noise seemed to her cacophonous, and she waited for someone to come to rescue or at least investigate, Russell or a neighbor or the cops or—a crazed fantasy—Cathy.

Nothing happened. She might as well not have fallen. She might as well not be lying crumpled on this filthy floor with a chair on top of her. She might as well not be separated from the love of her life, or going blind, or in a battle she didn't yet comprehend for body and psyche and soul.

She resisted the strong temptation to thrash mindlessly and scream for help. Scrabbling clumsily, she got to her knees with the chair still tied to wrists and ankles, then toppled sideways again. Her only conscious goal was to get herself *against* something, out of this borderless, dizzying space. This was a room, after all, and a small one; sooner or later, there had to be walls.

Hunched over, forehead braced against the floor since she couldn't use her hands, she twisted her upper body and rolled the chair from one side to the other. It slid a little, giving her disproportionate hope that the ropes might be loosening, but didn't strike anything. Her back ached fiercely, and the worn carpet was like sandpaper under her knees as she sidled to the right, fully aware that this might be exactly the wrong direction, a wall might be close on the left. Again she swung the chair. Again, nothing.

It took six more exhausting, crablike paces before she felt the proximity of something high and solid. She couldn't yet touch it, but the quality of air and sound changed, and she was certain—almost certain—that she was nearing a wall. This seemed a huge triumph, although what she'd do when she reached it she didn't know. One more time she gathered her strength and wrenched sideways, then flung herself hard to the right and to her giddy relief was jarringly stopped.

Testing, she knocked the side of her head against the vertical surface, starting close to the floor and working her way up as high as she could reach from spread knees. Not furniture. Not a box or anything similar she could visualize. A wall, surely.

She slumped against it. It held. She was panting, and her thigh muscles protested this prolonged stretching. The ropes had cut into wrists and ankles and into her sides, at least abrading if not actually having broken the skin. *Stigmata* occurred to her, and she snorted.

Gathering her strength and focus, she leaned as far as she could to the left, then heaved herself rightward and banged the chair into the wall. The thud was solid, no hint that the wood would shatter. She repeated the motion again and again, methodically battering, taking note of every slight shift in the position of the chair on her back like a carapace, every tiny alteration in the sharp pressure of the ropes. It was a wearing process, and her head and shoulders ached after the first two or three swings. But when she thought she heard an almost subliminal spider-webby sound in the back of the chair under and behind her left ear, adrenaline spurted through her and she put all her effort into a hard crash.

The shackle around her right forearm slipped. Leila froze, then very cautiously rotated the arm. It moved, not easily but undeniably. Leila visualized the cylinder of flesh and bone contracting inside the rope circlet. Her hand folded until, she hoped, it was hardly broader than her wrist. She slid her arm backward, but only a scant half-inch before her elbow was pressing against the frame of the chair. She pushed. The slat gave slightly. Longing to hammer with her elbow, she could manage no more than pressure, so diffuse it seemed passive and unlikely to be enough. But she gritted her teeth and pushed as hard and as long as she could.

The wood gave. For a moment she wasn't sure

what had happened. Almost silently, the broken slat fell through the loop of twine. The binding around her torso on that side slackened, and then, all of a piece, loosened around her wrist.

Hardly daring even to try, Leila slid her forearm backward. There wasn't much space, and then, at the widest part of her hand, the rope snagged. Against the temptation to despair she grimaced and bore down, trying to think what to do other than simply give up and wait for whatever Russell had in mind for her next.

Her body was not completely immobilized. There was no telling what effort might have what effect. She shrugged deeply, bringing her shoulders up high toward her ears and then dropping them low so that the shoulder blades pressed into the chair. She swiveled her head and contorted her face, surprised, now that she thought about it, that Russell hadn't gagged her. Her legs and ankles would hardly move, but she arched her feet, curled her toes.

Carefully, she wriggled and folded her fingers, both hands simultaneously at first but then focusing her attention on just the right, which seemed minutely more promising and would be more useful to her if she could free it. Muscles at the base of her thumb cramped. The hand was trembling, and she pressed it into the chair arm, angling for the slightest gap on top. She lifted her wrist and pulled back.

The rope slid forward a fraction of an inch. Leila held her breath and visualized her hand smaller, thinner, supple as Houdini's. The rope was at her first knuckles now, her sweaty flesh and gratifyingly flexible bones sliding backward in excruciating increments. Then, in what seemed a blaze of movement, her hand came free.

Now the urge was to celebrate, or at least to indulge in a moment or two of relief. She didn't dare. *Later,* she promised herself. *When I'm home with Cathy.*

It proved easier than she'd expected to loosen the corresponding knot enough to extricate her other wrist, and then, both hands usable, to untie her ankles. She allowed herself a smirk; obviously Russell had a few things to learn about hostage-taking. In a matter of minutes she was able to shuck off the rest of the chair and stand more or less erect. Groaning at the stiffness in her back, neck, shoulders, arms, legs, she stretched, bent, swiveled her head.

There was something on the floor, practically at her feet. Her purse. Leila crouched to retrieve it, nervous that with the next exploratory pat or slide of fingers into pockets she'd discover this was some bulging denim bag not her own.

The contents were familiar, though, and nothing obvious had been removed. Reflecting grimly that she couldn't have anticipated this urgency when she'd packed the bag, she took a rushed inventory: what in it could be used to escape? The tooled leather billfold that had been her mother's, still thick with one-dollar bills; the bus pass in its plastic sheath; house keys, which she'd heard could be used as a weapon; breath mints to stand in for a tooth-brush until she got home so if she asked somebody for help, halitosis wouldn't repulse them. *My God, the cell phone.* And, blessedly, eyedrops.

Knowing it would be smarter to call for help first, she fumbled the lid off the bottle, tipped her head back and squirted the cool liquid into the outside corner of her right eye. Immediate relief washed through her with the moisture across her dry eyeball, and she squirted again, excess fluid trickling down her cheek like joyful tears.

"Well. Christina."

Fighting the instinct to cower, Leila put the drops back into the side pocket of her purse and stood up to face him. "Why, Russell. Fancy meeting you here."

"I was just coming to get you."

"Is that a fact?"

He grasped her shoulder and she stiffened. He stepped closer and put his arm around her waist. Unwillingly she thought of how she must smell. Making it clear she had no choice in the matter, he guided her across the room and into the hallway, reached to pull the string for the bathroom light. "Let's get you cleaned up. We're going out."

"Out?" This seemed so unlikely she was sure she must be misunderstanding; he must have an idiosyn-cratic meaning for the phrase "going out."

He had turned on the water in the shower. She could hear that the stream was thin and guessed it wouldn't be especially hot. Still with one arm around her, he was leaning to test the temperature for her with his other hand. "We're going to fellowship, where you can be immersed in the Word."

"My clothes are—dirty." Despite herself, she was mortified by her urine-soaked and reeking skirt and underwear, sweaty shirt and bra.

"A short skirt wouldn't be appropriate anyway."

"Well, I don't usually carry a change of clothes to the movies."

"I brought you some."

"You brought me clothes?"

"My wife's. She'd be happy to contribute."

"Meaning you took them without telling her?"

"They might be a little small, but we'll make do."

Was this a jibe about her weight? Leila could hardly believe that, under the circumstances, she was even the tiniest bit insulted.

When he withdrew his hand from the shower stall, drops of cool water splattered her unpleasantly. "There. It's ready for you." Now he was pressing the small of her back. She shrugged in exaggerated obedience and stepped forward. Chuckling playfully, he grabbed the back of her shirt and tugged. "You won't get clean with your clothes on."

"Leave the room then."

"No can do." With an efficient motion she suspected of being practiced—maybe on his kids, or maybe, she speculated savagely, on his other hostages—he pulled her shirt up over her head. Her struggles against him resulted somehow in her arms coming out of the sleeves, and then she was standing in front of him in her bra, which—and this could not have been learned from his children, unless incest was among his many talents—he unhooked and pulled off. "Skirt now," he instructed. "And panties."

Out of dislike for the cutesy word, Leila always referred to that clothing item as underwear. She didn't correct him. Her hands went obediently to the zipper of her skirt, but she couldn't quite bring herself to pull it down until he reached to do it himself. Then she yanked the rest of her clothes off and turned her back to him, loathing the thought of him staring at her buttocks but preferring that to exposing her breasts and pubis.

"Here's soap and shampoo."

"What about conditioner?"

"I didn't think of that." He actually sounded contrite, and she was gratified to have won a point, however spurious.

"I'll definitely have a bad hair day without conditioner," she told him solemnly.

He seemed to consider it for a second or two, then dismissed it and shooed her into the shower. The cool trickle of water made her gasp when it hit her skin. The stall felt grimy, buggy; she didn't want to touch the sides, felt compromised by her bare feet on the floor.

The entire time she showered, he watched her,

holding aside the shower curtain, which, as it got wet, smelled even more strongly of new plastic. His prurience was incontestable, since there was no chance of her escaping from the stall. Leila launched into a bump-and-grind burlesque, thrusting her crotch at him, jiggling her breasts with soapy hands, leering. She expected an indignant command to desist, but he made no comment at all, and she felt so ludicrous that she switched her efforts to splashing him, which only made him wince.

The water turned rapidly from tepid to downright chilly. There was still soap in her hair when he turned the faucet off. Shivering and feeling even more exposed, she folded her arms over her breasts and pressed her thighs together. He passed her a thin, stiff towel and offered her a hand, which she ignored; she shook her head in an attempt to soak him as she stepped out of the shower.

"Here. Try these." Bikini underwear, silky with lace, a dark color. Leila stretched them between her forefingers and looked at him over the narrow waistband. "All I could find," he defended himself. She hoped he was blushing. They barely pulled on over her hips; the elastic indented the flesh and accentuated her belly.

Next he handed her a matching bra, a flashy wirecupped contraption that made her soft cotton, barely padded, flowered one seem like either a pre-teen's or an old lady's. She was able to get it fastened, though the cups were larger than her breasts and pointier than any breasts known to woman. "This is your wife's?" It was hard to imagine a woman who'd be married to Russell wearing such self-consciously sexy lingerie.

Not having taken his eyes off her, he held out a frilly white blouse. "Actually," he said, "some of these things are Stephanie's."

"Your teenage daughter gave you a set of her underwear to bring along for me to wear?" Leila tried to make some sense of this. If both his wife and his daughter actively and materially supported this endeavor, were there others? Was Russell the leader of some kind of cult, not acting alone, with reinforcements at the ready?

"Actually," he said, "I found them in her dresser drawer."

Fastening the dozen or so tiny buttons down the front of the blouse, Leila shuddered at the image of Russell pawing through his daughter's intimate apparel with the express intent of watching her, his captive, put it on. The placket gaped between buttons when she moved, the cuffs of the long, full sleeves ended well above her wristbones and she guessed the bra was showing through the white fabric. The skirt he'd brought wouldn't quite button, and there was a thick panty line when she smoothed her hands over her hips. "No slip?" she challenged.

"I didn't think of that," he admitted again.

She wanted to tell him she looked like shit and was not going out in public like this, but she bit her lip. It was, she thought, to her advantage to be among other people, even if they shared his fanaticism, and maybe someone would be alerted by her cobbled-together appearance. And there was always the chance that, outside this house, she could make a run for it.

While she blotted her hair, without much effect since the towel was already sopping, Russell got himself ready. He'd taken off his shirt to wash his face and neck at the splotched sink. He was wearing an undershirt, short-sleeved, modest, neckline above his collarbone; Leila hadn't seen a lot of men even partially undressed lately, but the undershirt struck her as further proof of his eccentricity. He pulled on another white shirt, tucked it in, zipped his pants and buckled his belt, adjusted the collar and cuffs. She didn't like being privy to his ablutions.

He turned toward her, and after a moment, just as she realized he must be holding something out to her, the teeth of a pocket comb scratched the back of her hand lightly, proprietarily. She jerked her hand back, then took the comb, ran it through her sopping, tangled hair. Soapy rivulets plastered the blouse to her back and shoulders. Russell didn't stop her from slipping the comb into the skirt pocket. Maybe it could be used as a weapon or a tool for escape. Or maybe it would just make her a neater captive.

"I heated up some soup," Russell said, almost

proudly. "Let's eat supper and then we'll go worship the Lord."

"I thought—" But she was hungry, and she shut up. He waited for her to move out of the bathroom, down the grungy little hall and into the kitchen. When she smelled tomato soup, singed, her stomach growled in uneasy eagerness.

# *Chapter Six*

He'd made the tomato soup with milk instead of water, the way Leila's mother used to. She hadn't thought of that in years. The memory stirred primal feelings of tenderness and safety. *Be careful,* she warned herself, but more than anything else she was hungry and about to be fed.

The slight burnt taste, from where unstirred soup had stuck to the bottom of the pan, hardly mattered. She was ravenous. Her mouth was actually watering; she'd always thought that was a figure of speech. The first few spoonsful tasted wonderful, warm and creamy and mildly tangy. Then her stomach cramped and, regretfully, she had to stop and wait for it to settle.

"And," he announced with a flourish, "we have a choice of crackers, club or onion crisps."

The two boxes, together with the two bowls and

water glasses, filled nearly all the available space on the little tabletop. A stack of more or less folded newspapers took up one whole quadrant; the smell of them was papery, inky and slightly rancid, as if something organic had been wrapped in them and left to rot.

The blandness of a club cracker would be more likely to soothe her stomach, but she couldn't tell for sure which was which and for a moment was paralyzed by trepidation that she might choose the wrong box.

Finally she took a deep breath and reached toward the crackers. But Russell, faster, intercepted her, as though which kind she ate really was a matter of significance. "Here, let me help you. Which would you like?"

Leila said stubbornly, "It doesn't matter."

"No, no, we want you to be happy."

"We? You and God?"

"That's right."

He was grasping a box in each hand, one mostly yellow and the other predominantly blue. She'd have had to fight him for them and did not have the stamina to take on his solicitousness, which, from him even more than from other people, masked something else. "Club," she capitulated.

"Good." Incredibly, she found herself smiling with pleasure at his praise and trying to understand what she'd done to please him so she could do it again. Was he reinforcing her for making the right decision, or simply for making one, despite or because of the fact that it was a bogus choice between meaningless alternatives?

He opened one of the boxes, took out a short stack of pale oval wafers and laid them beside her bowl. Without much interest, she wondered about the cleanliness of the table. The cracker she bit was crisp and salty, with mercifully little substance. Two of them she crumbled into her soup, then spooned up the resulting mush like baby food.

"Are you homesick, Christina?"

Staring at him in disbelief somehow was expressive even though she could see nothing more than an outline and the suggestion of features. What was the trap here? Was there a possible reply that would give him more information, more power? Warily, she settled on a parry. "What do you want me to say, Russell?"

But apparently it had been less a tactic than a segue, for he sighed and confessed, "I am. I'm homesick."

Curiously, outrageously, Leila felt a twinge of guilt that she was keeping him away from his home and family. Swallowing a clot of tomato-soaked crackers, she waved her spoon in the air and said brightly, "Hey, I've got a great idea! Why don't you go home?"

He laughed sadly. "My little one is just learning to walk. I hate to miss a step."

Further repulsed by every detail she was gleaning

about Russell Gavin's life—by the very thought of him as a husband and father before and presumably after taking on the project of her salvation—Leila nonetheless had a fuzzy idea that it was good to keep him talking. If she could talk about herself, too, get him to think of her as a person and not just as a target, it might wear him down. She'd look for a chance to work in a charming or inspirational story from her extensive repertoire about her kids at school.

A reminder of the past might be useful, too. Scouring her memory for a mutual experience from high school, the only period of their lives they'd shared and then only in the most general and peripheral sense, she came up with the names of two or three teachers he might remember fondly and a single incident senior year when his explanation of sines and cosines had suddenly made sense to her when nobody else's had.

Thus armed, hunger and thirst quelled if not satisfied, clothes clean and dry and not uncomfortable though ill-fitting, she was suddenly almost cocky. "I'll have some more of that good soup," she told him pleasantly, and held out her bowl.

He consulted his watch, and she was again reminded about this religious thing they were going to, a group of other crazies just like him. She'd be at their mercy. They'd likely do weird or downright harmful things to her. But she'd also be outside this house, in an environment Russell might not be able to control quite so thoroughly.

Both hopeful and scared, she felt her stomach roil again as Russell poured the last of the soup—thick now, clumpy—into her bowl. She wasn't sure she could eat any more, but since this might be the last food she saw for a while, she forced herself.

She'd begin with his family, the opening he'd given her. "How old did you say your youngest is?"

"Thirteen months on Saturday."

"That's a boy, isn't it?"

"George Paul. After Germaine's father, who died when she was a teenager."

Fleetingly Leila toyed with the possibility of pursuing that story but decided in favor of staying focused on him. "You have two boys and two girls?"

"Stephanie's sixteen, Alexander's twelve, Helene is seven, and little George." She saw him duck his head boyishly as he added shyly, slyly, "George was something of a surprise. Our miracle baby."

Angered and embarrassed as if she'd stumbled onto pornography, Leila did not want to know this, did not want to imagine Russell and Germaine Gavin making love, discovering the pregnancy, worrying over and welcoming the late-life baby. But she stored away both the facts and the impressions for possible future use.

He'd pulled something out of his pocket and was passing it to her, had probably been holding it out for several beats before she realized it was there. At first after she took it, reluctantly, she still didn't know what it was. A billfold-sized rectangular pouch, but flat and with a flapped opening on one of the longer sides; a gold glimmer—a monogram, she guessed—in one corner; leather, by the smell. "What is this?"

"Pictures of my family. I don't mean to bore you." He laughed modestly, quite as though they'd run into each other on the street after all these years and gone for a companionable cup of coffee to catch up on the rudiments of each other's lives.

Leila struck a pose, hand over heart. "Why, no, of course not, not at all."

Either he was oblivious to the increasingly surreal nature of the situation and her cheeky sarcasm about it, or his need was stronger to talk domesticity. Or it was a maneuver of some kind when he said with apparent earnestness, "I'd love to see your pictures, too, if you have any."

She wanted to snarl, "Of course I have pictures, Russell," but an instinct for self-protection—and for the protection of Cathy, which seemed at the moment much the same thing—kept her silent. He didn't press, but she anticipated he would, and then what would she do? In addition to several class pictures, innocent enough, there were several of Cathy and of the two of them together, including one of a campy French kiss taken in a fifty-cent booth at an amusement park.

If Russell hadn't already guessed the nature of

their relationship, he'd have no doubt once he saw the photos. Likely he'd take it as proof positive of her enthrallment to the devil, and who knew how that would twist and deepen his determination to save her from her sins?

This fancy leather envelope holding Russell's photos she found more than a little ostentatious. Plastic credit card windows were good enough for hers. She smirked, coughed to cover it.

But she couldn't hold on to her smugness when he confided proudly, "Alex gave me the photo pouch for Christmas last year. Ordered it from some fancy catalog. First present he ever bought with his own money."

Under the best of conditions, photographs were hard for Leila to see; the ones she carried were for showing other people, for occasionally touching like talismans. In this light, without contact lens or glasses—not to mention the spots and haloes and floaters starting to appear in her visual field from prolonged aridity—she wouldn't be able to make out much of anything.

She shook her head angrily and almost shoved the envelope back at him; after all, it was his fault she couldn't see the pictures. Then, petulance turning vicious, she started to pull the photos out, intending to throw them at him, maybe to tear them up.

Thinking better of it, instead she pushed the soup bowl aside and spread half a dozen pictures out on the tabletop. In the darker ones she could see nothing at all, not even shapes, but in three of them were discernible human figures with paler spots in configurations that could be faces.

She forced herself to gaze at them one after another, taking pains to bend close and tip them from side to side as she would if she really was examining them. Specific comments were too risky, so she made generic noises of appreciation—"Oh, how nice!"—whose blatant phoniness simultaneously repulsed and gratified her.

There must have been two dozen pictures in the envelope. When she'd pretended to look at all of them and carefully slid them all back under the flap, she took the chance of saying, "You have a great family, Russell. You must be proud," and realized, to her horror, that in fact she was feeling slightly less hostile toward the man who was, besides a dangerous fanatic, a devoted husband and father.

"After the Lord," he said simply, "they're the most important thing in my life."

"I can see that."

"I never thought I'd have a family of my own. I never thought anybody would love me the way Germaine and the kids love me." He took a breath and went on. "I was terribly lonely in high school. You were really the only person who was ever nice to me."

Leila shut her eyes and clasped her trembling hands between her knees under the table. Even so, her voice broke as she demanded, "So why are you doing this to me, Russell? Is this the way you pay me back for being nice to you?"

When for a moment he didn't answer, she dared to hope she'd gotten through to him. But then he stood up, leaned across the rickety table and took her face in his hands as if for a kiss. She braced herself, thought about spitting or biting. "Yes, Christina," he whispered urgently, shaking her a little. "Yes, exactly, this is what I owe you. A way out of your darkness and misery. A way into love and light."

"I'm not miserable!" she shouted at him, but sudden unwelcome doubt limned her voice; even she could hear it, and as a result her protestation was truncated, hollow.

Despite the good things in her life—Cathy first and foremost; to a lesser but still significant degree her job—it now seemed obvious to her that she was, in fact, fundamentally unhappy, had always been unhappy and was becoming increasingly so. For just a moment now, she entertained the notion that Russell somehow knew her better than she knew herself, that he could see into some core part of her that she would never before have thought to call her soul.

"I'm not miserable," she repeated, all but whimpering.

"Christina, Christina, Christina." It was an invocation. His hands on her face radiated warmth.

She held her breath until he let go, then sank back in her chair and pressed her palms against her cheeks where his palms had been. They were both breathing hard.

After a while he sighed and told her wistfully, "Stephanie has a band concert tonight. She's first chair flute. I've never missed a concert."

Leila softened her voice and did her best to look at him compassionately. "You're really close to Stephanie, aren't you?"

He nodded, and when he passed his hand over his eyes she wondered if he could be crying. Certainly his voice was shaky as he answered, "We're a really close-knit family, all of us. But Stephanie and I have always had a special bond."

Thinking of the sexy underwear he'd pilfered from Stephanie's drawer, Leila was suspicious of this "special bond." Was something unsavory going on between Russell and his daughter? Or merely—merely!—lust in the heart of the father? Was he hinting at a need to confess to her? And what would she do if he did? The more he talked the better, she decided again, although she wasn't sure how and her distaste was nearly physical. "Tell me about her." Leila couldn't imagine that he'd fall for this gambit; in his position, she'd disclose as little personal information as possible.

But Russell told her readily, "She's my firstborn. I've been present for the births of all my children, but Stephanie was the first baby I'd ever seen come into this world. I've seen a few miracles, but nothing compares to that, and I'm still not over it. But it's also because of who she is."

He stopped, and Leila prompted, "And who is she?" She made an effort not to sound sardonic.

He took a deep, happy breath. "She's bright and funny and immensely talented. She's interested in the wider world a lot more than you'd expect from a sixteen-year-old girl. She's generous and kind."

"And," Leila inquired, following an intuition, "does she share your religious beliefs?"

His sorrow was palpable, and Leila actually found herself feeling sorry for him. "No. She's turned away from the Lord. It is the tragedy of my life."

"What's she doing?"

He hesitated, shook his head. "What do you mean?"

"In what way has she turned away from the Lord? Drugs? Sex?"

"Oh, no, no. She's a good girl. But for the wrong reasons. She doesn't believe anymore. She doesn't accept Jesus Christ as her personal Savior. And without that, of course, she will not enter the Kingdom of Heaven." He cleared his throat, looked down.

Knowing it was unwise, Leila couldn't stop herself from arguing. "So, no matter what kind of life a person lives, no matter what good works they might do, they'll go to hell if they don't believe a certain way?"

"It's God's will that we live compassionate and loving lives. But entrance into His Kingdom isn't bought with deeds. It's a spiritual attitude. It's faith."

"And Stephanie doesn't have it."

He sighed. "Somehow we've failed her. I pray it's only a phase. And I pray nothing happens to her before it passes. I don't know how I could live with it if she was to die unsaved—" He stopped, unable for the moment to say more.

"It must be," Leila managed to say with a straight face, "a worry for you. I see a lot of parents who worry about a lot of things. It's hard."

"But there is also so much that's good," he hastened to assure her. "I only wish you could know the joys of family life, Christina."

"I do!" she'd protested before she thought.

There was an ominous pause of a beat or two before he informed her, "I saw the pictures in your wallet."

Leila was stunned. Had she imagined he wouldn't go through her purse? Her throat all but closed. Still she managed to launch into a giddy, desperate babble. "So you saw my kids. Aren't they great? Some of them are in college now. And I'm starting to have the children of the children I had my first years of teaching. Now *that's* a sobering experience!"

He gave a comradely chuckle. "Isn't it amazing? Everybody's so *young!* Doctors and judges and congressmen and preachers—they're *youngsters.*"

"Whippersnappers," she agreed, and laughed too loudly and too long,

"Your Big Five-oh is coming up, isn't it?"

For an instant she didn't know what he was talking

about. Then she gasped, "Oh, my birthday!" and pressed her knuckles to her mouth. Cathy'd been suspiciously noncommittal through all of Leila's coyly oblique references to her upcoming fiftieth birthday; suspecting a surprise party was being planned, Leila had been pleased and excited as a child. Surely, surely, she'd be home in time. *Please God,* she found herself thinking.

"September 10, right?"

She shuddered. "How'd you know that?"

"I remembered."

"You remembered my birthday? After all this time?"

"I remember a lot of things about you," he told her quietly. "I remember a sort of silky brown dress you used to wear. And I remember how you had to bend way over to see your papers on the desk, and your ponytail would fall in your face. You were so cute."

She started to breathe, "Jesus Christ!" but caught herself in time to substitute, "Wow."

He reached behind himself, apparently to the kitchen counter, and brought her purse onto the table. Its strap snagged his glass and Leila fervently willed the water to spill, but no such diversion occurred. He unsnapped the middle pocket and withdrew her mother's wallet, opened it, flipped through the credit cards to the windows that held photos. "Who's this?" He was holding it up, open to a particular photograph.

"I can't see it from here. I don't have my contact or my glasses," she pointed out testily.

"Oh, I'm sorry, Christina. Here." He worked the picture out of its sheath, as if he had a right, and gave it to her.

She didn't have to be able to see it to know it was of Cathy. She took it tenderly, laid it in her palm, bent her head over it.

Russell leaned forward. "That's the woman you live with. Who is she?"

"A roommate. A friend." It had been a long time since she'd had to obfuscate like that, and it felt like a terrible betrayal of Cathy.

"I saw you."

"What—"

"I saw you kissing her." He all but spat, ridding himself of the distasteful words.

"We're—*close* friends." High nervous laughter escaped her.

"What's her name?"

"Jezebel."

"Tell me about her, Christina."

"She's my slave. My *sex* slave. Everybody should have one. Anything I can think of, she'll do, and I have a *great* imagination. Sometimes she has ideas of her own. It's great, Russell. You ought to try it—"

He was on his feet. His chair crashed against the wall. The table teetered and something fell off, clattering. She stood up to meet him, ready to counter his attack with her own, ready to claw and punch and knee, suddenly confident she could best him and glad to have the chance.

But he took her in his arms. She brought her knee up into his groin; he gasped but held on. She pummeled his back with her fists, sank her teeth into his shoulder through the sweaty cloth of his shirt. He winced but did not retaliate. His embrace tightened, until she could scarcely breathe. He began to pray.

# Chapter Seven

A starburst of yellowish light strafed Leila's eye when Russell pulled open a dark door. Fondly and firmly clasping her upper arm, did he see it, too? Was it some kind of stage business to simulate a sign from God?

*Was* it a sign from God?

*Oh, stop that. Pay attention. Watch for your chance.*

Then she knew what it was. Her ophthalmologist had warned her about this. Too long deprived of moisture, her cornea was developing keratitis, a painful and rapidly progressive inflammation. The single earlier flush of rewetting drops had been too little too late. Unless she could get to a doctor right away, she risked losing what was left of her sight.

Primal, survivalist fury propelled her out of Russell's grasp. Twisting and ducking, she stumbled backward, caught hold of a pole she hadn't known was there, swung around it and lunged in what she hoped was a direction that would take her away from Russell and his crazy compatriots and into the public street.

Where there would, no doubt, be other sorts of dangers. Talk about out of the frying pan. What if her instinct for self-preservation was misguided? Maybe she ought to just stay where she was and see what happened. Startled by the appeal of that option (*Relax. Put yourself in someone else's hands. You know how to do that. Just do what you do with Cathy, only more so*), she faltered.

She couldn't afford to think like that. This might be her only opportunity to get away from Russell, and she had to get away from Russell.

She licked the tip of her little finger and touched it to the corner of her eye. This did bring relief from the dryness, but only briefly, and the pain and visual effects were unabated. From a streetlight or a warehouse security spotlight—she thought they were in a seedy warehouse district somewhere in lower downtown—light flashed across her eye again, the clearest thing she'd seen in years. The electric pain itself was all but visible and, jerking away from it, she collided with someone coming into the building. "Excuse me," she gasped, "I have to get out, I'm here against my will—"

"Easy, sister, nobody's going to hurt you." A full-throated female voice, small, soft, long-nailed hands over hers, heavy perfume that made Leila think *gardenia* although she doubted she'd actually recognize the scent of gardenias. The slither of something silky, almost slimy across her forearm; even as she understood it was a long fringed scarf, she thought *snake; snake handlers*, and her heart pounded.

"I *am* being hurt. My eye—I'm a *hostage*—" Why hadn't she rehearsed so she could make her situation clear in a few quick words?

"Of course you're hurt, sweetheart. Of course you're a hostage. We all are hurt, amen, we all are hostages, amen, without the grace of God, amen. You've come to the right place, amen."

Around them, from people she saw only as a fuzzy mass, rose "Amen"s and "Right on"s, but stimulating a response didn't seem to be the woman's intent. In her speech "Amen" apparently functioned as a form of punctuation, with no more emphasis than any other word.

Gathering herself, Leila grasped the stocky, padded shoulders and managed a shake, though the woman was considerably bigger than she was and her feet better planted on the floor. The small strong hands moved to her waist, gripping as if to hold her in place or to lift her up. "No!" Leila cried, as another stab of pain tore across the surface of her eye; this time unaccompanied by visual effects, the pain somehow seemed more awful, more intimate. "No, I'm not talking about that! I'm *his* hostage! Russell Gavin! He kidnapped me! At gunpoint!"

The big woman did glance to the left, where Russell must be standing, and her pressure on Leila's sides wavered, as though she might be wondering, considering. "Brother!" the big voice rang out. "Brother Russell, is it?"

*She doesn't know him,* Leila noted with surprise. Probably this changed things, but in what way?

Russell announced his name proudly, and the woman put it to immediate, cadenced use. "Brother Russell, Brother Russell Gavin, have you brought this lost child of God to us against her will?"

"Yes!" Russell declaimed. "Against her will, and against the will of the Enemy, which right now are one and the same."

Leila's first impulse was to parody, strike a wild pose or manufacture a fit as if of satanic possession. She thought better of it, then was tempted to deliver a passionate denial. But no one else seemed to find this public declaration of her alignment with the Devil shocking or even especially noteworthy. Other than a few scattered, all-purpose exhortations—"Father be with us!" "Jesus hear our prayers! "Oh Lord oh Jesus oh God!"—there was no reaction. They didn't turn into a righteous mob and rise up against her. They also didn't come to her aid.

"Sister Ardith, she's blind. I've brought her to be healed."

Now a murmur, more appreciative than sympathetic, buzzed from the asssembly. Pointlessly, Leila protested. Her voice, as clarion as she could make it, was nowhere near a match for Ardith's or even Russell's. "I am *not* blind! I have some usable vision! But I will be blind if I don't get to a doctor! What I need is medical care!" Her words, though accurate, were far less poetic than the way Russell and the others had put it, and she felt at a distinct disadvantage.

Through escalating discomfort of all sorts—physical, emotional, what she could only term spiritual—Leila struggled to keep her wits about her. The fact that Russell knew this imposing woman, although he wasn't known to her, suggested she was something of a public figure, perhaps someone with power to come to help Leila.

Ardith let go, but before Leila could squirm out of her reach, took her face in her hands. In the wrists laid against Leila's jawbone were strong, quick pulses, and the grip was both tender and firm. "Do you want to be made whole, sister? Do you want to see?"

"I *do* see." Light sparked in her eye, searing, and for a long moment she in fact saw nothing but the light. "I *am* whole," she insisted, but even to her own ears the declaration rang slightly hollow.

Ardith was looking at her closely, the way people did when they'd first noticed her eyes. "What's your name?"

Leila couldn't imagine why she hesitated, but the pause was long enough for Russell to step in. "Sister Ardith Ewing, this is an old and dear friend of mine,

Christina Luce. Christina, Ardith is a minister of this fellowship. I've heard her twice. She is gifted in the Word."

Ardith's nod was made to seem massive by the high black hairdo. The scarf around her neck reached well below her waist and glimmered. "Welcome, Christina. Worship the Lord with us tonight! Praise the Lord with us, and let us pray for you. You are safe from the Enemy here with us."

"Amen."

"Amen."

Russell's "Amen" was a passionate moan.

Ardith's fingers came to Leila's cheek and again she seemed to be appraising. Acutely aware of Russell's proximity and assuming he'd be monitoring her, wishing desperately that she knew whether he really had a gun, Leila tried to convey her desperation to the other woman by means of facial expression, telepathy, the look she imagined in her own eyes, all of which were almost equally theoretical to her. She couldn't tell where he was, exactly, or what he could see, but she risked mouthing, "Help. Help me. Help." There was a long pulsing moment. Ardith gave Leila's cheek a soft pat and started to turn away. Leila took a bigger chance and spoke in a whisper. "Please help me. He's holding me hostage. I need eyedrops and ointment. I need to get treatment. He won't let me have medicine." Even as she detested having to beg, she put everything she had into begging.

Ardith had turned back and now laid her finger-tips lightly on Leila's left eyelid. Amid distaste at being touched so presumptuously, Leila found a certain grim satisfaction in the fact that Ardith was ministering to the wrong eye, the one surely past healing, the one that had never hurt or seen. At the same time, she was strangely soothed.

"God made eyedrops, too," Ardith pointed out, and Leila's heart leaped.

Somebody murmured, "Amen." By now Leila had determined that this denoted mere aesthetic participation and not necessarily agreement, a sort of call and response independent of content.

Glancing triumphantly in Russell's direction, she couldn't tell whether he'd taken Ardith's point. In any case, nothing changed. Her eye was still painfully and dangerously arid.

Ardith and the others moved away, and Russell was trying to lead Leila somewhere. She pulled back. After a moment he seemed to decide, ludicrously, that offering her his arm might assuage her discomfort and make her feel more secure. She didn't take it. He said, "The service is about to get underway. Let's go sit down." Haltingly she started in the direction she thought the others had gone, but Russell said, "This way, Christina," and took up her hand in a tight grasp she didn't even try to break. When, knowing better, she actually relaxed a little once she'd surrendered to his help, she had a new and probably useless insight that this was the reason unsolicited assistance was so threatening under any circumstances: In the short run, it made things so much easier, but at an unacceptable price.

In a big warehouselike space, under unshaded bulbs high in the rafters whose pinprick light hurt her eyes even when she wasn't looking up at them, three long folding tables made an open square. Hymns from a tape or CD player somewhere had, she realized, been playing in the background all along; just now the volume had been turned up.

Most of the metal folding chairs around the perimeter of the tables were already occupied. Many people were singing softly along with the recorded music. Leila's knowledge of hymns was scant, but she'd have sworn some of the singers were humming or murmuring songs different from those being played, and for some reason that was stirring, disturbing. One rich contralto laid in a nearly subliminal line under the rest, like the heartbeat bass of an otherwise inaudible rock song.

Because Russell was propelling her faster than she usually moved, the collision of the side of her foot with a chair leg was hard and loud and caused her to stumble. Russell apologized disproportionately, and several people called, "Are you all right? Is she all right?" It wasn't the first time people who didn't know any better had fussed about the wrong thing.

Hastily she sat down in what she hoped was an empty chair, and Russell took the one to her left, where she couldn't see him without turning her head three-quarters of the way around. She could feel his body heat, though, and hear his heavy breathing.

He took her hand. She thought it was a bizarre expression of affection, or a way of keeping track of her, or something to do with the service, and she pulled out of his grasp. He took her hand again and pressed it into his lap. Repulsed, she clawed her fingers and waited for his hard-on to come within reach.

The cylindrical object she was forced to feel, though inside his pants and decidedly phallic, was metal rather than flesh. It took her a moment to realize it must be a gun. She had never touched a gun before. He wouldn't let her pull her hand away. He moved her palm along what must be the barrel, made sure her fingertips explored and identified the trigger.

Someone brought Styrofoam cups of water. "Here's a cup of water," Russell explained unnecessarily, even positioning her fingers around the cup. She recoiled, but she was thirsty, and the water, though tepid, eased her dry throat. She drained the cup, wanted more. Someone refilled it. Pressure starting in her bladder reminded her that she didn't know where the bathroom was, if there even was a bathroom in this place, but thirst won out and she gulped the water. A blade of bright pain slashed her eye.

She'd been led to expect Ardith to preach, but it was a man's voice that called, "Let us raise our hearts and our voices in prayer!" Out of the small crowd, she assumed, or from some hidden place in this building that functioned as backstage, he'd come to stand in the partly enclosed space created by the tables. No pulpit, no pews, no choir or organ or hymnals; he was dressed not in a robe or even a suit but in jeans and a denim work shirt, tennis shoes, hair tied back in a ponytail. Leila could tell that his feet were braced sturdily apart in much the same stance Ardith had taken, arms upraised, face uplifted.

Noisily Ardith pulled up a chair, making a place for herself between Leila and the cigarette-smelling man on her right. From the first whiff of gardenia perfume, Leila felt unreasonable relief, which made her realize she'd already come to regard the woman as an ally. Obviously this was another trick intended to keep her off-balance.

A really rather accomplished performance artist, the preacher was exhorting now. "Father, be with us tonight, amen, as we gather here in Your name, amen. Father, we lift our voices and our hearts to You in praise, amen, and in supplication, amen, that You may show us all the light, amen, and heal us all, amen." Nearly everyone was calling out, murmuring, chanting. The contralto had begun "Amazing Grace," and Leila found herself singing along, surprised by how much of it she knew and how compelling it was. It didn't take long to get to "I once was blind but now I see." Singing that, she flushed and cringed but finished the verse.

109

Even as her dread and revulsion grew, and comprehension of the magnitude of the danger she was in, Leila could barely contain her derision. Didn't these people realize how silly they made themselves, what easy targets for parody and caricature?

Cathy would have a field day. Leila almost smiled to think of it, though it made her ache for the comfort of that clear, confident world view; Cathy was so sure of things that it was easy to be sure, too, by proxy. All organized religion, even the paganism and goddess worship some of their friends espoused, Cathy vehemently and vociferously scorned, and Leila'd come—from no particular position of her own on the matter—to more or less agree with her.

So it was as much for Cathy as for herself that she stayed observant, collecting impressions to take home like souvenirs while at the same time being on the alert for information that would aid in her escape. She paid attention to the cadences of the preacher and his congregation, so she could recreate them for Cathy. She stored impressions of the room: the hard echoes; the sensation of being in a small, intensely self-referential group in a vast space; the damp-concrete smell; the peeling veneer on the table edge under her nervous fingernails. Inspired by thoughts of Cathy—who, of course, would never be in a situation like this, because she could see—Leila was fleetingly but sorely tempted to burst into a raucous solo, maybe "Yummy Yummy Yummy I Got Love in My Tummy" or "The One-Eyed One-Horned

Flyin' Purple People-Eater," both of which seemed relevant.

The preacher had sunk to his knees. "Oh, Lord, oh, my Lord, we ask Your help and protection, amen, in this sinful world in which we live. We give You thanks for our very lives, amen! We sing Your praises with every breath of our being, amen! We ask Your forgiveness of our sins, amen, and we ask Your blessings upon us, amen. Thy Will, Thy gracious and mysterious will, be done."

Ardith's thigh pressed against Leila's, transferring an electric trembling. Leila edged away, but Russell was close on the other side, and she'd rather be touching Ardith than him. Under the preacher's cries and calls, shouts and near-whispers, the woman was chanting in a language definitely not English. The rhythm of it seemed ancient and pre-verbal, or at least not commonly spoken; Leila thought at first it might be Latin.

Still on his knees and with clasped hands upraised, the preacher crawled sideways and began making his effortful way along the row of congregants. "Jesus, come into the heart of your son Walter, amen, who has been wandering lost and anguished on the streets of Gomorrah. Let him know he is not alone, amen, we are none of us alone."

A ripple of amens rose like mesh around his prayer. A man, presumably Walter, crooned, "Yes, Lord, oh yes, Lord."

The blur that was the preacher as Leila tried to

keep him in view moved to the right one place, where he pleaded, "Jesus, come into the heart of your daughter Betty Jo, amen, who needs Your intimate presence in her marriage bed." Betty Jo was sobbing.

His plan must be to work his way around, calling Jesus into the heart of each person by name and individual circumstance. Leila tried frantically to formulate something she could say to him when it was her turn, something she would whisper or scream, that would make these people understand what was happening here.

But Russell had a gun. He was crazy, and possessed by holy fervor. There was no reason to think he wouldn't kill anyone who got in his way.

The chanting from the woman beside her hadn't changed in pitch or volume or pace, but in some indefinable way it had intensified to a level Leila was finding very nearly intolerable. Was it Hebrew? Or some other biblical language—she flailed for possibilities—Sumerian? Corinthian? It hardly seemed like language. She thought of the Tower of Babel, barely remembering the story.

Longing to get away from it, Leila swiveled her head toward Russell, as if he was not a greater and more explicit threat. Her right eye blazed and burned. The eyeball actually felt swollen. Both eyes filled with tears. Not wanting to call attention to her weeping for fear someone would think it evidence that she was moved by the Spirit, she didn't wipe the tears away, and they left a fine dry crust of salt on her lashes and cheeks.

Through the extra film of the tears, which acted fleetingly and with much distortion like a magnifying glass, she thought she saw Russell's eyes closed and his fists clenched on the table in what she took for rapture. Maybe he was in some sort of trance, not entirely aware of this world anymore. Cautiously she began to slide her chair backward, wincing at the clatter of metal on concrete.

"Lord God, come into the heart of Your daughter Ardith, that she may surrender to Your will the life and soul of her beloved daughter."

Ardith's chanting did not alter. Fierce and focused, each syllable precise, it gave the overall impression of being vastly articulate although it was utterly incomprehensible.

Suddenly Leila realized what this must be. The woman was speaking in tongues. Was there a gunny sack of snakes in the shadows somewhere, too, waiting to be handled? Had it been only water in the cup? She shuddered, surprisingly unnerved by something she'd have expected to dismiss as simple sham.

Russell hadn't moved. She had slid her chair back far enough now to be able to stand up. Did she know which way the exit was? Were there steps in the way?

But the preacher had crawled to a position in front of her now, and he grabbed her wrists. "Jesus Christ, our Lord and Savior, we pray that You'll come into

113

the heart of our sister Christine tonight, amen, and, if it pleases You, heal her, amen."

"Christin*a*," she corrected him, and could hardly believe what she'd said.

The preacher drew himself up. "The Lord knows your real name, sister. Not to worry!" He let go of her wrist, but only to stretch out his hands, slightly clawed, toward her face. Because she'd shoved herself back from the table, he couldn't quite reach her. Having saved herself even that much gave her confidence.

Ardith was still speaking—praying, witnessing, performing, babbling nonsense. Russell was talking, too, but in English. Leila caught "unclean" and "an abomination in the eyes of God."

Wailing and gesticulating, the preacher swayed back and forth on his knees. At times he looked to Leila tall and bulky, imposing; then he'd disappear from her view entirely, and she guessed he must be prostrating himself on the floor, maybe even beneath the table. She tucked her feet safely back under her chair.

Because she couldn't pinpoint the source of the music, now blaring, it could have been coming from nowhere and everywhere—from the walls and rafters, from the wraparound city night, from another dimension. Shouts and what sounded like incantations rose and mingled like flames, and people were up on their feet or down on their knees.

Amid this rising, ecstatic cacophony, Leila was

afraid. The gathering fervor itself frightened her; a vague distrust of any fierce belief system was what had kept her from joining the anti-war movement in college and gay rights or feminist causes later, and this was already taking on a life of its own, a mob mentality. Cathy would say this was dangerous hokum. As usual, she'd be right. But she'd also be missing something.

Leila was most afraid of Russell, on his feet and crying out now as if the preacher were pulling something out of him. "Jesus Lord, reveal Yourself in the heart of our brother Russell, come to us from far away to fight the battle of his life." She was afraid of the gun. He seemed to be palming it now, almost openly. Did anybody else see it? Was she seeing what she thought she was seeing?

She was afraid of Ardith, who gave every appearance of being utterly transported by the nonhuman language she must surely be making up as she went along, hands gripping the edge of the table, body shaking. Afraid of the person she'd just become aware of squatting behind her, reeking of booze and garbage. Afraid of what was happening to her eye. Afraid to try to leave this place alone, but more afraid not to. Afraid of the gun Russell might or might not have, and how far he might or might not go to keep her here.

Russell had left his chair. She felt his absence as newly opened space beside her. She edged to the left so that she was no longer touching Ardith, pushed

Russell's empty chair away to make room for her knees.

Moved by something—maybe the impudence of a chastised child, maybe a parrotlike instinct for mimicry, maybe envy—she was tempted to leap to her feet speaking in her own set of tongues, knock her chair over, fall over Russell, join the preacher on the floor. She did stand up. Crowd noise and music rose with her.

Not daring to make her move until she located Russell, she squinted, tried to focus through three or four flashes like silent fireworks, like what she imagined bombs would look like in a murky sky.

Then she heard him in the space bounded by the tables, beseeching and praising the Lord with a vehemence that, if less than the total abandon of some of the others, was nonetheless a shocking departure from the reticence and control she'd so far seen in him.

Suddenly there was quiet. The taped hymns stopped. Ardith wasn't chanting aloud, although there was a rhythmic whispering that might be coming from her. The preacher's soft prayer and Russell's bleated amens stood out in raised relief. Heart pounding, Leila stood still.

Then, as if at a signal, three things happened nearly simultaneously: The music took up again with a huge cymbal crash, all voices in the cavernous room lifted in shrieks and moans and Leila's right hand fumbled against a section of wall that moved outward and revealed itself to be a door. Divine intervention or literal blind luck, she'd take it. She stumbled outside.

# Chapter Eight

"Urine-smelling alley" was such a cliché that Leila had trouble believing she was actually in one. Like so much else happening to her, this was wildly disorienting, and she had an urge to laugh incredulously. Creeping along, her eye calmer now in the dimness but her vision almost useless, she speculated a little giddily that this must be an odor all its own, recognizable as human excrement but with a particular edge to it, presumably from wet concrete and brick, saturated newspaper, anointed garbage. After this, she'd know the odor of alley pee anywhere. Now, there was a usable skill.

*Like snow unto an Eskimo,* she thought wildly, *so is piss unto a blind woman.* "Jesus H. Christ," she said, almost aloud, was shocked and shamed by the blasphemy spilling out of her mouth, then by the shock and shame themselves, which, until Russell, would never have crossed her mind.

Apparently this alley was narrower and more hemmed in than those in her neighborhood, for the quality of the air and of ambient sound was different. On at least one side, her left, was a solid wall considerably higher than her head; she'd sensed it well before brushing against it with shoulder, elbow, hip, though it remained completely invisible even when she was in continuous contact with it.

As if to catch her breath, though not from physical exertion, she leaned for long moments against the wall. Probably this was unwise, if Russell was chasing her. But he could just as easily be coming from the other end of the alley in order to intercept and trap her, in which case proceeding would turn out to have been unwise, too. Or she could have gotten herself turned around and be heading the wrong way, straight into his exorcistic arms. He'd say it was God leading her.

The need to know whether there was also a wall on the other side of the alley suddenly became urgent, for no good reason other than a visceral curiosity and some vestigial need for tactile symmetry. She had to talk herself out of veering to the right into open space bounded only by the cluttered and uneven pavement under her feet. She was disoriented already; if she did that, she'd be thoroughly lost.

The wall was sticky. Before she could stop herself she'd imagined several unpleasant reasons why that might be so. Touching it was repulsive, but she was reluctant to try maneuvering without it against the back of her hand. It hadn't been designed as a guide, of course, and there were obstacles—pipes and cables up the outside of the building, hard crumbling piles of what might be construction debris or just junk. She moved haltingly, though she yearned to run and, indeed, in every way but literal speed felt as if she were running. She moved in the way she'd always despised and struggled to avoid: shuffling, hand extended protectively in front of her, shoulders stiff, head unnaturally angled. Like a blind person.

She had no idea which way to go or not to, or how she'd know which way she was going, could think only: *away. Get away.* She wasn't even certain which way was "away"; she wouldn't have thought it possible to get turned around in an alley. Behind her, glad voices rose, and rousing music with a decidedly religious tone, telling her at least what to keep at her back.

Something scurried. She froze. Had she really heard it, was it really rats, or was this just another part of the cliché—after dark in an alley reeking of urine and garbage, there must of course be rats? She didn't hear it again. There were other noises.

Terror was only barely tamped down by almost unbearable frustration. She moved again in the direction that felt like forward, although the relativity

implied in such terms—forward, backward, sideways, up, down, in, out—was all but nonexistent
here.

A figure materialized out of the gloom more or less
ahead of her, distant and then, in a split second, close
enough to touch. Telling herself it was unlikely that
she'd be seeing something with even that much clar-
ity in this less-than-half light, she reached out, came
into contact with nothing.

What a stupid thing to do, she berated herself; her
first-graders knew better than to get close enough for
a stranger to grab them. This particular evolutionary
benefit of visual acuity hadn't occurred to her before:
it was considerably riskier to gather information by
means of touch than by sight. One more way in
which she was maladapted, a clumsy cow in the
china shop of life.

*Oh, please,* she scoffed at herself, but without
much effect.

The multiple-haloed figure had vanished, more
likely hadn't existed in the first place. Seeing something that flat-out wasn't there—which was to say,
hallucinating—was a new variation on not seeing
much of anything that was. Tempted to collapse and
give up under the weight of self-loathing and self-
pity, she kept going.

The alley seemed endless. She stumbled over
something appallingly soft, caught herself against
something that abraded. Was she bleeding? Did she

now have an open wound that would let contamination into her body?

The eerily joyful sounds of the prayer meeting had now been fuzzed over by nighttime city din. A siren yipped, and for a moment she listened hopefully, even prayerfully, but it wasn't coming to her aid.

The wall ended, though the alley did not. Apparently the building took up only part of the block; that was to be expected, of course, but she hadn't expected it. When her trailing fist plummeted into open space, she jerked it back hard and scraped knuckles against brick, flinched, flexed her fingers, groped for anything that might extend beyond the wall to keep her on course, approximate as that course was.

There was nothing. Her wounds stung. She curled both hands into her waist, imagining blood on Stephanie's white blouse. She took a deep breath and set out into the void.

Under her second step the pavement gave way. A hole, a gap in the asphalt and underlying dirt and bedrock—or just a change in the surface she was walking on—it threw her. Falling, she cried out.

She was caught, saved. Someone caught her. Arms around her, breath on her cheek. A voice, comforting and steadying, speaking in some sort of meta-language beyond or behind or under words. Moisture welling in her eyes: not just tears, though certainly there were tears, but also something stronger, more viscous; oddly, her mind played back her ophthalmologist's careful explanation of the normal lipid and musim layers her eyes all but lacked, the function of which was to make tears adhere instead of just rolling off and—in what seemed but was not contradictory—further drying the surface of the eye.

A visual image, hazy and featureless but in no way dim; vividly amorphous, brilliantly inchoate. Then, gradually, a face. Eyes, in which she could clearly, magically, see the look of enormous love. Golden brown, the first time in her life she'd ever seen for herself the color of someone's eyes; Cathy's eyes were brown, too, but she knew that only because she'd been told, because no matter how close she got she couldn't bring them into focus. Never having seen for herself how emotion showed that way, she wondered now how she knew that the expression in these brown eyes was love.

Then, nothing.

Nothing visual beyond disorganized flashes and pinpoints. No tactile sensations other than close gritty air, the uneven and shifting surface underfoot, discomforts in various body parts. No human or extra-human voice, only the roar of highway traffic far enough away to be all one sound, a blatting car alarm (which quickly stopped, meaning, she presumed uneasily, that someone was there), music with indecipherable lyrics from an open door or window.

Her extremities tingled from the near-fall. Her field of vision teemed with explosive light and color, but the relative absence of pain this time made the effect less threatening than revelatory, though she couldn't guess what it revealed.

Suddenly headlights were approaching from a confusing angle to her right and slightly behind her, where no cars ought to be. Unless she was no longer in an alley; maybe this was a parking lot or a street and she'd missed the transition. Or maybe Russell and Ardith and the ponytailed preacher were chasing her, cutting across and thereby corrupting the predictable grid of blocks and bisected blocks to hunt her down.

The car could be going anywhere, was going everywhere at once. Its headlights broke sharply across her vision, and the squawks of its horn were erratic. She didn't know which way to move to evade it, and panic took up the split second available for making a decision.

The car was upon her. Her entire visual field turned painfully white. Unable to protect herself in any other way, she shielded her eyes with her hand, but the glare slashed underneath; she shut and then covered her eyes, but the glare punched through.

Utterly in the open, she hunkered down and waited.

The headlights swerved off her; she felt their absence like cold. The car moved away, tires crunching, engine whining. Realizing she never had heard any evidence of a human being, she nonetheless struggled to her feet and raised her arms to hail whoever was there, now desperately not wanting to lose this potential rescuer. But the car turned a corner—what corner? the intersection of what and what?—and was out of sight and, more crucially, earshot.

She could stay here, wait for something that would help her decide what to do—daylight, Russell, an unknown attacker, an unknown rescuer, blindness, a reprise of the hallucination. Or she could keep moving in hopes of coming to someplace she recognized, if not in specific then at least generally—a major thoroughfare, an open store. Staying there was tempting because it required so little of her. Unsure what would be required of her by moving on, she moved on.

Warm wind had picked up. Trying to hone, instantaneously, the sensitivity of the soles of her feet so she could distinguish through shoe leather what she was stepping on—gravel, pavement, grass, dirt, garbage, the body of a rat, the body of a street person, Russell in wait like a gargoyle—she did perceive a dip in the surface that might signal the end of the alley at a street, and, for no good reason, she turned right rather than left.

An indeterminable distance ahead was a streetlight, pinkish, streaking and pulsating no matter how obliquely she peered at it. She pointed herself toward it, stumbled over what must be a curb, veered back up over it so as not to be walking in the street.

A car sped past, rap music thumping. She caught the word *bitch,* repeated again and again, part of the rhyme scheme, the basis for the contagious beat. Stopping and squinting, she saw the car turn through the mauve pool cast by the streetlight. So that must be an intersection, worth getting to. The urge to hurry returned, but increasing her pace even slightly made her feel too precarious so she slowed again, slid her feet over cracked concrete and weeds, found a chain-link fence to run her right hand along for a time.

Now she was at the intersection. This was a bigger street, more traffic, another stoplight off to the left at what must be the next corner and a configuration of building lights there that could be a convenience store or some other establishment open this late. Hope geysered hot into her throat. The single-block trek took a long time. With the wide street on her right and nothing particularly solid or continuous on her left, the sensation of exposure was nauseating and renewed a buoyant yearning for Cathy, for Cathy's plump elbow to grasp and Cathy's sure steps to follow.

A screech above and ahead sent her jumping back, heart racing. It took her a long few seconds to realize it wasn't another car bearing down on her but a metal street sign noisily swaying in the wind. She couldn't read the sign.

She could, though, tell when the light changed from red to green, one advantage of traveling after dark. Crossing the street and then a narrow parking lot, she tried to ascertain whether the fluorescent ceiling lights in the building meant it was open for business or were just for night security. Feeling acutely conspicuous, she went from pane to pane along the glass front of the building until she found a handle. The door was locked. With what felt like great courage, she knocked. No response.

Maybe there was a phone. Trembling, she felt her way from the door across the glass panels again, onto a smoother wallboardlike surface, then onto something rough and hard like cement block. At the end of the building she forced herself to go around to the back, though it seemed, illogically, far more dangerous than the not-much-more-illuminated front. She encountered pipes, and a head-height box that was probably something electrical, but no phone.

Able to move slightly more quickly the second time she traversed the territory, she reversed her path until she came to the other end of the building and, reluctantly but without pausing, turned that corner. Something attached to the wall at knee level—an air hose? A bike rack? No phone. To be thorough she ought to search the fourth side of the building, too, but she couldn't do it, and rationalized by telling herself it was unlikely there'd be a phone hidden away back there.

She pressed her back and her hands flattened behind her back against the glass and just stood there, agonizingly aware that by not moving she could be either increasing or decreasing the chances of being assaulted or recaptured. Suddenly, belatedly, she was physically exhausted. It wasn't cold, so maybe she could find a spot to lie down. The thought of sleeping out in the urban open shocked her, but dully through the fatigue and in context of everything else amazing that had happened to her in recent days.

She couldn't distinguish one place from another, couldn't reliably gauge whether here'd be any more comfortable or any more concealed than there, so finally she simply found something to lean against and sat down. The ground was hard but not especially pebbly or otherwise rough, and there was room to stretch out her legs. As she was settling into a crevice of sorts between one structure and another at her shoulder, her eye flared, and she gasped and covered it with a cupped hand.

The pain subsided. The flashes dimmed. She let out her breath and lowered her hand, leaned her head sideways into a hard structure that for the moment seemed welcoming. With a distant, amazed appreciation of human adaptability, she noted that she was actually drifting toward something like sleep.

"Amazing Grace" was playing through her mind. The melody was hypnotic, the words intensely poignant. "I once was lost but now I'm found." The broad allusion to her current situation should have made her laugh and groan as at a bad pun, but in this altered state of consciousness the song seemed personally profound, both sinister and appealing. "Was blind but now I see."

"Follow me and you shall enter the Kingdom of Heaven."

"Hey."

"I am the Way, the Truth and the Light." A gentle hand over her eyes like a warm, moist blindfold.

"Hey, bitch." A blow against her side.

Not sure whether she was actually awake but abuzz with adrenaline, she struck out with fists and feet against both intruders, connected with something. A boot came down hard on her instep. Her wrist was caught and twisted. She dug her nails into flesh, kicked the throbbing foot up into a malleable crotch, heaved herself up and ran.

She was on pavement, then not, then on a less stable and more cluttered surface, then on pavement again, all in a dozen irregular paces. Her toe stubbed hard against an obstacle, and then her other foot went off a step or ledge or curb, not a long drop but enough to jar. She made an effort to quell her distressed panting in order to listen for footsteps behind her, heavy breathing.

When she smashed into a chain-link fence—scratched her neck on the sullen fringe of twisted heavy wire along the top edge, bruised a knee against a post and bounced back with a grunt and a loud twang—she righted herself and slowed. If she was going to save herself, without help or guidance or anybody to hang on to *(oh, Cathy),* it would not be by means of speed or, for that matter, any physical attribute. *Brains,* she told herself, almost jauntily;

*brains, not brawn.* But, in truth, her mind was no better suited for this sort of thing than her body; teaching little kids reading-readiness skills was the most strategic planning she'd ever practiced.

Actually she was no more lost than she'd been before, but the sensation was of winding deeper into a labyrinth. One way and then another she turned, but each change of direction might be cumulatively canceling out those that had come before. She must be in the street now, because a car passed too close, and somebody yelled, "Get off the street, slimeball! We don't want to look at you!" out the open window, which almost made her laugh. Not until it was too late did she think of calling out for help.

Now there was something vaguely familiar about her surroundings. Wary of sacrificing vigilance to premature relief, she nonetheless let optimism rise as she thought she recognized a row of buildings, the flat illumination of a security light and the dulling and narrowing of sound, a door. Voices behind the door.

Waiting to receive more information, she stopped. Her eye blazed, went nearly blank. Russell put his arms around her from behind and cried out in praise, though certainly not of her. "Thank you, thank you, Father, for bringing our Christina home!"

# *Chapter Nine*

Russell had hold of her hair. "I am the Way, the Truth and the Light," he was chanting, and they walked to that rhythm, marched to it through dark places and places with steps. He had twisted her hands behind her and pulled them up too high so that her shoulders and wrists ached, and he was pulling her along by her hair, bringing tears. "I am the Way, the Truth and the Light. I am the Way, the Truth and the Light. I am the Way—"

"Let me *go!*" Wrenching sideways, she heard inside her skull the terrible sound of hair tearing from its roots.

His grasp on both her hair and her wrists tightened, in an almost friendly way, as if he wouldn't want to lose her, wouldn't want her to get lost. "I am the Way, the Truth—"

"God *damn* you! God damn you to hell!" It was

not an epithet she'd have thought to use before, but here and now it was exactly what she meant. She stuck her foot out in front of him and he tripped, but he didn't let go; she was pulled down and sideways, neck and shoulder muscles straining, scalp throbbing as if from open wounds. They didn't quite fall.

By now the cadence of his chant had acquired a certain infectious lilt. "I am the Way, the Truth and the Light."

To keep herself from mouthing the words, she demanded, "Where are you taking me this time, Russell?"

"You're not to know that," he told her sternly.

"Who says? God? Jesus?"

Not to be baited, he launched again into, "I am the Way, the Truth and the Light," as though to shield himself from some sort of temptation. For a few minutes they all but goose-stepped along to the grimly comic beat.

"Fine." The thought was like a voice in a thunderbolt. "Fine. Whatever. I give up."

She yelled, ducked and pivoted hard into him, leading with her elbow into his ribs. He grunted. His grip on her hair was not dislodged, and the pain at the roots cracked, the tendons in her neck pipped and sang like rubber bands.

They were walking much too fast. Although Russell held her tight, she felt as if she were careening out of control; she kept stumbling, flailing to right herself and not being sure whether she had or not, then lost her balance entirely, gave it up, so that Russell was the only reason she was on her feet. He forced her upright. He pulled and pushed her along, and in some peculiar kinesthetic way her body, at least, began to trust that he knew what he was doing, he would get them where they were going, he would keep her from falling or colliding with anything on the way. He would protect her from getting lost. She was not quite ready to surrender, but once she did, once she made that decision, she would not have to make any more.

She shoved her hip into his and twisted away, managed to loosen his grip on her wrists enough to ease the strain on her arms though she didn't come close to freeing herself. He yanked her hair. She cried out. "Hush," he warned her, and yanked again; the pain spread like flame across her scalp.

Surely there were other people on the street, walking or in cars or in buildings. Had no one noticed them? Could no one tell that she was in jeopardy here, being kidnapped, being held and maneuvered against her will? She took a chance and called, "Help! Help me!" before Russell moved his hand to the back of her neck and squeezed.

"*I* am the Way the Truth and the Light," he muttered fiercely, with a slight sinister alteration of the emphasis and the rhythm. He shook her once, hard, and it was clear to her that he could and would break her neck if he did not have other plans for her. It was also clear, chillingly, that this was nothing personal; it was not she herself—Leila Blackwell or Christina Luce—whom he intended to destroy, but the Devil in her.

For a scintillating instant, she considered believing he was right. Satan was a literal presence, a monster of almost but not quite the highest and deepest order, who could take up physical residence inside a person's heart. God was a supernatural being in whom one could take up residence. Satan was simple, unalloyed evil, literal and real, in no way symbolic. Jesus was pure goodness, metaphorical only in his human guise. A person could choose. A person could make one choice: follow Satan or follow Jesus. Serve evil or serve goodness. Travel in darkness or travel in the light. One decision.

*Christina Luce.* She placed the name in her mind. It glowed and hummed, and she thrilled to the knowledge that it was hers for the asking. *Christina Luce.*

"Christina," he began.

"Leila," she insisted, but her heart wasn't in it. *Leila Blackwell* no longer applied to her, and she couldn't yet claim *Christina.* Her ears rang with the horror of having no name, and her eye blazed with invisible fire.

Russell had stopped chanting and made no other attempts to address her directly. She could hear him murmuring, and his breath came hard and fast. Praying, she supposed. Speaking in tongues. She was pierced by a yearning to *understand,* to be included, to be able to contact a higher power like that. *Teach me. Take me.* It was as though some consciousness not her own, some other will, had injected the supplication into her mind, but once it was there it seemed like her own.

"Here we are." They turned sharply left.

They had not gone far enough for this to be the same house, and she was certain, though she couldn't have said how, that they'd have turned right if they'd been going there. Exorbitant confusion made her want to stop, at least hesitate, but she was not allowed. There were steps where there shouldn't have been steps, a door opening in instead of out, but then the space into which she was propelled did smell familiar, an odor very much if not exactly like the body odor, so to speak, of the house where Russell had held her captive.

He let her go to shut and lock the door. She just stood there. He laid a hand on either side of her head, and for a terrible moment she thought he was going to kiss her and braced herself for it, thought frantically about biting, about meeting his tongue with her own. He held her face and looked at her for a long moment. Her eyes hurt and she closed them; in the minimal light, she couldn't have met his gaze anyway. He slid his hands down her jaw and neck to her shoulders, where they paused, caressed, shook her a little. Then down her arms to her wrists, to her hands; her flesh cringed and tingled in his wake. He took her hands. "This way," he said softly, and she wondered why he wasn't using her name.

Down more steps, these steep and narrow and, she could tell, unlit. A basement, by the dank and dirty smell of it. A cobweb trailed across her mouth, softly sticky. There were noises, the suggestion of noises that stopped when she turned her attention to locating and identifying them. Through what felt like a maze but might not have been. Past what felt like hands and tails and teeth but could not have been. Into what felt like hell.

"Russell?"

"Hush," he whispered, as if not to disturb someone or not to give himself away. He managed to pat her back while still bending her wrists up almost to her shoulder blades. Comfort in the midst of inflicted pain. Out of suffering and despair, the hope of salvation.

Sharp bright pain flowered in her eye. Instinctively her hand jerked to cover it, but Russell held her fast. She moaned. The candle had gone out, or had been moved or moved of its own accord outside her very narrow range of very dim vision, and she could see nothing at all now, not the walls pressing in on either side of her or the lowering ceiling, not Russell beside and behind her, not her own feet taking her to her doom, not whatever lay ahead of her, though she was sure something did. Maybe she'd lost her last tendrils of vision. Or maybe there was no light down here, and Russell had no need to see. Something was going to happen. Something was being prepared.

Russell sank to his knees. She had no choice but to fall with him. He straightened and steadied her so that she was kneeling and her hands were joined with his in front of her now, his arms around her. The surface under them—floor? Ground? Substratum?—was both hard and pliable, layers of filth over concrete, of sediment over bedrock, of sin and temptation over Truth. The juxtaposition of the two sensations was somehow especially awful. Her eye blazed with dry fire. She thought she was going to be sick. Softly, Russell commanded, "Pray."

Thinking he was announcing what they were going to do next, she waited. Her knees were already beginning to hurt. He'd let her hands drop slightly and the pain in her shoulders had lessened, for which she was intensely grateful.

He prodded her, a sharp object into her side that was probably nothing more than his finger but that frightened her, made her cry out. "Pray, Christina."

"I—I don't know how." It seemed a terrible thing to admit.

"Pray for your sight. Pray for your soul. Tell the Lord what you will do to get your sight and your soul back."

"I don't know how. I don't know how to start. I don't know what to say. I don't know—"

When Russell took his hands away from her, she was shocked. She swayed and trembled in open space and actually reached out for him. He lit a candle and set it down in front of them. She could see only the flame itself and the haloes her damaged eye created out of it; there was no illumination of anything else. The flame swelled, and its companion flames, whose existence resulted entirely from the abnormality of her retina; was it accurate to say that the halo flames didn't exist, when she perceived them more clearly than just about anything else? The smoke was thin and sharp as braided glass. There was a minute sucking sound, as the fire gulped air. She thought almost reverently of the fire hazard; if the fire caught and spread—if someone knocked the candle over; if the fire was passed from the wick to some larger flammable thing in a symbolic religious ritual, if the flame took it upon itself to grow—there would likely be no escape route that she could find. Would it be accurate to say there would be no escape route, if it was not accessible to her?

Russell's voice came from a lower angle now, and she knew he was kneeling, although that wouldn't have been something she'd have thought of under other circumstances. "Christina," he exhorted. "You have to pray."

"Why?" she stalled. "Doesn't God know what I want? Doesn't He know what's in my heart?" Her voice was hoarse and hurt as she forced it out.

"He wants to hear it from you."

*How do you know?* she thought, but without conviction; in truth, she had almost no doubt that he did.

Clumsily, never having done this before and curiously ill at ease, she got down on her knees. It was an unnatural position. Hoping her awkwardness would not be taken for parody, by Russell or by God—or, for that matter, by Satan, whose reputation as an opportunist even she was aware of—she clasped her hands in front of her and bowed her head. She was seized by a terrible fear of doing something wrong. "What—how do I start?"

"Address Him. Say His name."

She was not sure she could do that. Naming something carried a power and a powerful acquiescence that rendered her unable to speak. *Blind and dumb,* came the hysterical thought; *What's next? Deafness? Loss of my sense of touch?* Indeed, it did not seem to her that she was feeling the basement floor under her knees and shins the way she should be, or the pain in her eye; she was hearing a cacophony that could be everything or nothing, and her nasal passages were blocked so that she could scarcely breathe let alone smell.

"Call him Father," Russell instructed.

"Father!" burst out of her. "Father, help me!"

"Tell Him what you'll do if He does."

"I will renounce evil! I will renounce Satan!" She doubted she'd ever used the word *renounce* before; how did she know to use it now? How had she come to be conversant in such matters as evil and the devil? She was sure she didn't believe in any of this, but saying the words and making the motions made her tremble with what she could only assume was awe. "I will ally myself with the forces of light and renounce darkness! I will follow Thee!" She had never used the word *thee* before, either; it had a strong, meta-language quality.

"And your name?" Russell prompted.

"My name!" This was hard. This was the test. She gathered herself and cried, "My name shall henceforth be Christina Luce! Leila Blackwell is dead!" *Oh Cathy*.

"Praise the Lord!" Russell moaned, and then all but screamed. "Praise the Lord! Praise the Lord! Praise the Lord!" until he was not speaking those or any other ordinary words but something else, some language beyond language, and Christina was transported.

She longed to speak like that, in tongues belonging not to her or to anyone else but God, to address the Lord directly like that without intervening interpretation or nuance. "Praise the Lord! Praise the Lord! Praise the Lord!" she chanted and murmured and shrieked along with Russell, matching cadences and tone to his as best she could, but she wasn't pulled over into that next realm. *That will come later. Have patience*. The promise came to her like fire, and it did seem possible that she'd been spoken to. *You've taken just the first step. There are many more.*

After a while she realized that Russell was no longer praying with her. When, with considerable effort, she quieted herself, there were no voices in the space she occupied, human or otherwise. The candle seemed to have been snuffed; the darkness was utter and far more terrifying than she'd have expected, given that she lived in near-darkness all the time. She held her breath and listened. Nothing. She reached out one hand and then the other, very cautiously, and encountered nothing. No walls. No crawling or nibbling sounds now; silence thick and layered as if it had once been inhabited but was no longer. No human being: no body heat, no odor, no sound of breathing or of footsteps overhead. No god or devil. She was, apparently, quite alone.

Would she die here, or be reborn? Would she go blind, or for the first time in her life receive full sight? Would she emerge transformed, or never emerge at all? Was there any possibility of escape? What would she be escaping to?

*Cathy.*

Who wasn't here. Who didn't even know where she was. Who surely could have found her by now if she'd really wanted to. Who maybe wasn't even looking. Whose love for her, if it existed at all, might well be proof and emblem of—

This was absurd. This was outrageous. *This* was proof and emblem of her own weakness of character; had Russell already broken her down, brainwashed her, shaken her faith in the things she knew to be true? Or was it God who'd done that, some petulant god, determined that nobody else could have her love if He couldn't?

She dropped to her hands and knees in what might

have been taken for an attitude of obeisance but was, definitely, not. Her well-tuned mechanisms for culling information from the environment, whether or not it turned out to be useful, went into operation now, and she gathered that the floor was more likely hard-packed dirt than concrete, the space she was in was bigger in circumference than the span of her outstretched arms but not by much, the ceiling was thick and low and somewhere there was an open exit that minutely thinned the air.

But she could not find it. Bringing to bear a fierce concentration, she employed every technique she'd ever known or imagined: used auditory and tactile cues. Crawled, stood and turned very slowly in place with arms outstretched, edged in what she thought was one direction and then a few degrees in what she thought was another. She could find neither the walls that confined her nor the opening she knew was there.

She was not alone.

She stopped breathing, held herself absolutely still. She sent her mind out past her pain and fear and disorientation in time and space and need to escape and need to stay here forever, in under her own heartbeat and longing for Cathy and was immensely aware of another presence, here, in this basement room; here, in her life as far back and as far forward as she could fathom. Beyond evil or good. Beyond dark or light. Simply infinite. Simply eternal.

She was not alone.

And then she was. Then the presence vanished, or absorbed itself again, or hid from her in plain view, or had never existed at all outside her overheated mind. She was alone.

# *Chapter Ten*

"Thirsty."

"Thirst for the Light, Christina."

"Thirsty."

"Thirst for the Truth."

"Water."

"Christina. Christina Luce."

Long silence. Hours, days.

"Hungry."

"The Word will nourish you when you choose to take it in. The Truth is sustenance enough."

Long absence.

"Hurts."

"The suffering of the flesh is as nothing compared to the eternal suffering of the soul in the fires of Hell. It is as nothing. Nothing."

"Oh, God. Hurts."

"Oh, God, oh, God, oh, God, oh, God, oh God oh

144

gonomone moricabanay ilium ilianum moravis."

"God! Please! God! It hurts!"

"Ama amada amadane dama ane intilbe."

"Help me! Please, help me!"

"Christina Luce."

"Christina Luce."

"Christina Luce."

A third voice? Was that a third voice?

"Christina Luce."

"Yes, yes, my God, I'm here."

# *Chapter Eleven*

"Christina, wake up. We're having company for dinner tonight. We have preparations to make." He was buoyant.

She stirred. *Where am I? Who is this man, leaning too close over me, smelling of chewing gum, pushing at my shoulder as if he had a right? Who's he calling Christina?*

"Come on, sleepy head, up and at 'em. You've been napping all afternoon. It's time to get ready. Ardith will be here soon."

She groaned and fumbled for something to cover her head, blanket or sheet or pillow, found nothing and realized none of her body was covered, except by underwear and a shirt that had bunched up under her. She sat up. Her eye hurt. Her head swam. She tugged the shirt down as far as it would go, which was not very far. "What?"

146

Russell was bustling now somewhere out of her range of smell and touch and certainly sight, in the far reaches of the small stuffy room. "Here, put these on for now." A loose bundle landed on her lap— pants; she felt the zipper, the inseams. "We'll get cleaned up after we get the house in shape."

"What?"

"Get dressed."

"Russell—"

"Get dressed. We only have a couple of hours, and there's a lot to do."

Struggling into the pants, which seemed to be ones she'd worn before and smelled filthy, she demanded, still groggily, "What are you talking about, company? This is bizarre."

"Ardith's been a servant of the Lord a lot longer than I have. I invited her over to help with our project."

There was no hesitation or other sign that he knew how surreal his choice of words was. She snorted. "You mean, like a home-improvement project?"

Russell laughed delightedly and clapped his hands. "Yes! Christina, yes! A remodeling, a renovation, a restoration of the home you are offering to the Lord!"

"I'm sorry I brought it up."

"Ardith's a nice person. You'll like her. There's cleaning and cooking to do."

"What are we doing, playing house here?" But she

was sitting up on the edge of the bed, waiting for her head to clear.

Together, they cleaned house. She kept thinking how crazy this was, and waiting for a way to slip through the new pattern of activity and escape, but Russell never let her leave his side. They did everything as a team. After a while, peculiarly, she got into it; there was something satisfying, soothing about scrubbing the kitchen counters until at last they weren't sticky, concentrating on sweeping the floor by use of a mental grid so that she didn't miss a spot, imagining caked dust disappearing under her lemon-sprayed cloth. Russell felt it, too. He was whistling something which, though it was probably a hymn, had a catchy melody; she had to actively resist the impulse to hum it herself.

Together, they cooked. He chopped the vegetables and diced the meat, and to her protest that she was perfectly capable of doing that, she did it all the time at home (*what am I doing? Why do I give a shit what he thinks of my competence?*) he replied that he didn't want her to hurt herself. Also, of course, he didn't trust her with a weapon even as puny as a paring knife, and with good reason. Her job was to put the ingredients in a pot and cover them with water.

"I bought spices," he told her, rummaging in a paper bag, proud as a child. "Onion salt, garlic powder, marjoram and anise."

"Anise?" She guffawed. "For beef stew? Anise is licorice."

"Well. I didn't know." He sounded a little miffed.

"And onion powder or flakes would have been better. Keep the sodium intake down."

"Oh." She'd hurt his feelings, and she felt bad. This was becoming truly surreal.

Reaching in his direction, she located the spice bottles in his hands and took them from him. "It'll be okay. I won't use the anise, but the rest will work. We could have used some sage."

"Sorry."

"It'll be okay."

"I bought some rolls at the bakery. I'd have got the brown-and-serve kind, but I didn't know if the oven worked." She cringed. It was a point of honor with her and Cathy always to make things from scratch. "And," he added with an audible flourish, "brownies for dessert."

"You thought of everything, didn't you?" She meant it sarcastically, but he took it as a compliment and thanked her shyly.

With the stew simmering, already filling the stale, shut-up-too-long little house with good smells, Russell said, "Ardith will be here in an hour or so. I told her six o'clock, and she's always early. So you and I better get ourselves cleaned up now."

"If it's all the same to you, I'd just as soon look like what I am," she told him grimly. "A captive."

He ignored that. "Come on. Let's go take a shower."

"*A* shower?" She stumbled after him as he tugged at her hand.

"We'll shower together. I know better than to leave you unsupervised. Unless I tie you up, and I don't want to do that all the time."

"Russell. Trust me on this. I am not going to get into the shower with you."

"You can't see me anyway, so it doesn't matter. And I've already seen you." Expecting a chortle or some other salaciousness, she bristled, and was thrown off when none came. His back to her, he began taking off his clothes.

"Russell, this is—"

"We don't have time to debate it. We don't want to be in the shower when Ardith gets here."

"Why not? Because she might think it was crazy? Or immoral? Or disgusting? I can't imagine why anybody would think that, can you, Russell? I mean, *everybody* takes showers together in order to save their souls. *Everybody*—" She could not avoid seeing the wan globular scallops of his buttocks. Her throat tightened to hold down nausea. She stopped and caught her breath. "What if God restores my sight all of a sudden while we're in the shower?"

He swiveled to face her, holding the bundle of his dirty clothes in front of his crotch. Even without it, she couldn't have seen anything as detailed as his penis, but she turned her eyes away anyway, then pointedly brought her gaze back and stared. There was a pause while, apparently, he considered her suggestion, and ribald disbelief nearly made her laugh out loud.

Then he gathered himself together and became decisive again. "Christina, you have a choice here. You can get undressed and get into the shower with me, or you can take a shower with your clothes on. Which is it going to be?"

"I'm not getting into the shower with you. I'll wait here in the bathroom. I won't try to escape." But she would, of course. Already she was figuring when would be the most propitious moment to dart out of the bathroom—when he'd just gotten into the shower? When he was soaped and shampooed? Not now, not yet; she edged toward the door while the noise of the water changed as he adjusted the temperature.

Then he grabbed her. Ready for him, she wasted no time. She slammed her knee up into his groin. He yelped and doubled over. In the narrow space between the shower and the toilet, his chin came down on her shoulder. She tried to tangle her hands in his hair, but it was too short, so she seized his ears and twisted. Again he cried out, and, in an overheated sort of way, she noted that even under these circumstances he didn't swear. Largely in reaction to his abstinence, she let loose a stream of profanity as obscene and sacrilegious as she could make it, pairing the Lord's name and graphic sexual references in numerous creative ways.

This, she realized too late, was the wrong strategy. It energized him. He butted his head into her chest and forced her back against the wall, then slid one arm under her knees and the other under her arms and tossed her into the shower. They both fell on the slippery, loose tile. Her screams of rage and his grunts echoed. Managing to get up onto his haunches, he squirted a huge dollop of shampoo onto the top of her head. Soapy water streamed into her eyes, stinging like fire.

Once she gave in, her self-consciousness and outrage were diluted by the simple pleasure of getting clean. Russell made no lascivious moves. She turned away from him when she stripped off her soaking clothes but really didn't much care what he saw. He handed her a washcloth and soap and she luxuriated in lathering her body. She felt almost playful. She had the crazy impulse to sing.

She washed and rinsed her hair twice and was starting on a third time when he took the shampoo bottle away from her. "Hey," she protested, "I'm not done with that." He shut off the water, and abruptly the oval enclosed by the shower curtain turned into a vaguely threatening space. She backed away from him, her heel knocking over something that sounded like glass breaking on the tile floor. She half-expected him to come after her, but instead he pulled open the shower curtain, letting in unpleasantly cold air that she knew was cold only by contrast. Goose-flesh rose, and she tried to cover her breasts and genitals with her arms.

He stepped out. She thought she'd stay in here as long as she could, hiding. "Hurry and get dressed," he ordered, handing her a thin, unclean-smelling towel. "Ardith will be here soon."

In fact, neither of them was dressed when they heard a knock at the front door. She deliberately slowed down, thinking that a state of obvious dishevelment might tip Ardith off that something was wrong here. Russell's breathing quickened as he rushed to fasten his clothes, comb his wet hair, tie his shoes. The knock came again. "Get dressed," he hissed at her. "Your clothes are hanging on the hook on the back of the door. Get *dressed*," and went out, leaving her unsupervised and unbound.

Suddenly she wasn't sure she could get dressed without help. At the same time, she was immediately thinking about escape. Clambering up onto the toilet seat, which was loose, she could just reach the single small window with her fingertips and determined that it was constructed of four glass bricks, utterly unopenable.

The house must have a back door. If she moved fast, without taking time to get dressed, she had a slim chance of finding it while Russell was answering the front door.

Nightmare images welled up of being out in public naked *and* all but blind. Could she do this?

153

Russell pushed the door open and whispered, "Don't try anything tonight, Christina. I'll have the gun the whole time."

That decided her. Heart thudding, breath ragged, she felt with careful haste for the clean clothes Russell had set out for her—a T-shirt she might even have chosen for herself; pants and a complete set of frilly underwear, including a bra. The underwear would go on quickly. While she put it on she tried to envision the layout of the house, of which she had only the vaguest impression, and to choose which way she should try on what would surely be her one chance before Russell got back. The enormity of the risk nearly made it impossible for her to choose at all, but she forced herself to ease the door open a finger's width, still not sure which way she'd turn but committed to making a choice, right or wrong.

The door didn't creak when she pushed it open enough for her to squeeze through. She heard Ardith and Russell exchanging pleasantries, quite as though she were merely a dinner guest.

"We're blessed that you could come this day."

"I'm blessed that you invited me. What smells so good?"

"Beef stew," Russell told her proudly.

"Really? I wouldn't have guessed beef stew. It smells wonderful."

It all sounded so normal that for a disorienting moment she wondered if she could somehow have misinterpreted all of this. Of course she hadn't. She was the captive of a crazy person who'd just brought in another crazy person as reinforcement. This might well be her only opportunity to get free. The hall felt narrow, although when she reached in front of her she didn't touch the opposite wall. She strained to sense which way lay an escape route, in the unlikely hope that there'd be a difference in the quality of the stuffy air or the ambient sound in the direction of an outside door, but there were no clues. Flattening her hands against the wall behind her, she took a deep breath, pushed off and turned left, instantly convinced the exit lay to the right but with a sinking heart knowing it was too late to change her mind now. She moved as quickly as she could along the corridor, her pace still maddeningly slow, fearful of steps and dead ends and of being caught. Fearful, too, of finding herself outdoors, free and at a terrible loss as to how to get herself home.

"Please," came Russell's voice, closer, louder, booming, from someplace she couldn't pinpoint so that it seemed to be coming from everywhere at once like the voice of God, "make yourself at home and I'll let Christina know you're here."

Heart in her throat, she took a single rushed stride forward and banged into a wall. Too late to cushion the impact, she put her hands up and came into immediate contact with the palm-wide ridge of a door frame, a loose scarred-metal doorknob with a dead bolt turned to the horizontal in the middle of it. Her hand was shaking and the bolt was stiff, but she managed to get it vertical and turn the knob. The door opened easily. Fresh air swept in, a bit of a breeze, the fragrance of rain on pavement. It was not quite pitch black out there; she could discern variations in the darkness too slight to be called light or to help with navigation, but enough to make navigation seem possible. Holding on to the door jamb, she stepped over the threshold, grunting as her foot hit the ground sooner than she'd anticipated, feeling with hands and feet for obstacles and markers without slackening her pace.

Russell caught her by the back of the neck. "Christina, Christina, Christina," he admonished, shaking her a little. "You can't go out in public half-dressed like this! And besides, dinner's almost ready and our guest is waiting."

He didn't hurt her. He didn't really even force her. Later she would go over and over that moment, that quick succession of moments between knowing he was behind her in the doorway and standing in the bathroom getting dressed under his palpable gaze and the glint and click of what he assured her was a gun. What if she'd bolted? What if she'd screamed? With Ardith there, how far would he have gone in order to hold her? Why hadn't she tried?

The bra was a size or two too big in the cups and too tight around the chest, made for an altogether different body type. The lacy, beribboned, bikini-style panties came too low under her belly and too high on her thighs; she knew she'd be squirming in them all evening. The pants were too long and too tight around the waist; she left the button undone. The T-shirt fit well enough, though it was tighter than she'd have liked. "You look nice," he said. "Let's go."

"Where's a comb?"

The ensuing silence caused her to wonder if asking for a comb was against his crazy set of rules somehow, or if he hadn't understood what she wanted. She was about to repeat the question when he said, "Here," and she realized he'd been holding a comb out to her, his hand and the object in it below her field of vision. What else might he be doing in what he'd think was plain view that she'd be missing altogether? She took the comb. Its teeth felt encrusted, and she grimaced, but she ran it through her wet hair anyway, not even trying to do anything but keep it out of her face.

"You look lovely," he said. "Let's go."

"You lead. I'll follow. That's easier for me."

This was her standard way of getting around, allowing her to watch people's feet, if they were wearing light-colored shoes, and tell when there were steps or corners or obstacles. But of course he wasn't about to trust her. "No. You go first."

Though she'd always been bad at judging distances, she knew it couldn't have been far from the bathroom to the living room; this was a small house. But getting there seemed to take an eternity. What was she so cautious about? Falling? Getting lost?

Appearing handicapped? She inched along, shuffling her feet and holding a hand out in front of her like a cartoon sleepwalker. Every now and then she'd find herself stopping altogether, and Russell would nudge her in the small of the back with something hard, and she'd jump forward, every time, as if she didn't expect it, as if it really was a gun. Which it might be, but she couldn't imagine that he'd really shoot her, especially with Ardith in the house. Whether because of the threat or simply because, in the long run, moving ahead was preferable to staying with Russell in the narrow corridor, she did eventually emerge into the living room. She didn't know where Ardith was until the other woman spoke and came to her.

"Christina, hello. It's so good to see you again." Her hand was taken and encased between Ardith's. Redolent with waxy perfume, very black hair high and stiff, a gaudy purple and silver scarf draped in some complicated way over her upper arms, the woman occupied much more than her share of space. Repulsed, Leila pulled away.

Russell was nervous. "Come on into the kitchen. Dinner's ready. I think." He laughed.

Ardith took her arm. Such a gesture from someone she scarcely knew was always presumptuous; under the present circumstances, it was downright aggressive. She pulled away. Ardith exclaimed, "Careful!" and Leila stopped, having no idea what she was to be careful of, inhibited more by the imprecise warning than if Ardith had said nothing. Some insubstantial piece of furniture, which would hardly have caused injury even if she had stumbled over it, was moved out of her way. "Okay," Ardith advised. Leila proceeded. Ardith hovered, quite as though Leila had never moved in this place before and as though a mistake would be catastrophic. She couldn't restrain herself from putting a guiding, protective arm around Leila's waist. Leila jerked away, and Ardith, misinterpreting, exclaimed, "Oops! Be careful!" and took hold of her again.

This was more than an annoyance. This felt like a matter of survival. Ordinarily she might capitulate, allow her right to self-determination and her carefully developed operating systems to be compromised by persistent misguided "help" in order not to appear petulant, not to create a scene. Under these circumstances she couldn't afford to lose any more ability to function, and creating a scene might be just the thing to do.

Placing a firm hand on Ardith's wrist, she removed the other woman's arm from her. "Don't do that."

"I'm just trying to help—"

"I get to say what's helpful to me. That's not helpful. I get to say what I need."

Ardith could not quite give it up. "I'm afraid you'll fall. I'm afraid you'll run into something."

"Believe me," Leila said pointedly, "that's the least of my worries at the moment."

Ardith chuckled as though she'd made a wry little

joke, and Russell broke in with, "Let's eat, ladies, shall we?"

There followed an hour or so of surreal charade. Ardith said the stew was delicious, and Russell preened; Leila could hardly taste it. She could not drink the weak coffee he made, though he pressed it on her. It was Ardith who kept the small talk going, and a few times, out of a ludicrous politeness or an even more ludicrous desire to be included, Leila found herself tempted to join in, particularly when Ardith made a point of addressing a comment to her. But she concentrated on making her distress obvious, hoping Ardith would notice and wonder. She said very little. She ate almost nothing. She mouthed "Help" at Ardith when it seemed to her that Russell might not be looking.

At one point he took her hand under the table. It was so much the way she and Cathy often held hands that at first she mistook it for a bizarre expression of affection or we're-in-this-together camaraderie, and disgustedly she shook him off. But his hand was back immediately, tight around her wrist, guiding, insisting. Was he really going to put her hand on his crotch? She half hoped so; she'd squeeze his dick as hard as she could and see how well he could maintain his pleasant facade. But it was the gun he wanted her to feel. At least it felt like a gun, hard, the right shape. He forced her index fingers to what must be the trigger, though she wasn't certain, having never touched the trigger of a firearm before.

Then he let her go to pour Ardith a second cup of coffee.

As he set the full cup down, bitter aroma and a small thud, he finally declared his intentions. "Ardith, we asked you here tonight because we need your help."

"And here I thought it was for the pleasure of my company." The husky voice carried a hint of something like pique, although she was smiling.

Russell went right past that. "The Spirit of Infirmity and the Spirit of Deception are on Christina. They are too strong for me alone. Will you help cast them out?"

"What?" Leila sputtered. "Wait—"

Ardith said, "That would take some thought and some preparation. It's not something you just rush into. The Enemy is strong, and he's no fool."

"Oh," Russell said, "I know."

"Have you seen Satan, Russell? Have you encountered his demons?"

There was a pause, and then Russell said softly, regretfully, "No. I know they're present among us, but I have not seen them."

"Oh, you have," Ardith assured him. "We all have. You just haven't been aware of it. You have to be careful. You have to read and study the Word. The Enemy's slippery. He assumes many forms."

"Christina," Russell informed her, "lives in sin."

"We all live in sin, brother," Ardith answered

readily. "That's human nature. That's why Jesus lived and died."

"Christina is"—he could hardly say the word—"*homosexual.*"

There was a pause, and then Ardith said, very sadly, "The Word teaches us to hate the sin and love the sinner."

Leila spoke up. "I'm lesbian. I love another woman. We've been together a long time. We love each other. How can that be wrong?"

"Homosexuality is an abomination in the eyes of the Lord," Ardith explained gently. "The Word is really clear on that."

*Abomination* was not a word Leila had often used, and in her rather vague construct of a Higher Power, which was rapidly becoming clearer as a result of her forced proximity to Russell, it seemed highly unlikely to her that God, whatever that was, would take any notice of her sexual orientation. Unlikely and offensive in a way she could only call spiritual: A God who cared about such things—a God referred to as "who," a personage, a God understandable in human terms—wouldn't be worth worship.

To Ardith's reasonably inflected declaration, Leila could come up with no response more cogent than, "Oh, please." This seemed an egregious betrayal—of Cathy; of herself; of her sense of God that was emerging in this place, against her will and certainly against Russell's—but it was the best she could do, and anyway the conversation had gone on without her, a debate over her eternal soul that had nothing to do with her.

Her eye had started to hurt again, a deep ache instead of the surface sting she was used to. When she became aware of the nature of the pain, it already seemed to have been going on for a long time, and quickly it claimed nearly all her attention, so that the exchanges between Russell and Ardith—statements, exhortations, appeals by the sound of them; explications with no context she could identify and nothing by which to orient herself; arguments that made no sense to her from one side or the other—came to seem like speaking in tongues. Her eye hurt. Deep in the socket, deep inside her head, her eye hurt. What did this mean? What might it reveal or portend?

"Christina?" Ardith was speaking loud and close, as if her hearing were also impaired. Ardith's breath smelled of spearmint. "Christina, would it be all right if I laid hands on you?"

"What? No!"

"Christina—" Russell began sternly, but Ardith cut him off.

"We don't force people to God. We show them the way. We invite them. The rest is between Christina and God."

Russell insisted, "She is marked by the Devil. Look at her eyes."

There was a pause while, presumably, Ardith did so. Her eyes pulsed. When Ardith spoke again, there was a new, cautious quality to her voice, at the same time that she spoke very firmly. "The Devil has many disguises, Russell. He's clever. If we don't really listen to what God tells us, we can easily be fooled."

Russell subsided, though not willingly; Leila imagined he was only biding his time. To her, Ardith now assumed the form of an ally, and, although she knew this might well be a deception, she felt herself leaning toward the charismatic, kindly woman, silently begging her for help, silently pledging some unknown commodity as barter.

As if in response, Ardith spoke to her again. "Christina. May I pray for you?"

Could this hurt her in some way? If she gave permission, what would she be acceding to? If she denied permission, what would she be missing? Nothing, probably, to both questions, but it seemed an important decision, and one utterly without context. She hesitated, then finally said, "I guess," and Ardith took that as agreement.

"Thank you," Ardith breathed, her voice breaking in such gratitude that Leila feared she'd bestowed on her an unintended gift. "Russell, shall we pray?"

Russell and Ardith knelt at Leila's feet. The urge to join them on the floor was strong, but she resisted it. Not entirely coherently, she thought if they were transported by prayer and she stayed alert, she might be able to escape. She sat on the edge of her chair and planted her feet firmly on the floor.

"Oh, Heavenly Father," Ardith began conversationally, as though talking to a friend. "We're just here to ask that you heal your servant Christina." The words and phrases quickened, became richer and more tangled. "We ask that You lift from her the Spirit of Infirmity and take her to Your bosom." Her voice rose and deepened until she was joyously beseeching. "In the name of Jesus Christ Our Lord and Savior, we ask that You make Christina whole!" and all three of them cried out.

# Chapter Twelve

"Oh my God!"

Russell, chanting and swaying with his hands constantly moving but always somewhere on her, Russell started.

"Oh my God, I can see!"

On his knees, Russell rose over her and took her face in his hands. His hands were sweaty. He was breathing hard from the physical and spiritual strain of having been praying over her for so long.

"Heavenly Father, oh, Lord, in the name of Jesus Christ Our Lord and Savior—" his prayer—nonspecific now and jumbled, but still words, still not over the edge into tongues—intensified as he brought her face very close to his to peer into her eyes, which with great effort she managed to keep wide open.

Her right eye writhed as if under the brilliant blue of an ophthalmologist's exam, and even her left eye, which seldom reacted to anything, burned and twitched. Wildly, she imagined it growing before his eyes, swelling to normal size and shape, at last filling out the socket.

"I can see!" she whispered. Her mouth tasted awful and she knew her breath must smell as bad. She blew it into his face and he did not flinch. "Jesus Christ our Lord and Savior, I can see!"

For what must surely be most of a day or night, they had been working with what Russell called "The Word," never "the Bible" or even "Scripture." He'd hold up a placard on which he'd painstakingly inscribed a verse or two about blindness in particular or the work of the Devil in general, and wait, every time, for her to tell him she couldn't see it. Then, sorrowfully, he'd read it to her:

Be strong, fear not, behold: Your God will come with vengeance, even God with a recompense. He will come and save you.

Then the eyes of the blind shall be opened, and the ears of the deaf shall be unstopped.

Then shall the lame man leap as an hart, and the tongue of the dumb sing. For in the wilderness shall waters break out, and streams in the desert,

And the parched ground shall become a pool, and the thirsty land springs of water. In the habitation of dragons, where each lay, shall be grass with reeds and rushes.

And a highway shall be there, and a way, and it shall be called the Way of Holiness; the unclean shall not pass over it, but it shall be for those. The wayfaring men, though fools, shall not err therein.

No lion shall be there, nor any ravenous beast shall go up thereon, it shall not be found there; but the redeemed shall walk there.

And the ransomed of the LORD shall return, and come to Zion with songs and everlasting joy upon their heads; they shall obtain joy and kindness, and sorrow and sighing shall flee away.

She'd be required to recite the passage back to him. "Not to me," he corrected her. "To the Lord." Memorization had always come easily for her, but now fatigue, anxiety, hunger, sleep deprivation and the incredibly high stakes all combined to make it nearly impossible. She'd stumble. Her mind would go blank. Thinking she knew exactly what to repeat and how, she'd make a mistake, every time.

Yet the words—the Word—did have an appeal that disturbed and drew her. The evocative, often lush imagery did set her blood racing. The yearning to be made whole in the eyes of the Lord—and to know not only what *whole* was but also what and who and where the Lord was—resonated for her in a place she had never acknowledged. The direct cause-and-effect connection between righteousness and physical healing did make horrible, wonderful sense.

How God anointed Jesus of Nazareth with the Holy Ghost and with power; who went about doing good, and healing all that were oppressed by the Devil; for God was with him.

"Oppressed *of* the Devil," he corrected her, and made her say it again.

The drill had been going on all day. She had the impression that it was before dawn when he'd tugged at the wrist-tether to get her out of bed; she'd not been asleep, exactly, but inertia had been pressing her into the mattress and her arm tied to his had been dead weight, from lethargy rather than any overt resistance. "Rise and shine, Christina," he'd cheerily cajoled. "We've got work to do."

She'd mumbled, "Work?"

"Holy work. The Lord's work. Come on, come on, lazy bones. Up and at 'em." Vaguely, she'd been impressed by his dedication to the cause—which was, in some weird way, her.

He had not mentioned breakfast, and when, some time later, she'd announced her hunger and thirst, he'd paid no attention. The ambient light had brightened and the temperature and outside noise had gradually increased while they'd worked and worked, so she'd known time was passing. She'd been weak and dizzy. Her eye had crackled.

169

It must have been mid-afternoon when she heard herself say, as if from a considerable distance:

Happy is he that hath the LORD of Jacob for his help, whose hope is in the LORD his GOD;

Which made heaven, and earth, the sea and all that therein is; which keepeth truth for ever;

Which executeth judgment for the oppressed; which giveth food to the hungry. The LORD looseth the prisoners;

The LORD openeth the eyes of the blind; the LORD raiseth them that are bowed down; the LORD loveth the righteous;

The LORD preserveth the strangers; he relieveth the fatherless and widow; but the way of the wicked he turneth upside down.

Russell had let out his breath and punched the air. "Yes!" He'd hugged her, and she'd been appalled by the rush of pleasure she felt at having pleased him. "Yes, Christina, you did it! Good job!"

"So now can we stop?"

"How's your eye?"

"It hurts. It's dry. I need eyedrops."

"How's your vision, I mean?"

She'd blinked, looked around, winced. "The same. No miracles."

He'd sighed in disappointment and weariness. "Then, no, we can't stop."

"Russell, I need to eat something. I need water."

"Fasting helps us to achieve direct contact with the Lord, because it goes against the flesh, which is where sin resides."

"Passing out from hunger and dehydration won't bring me to spiritual enlightenment. Trust me."

"Tell you what," he'd told her, slyly. "When your sight is restored, you may eat and drink."

"But I have no control—"

"You do, Christina. You do. That's the whole point. Give your heart and your soul to God, and you shall be healed."

And Jesus stood still, and called them, and said, What will ye that I shall do unto you? They said unto him, Lord, that our eyes may be opened.

So Jesus had compassion on them, and touched their eyes; and immediately their eyes received sight, and they followed him.

"Oh my God!" she screamed again now. "I can see!"

Russell's trembling made her head shake and her ears ring where the heels of his hands pressed too hard. "Praise the Lord," he began to murmur, then to chant and then to declaim. "Praise and honor and surrender to the Will of God!"

"Praise the Lord!" she echoed, hoping she was getting it right, the cadence and inflection, the attitude. She risked elaborating: "Thank you, God, for now I see!"

Russell was weeping. Thus encouraged, her own tears readily welled and sobs rose from deep in her chest. Russell moved his hands from her head to her shoulders and pulled her to him; she held on to him, and for a long moment the two of them wept in each other's arms.

Then Russell said, "Read this."

She didn't immediately understand what he meant. Momentum established, she kept on crying and shaking. "Praise the Lord! Oh, God, praise the Lord! Praise the Heavenly Lord!" She could feel that the words were trembling on the brink of exalted nonsense, and it was quite possible to believe that she herself wasn't uttering them at all, that she was only a conduit, only a vessel, only mouth and eyes.

Then through the fervor came the realization that he had taken one hand away from her shoulder and was holding something up. It must, of course, be one of the placards on which he'd inscribed the Bible verses that she'd been required to memorize. But which one? Which one? Suddenly she could remember none of them at all, and the jumble of words and phrases that rose in her mind seemed to have no way in.

The blind receive their sight, and the lame walk; the lepers are cleansed, and the deaf hear; the dead are raised up, and the poor have the gospel preached to them.

172

And blessed is he, whosoever shall not be offended in me.

In one terrifying motion, Russell stood, bellowed and struck her in the center of the forehead. She fell backward and off the sagging couch onto the floor. He knelt over her, hands everywhere, rancid breath everywhere, voice and words everywhere. "Demons! Satan's demons! In the name of Jesus Christ and all that is holy, I command you to leave this woman! I command you to set her free!"

Nothing happened. Nothing left her that she could tell or that he acknowledged. But Russell was on a roll.

Through the days and nights that followed, she fell backward and sideways a lot. He hit her. He pushed her. Railing and panting, he'd grasp her head in both hands as though he meant to twist it off her neck, pressing his thumbs into her forehead as though to punch a third and fourth eye through her skull, then wrestle her down. She'd scratch and kick, sink her teeth into his flesh until she could taste blood, scream obscenities and blasphemies and prayers, but he was impervious. He murmured and shouted and came close to something like singing. He fell with her to the floor.

"Slain in the Spirit," he called it, and in the spaces in between attacks, when he paused for breath and held her more calmly though no less firmly, he explained to her that this was a miracle, how lucky she

173

was to be receiving God's love in this way, how any minute now the demons would flee and Satan would be vanquished and her sight would burst open. Then he'd come at her again, and it got so that, at his first touch or the instant before, she'd sometimes collapse of her own volition or out of a mutated instinct for self-preservation, and then he'd fling himself down beside her, lay hands on her somewhere and give soul-felt thanks.

In the midst of the actual and imminent physical violence, hunger and thirst gradually asserted themselves, and then rapidly became more critical than any other threat. Russell hadn't eaten or drunk anything either since this siege had begun, and she guessed he'd probably lost track of such trivialities in the midst of his all-consuming higher purpose. Once when he came at her, she found herself screaming in his face, "Russell, Russell, food! Listen to me! Food and water!" but it was as if she were speaking in evil tongues, Satan's meta-language; if anything, his fury intensified, and his blow—from a closed fist this time, surely—made her head spin.

She flung her arms around his neck and pulled him down with her, and for a while they lay there, catching their breath. Her ears rang. Her headache was fierce, the bright pain in her eye like blood-red strikes of lightning.

But hunger and thirst were the most immediate threats to the life of the organism, and without any conscious decision she began to work her way toward the kitchen, where primitive awareness told her both could be slaked. She crawled. Russell put his weight into her back and flattened her onto the gritty floor. She struggled to her feet, dizzy, and took a step in what something like instinct told her was the right direction, making it a point to fall that way when he pulled her feet out from under her.

"Hungry," she gasped. "Thirsty. Please."

"We must fast and pray," he told her. "Fast and pray. Fast and pray. Fast and pray." With obvious effort he stopped the preseveration and took a shallow breath. "Fasting works against the flesh, which is where sin abides."

"Hungry. Thirsty. Please."

"No food or drink shall pass our lips," he pledged, "until God restores your sight. That shall be our sign." He hugged her. Her body recoiled, then collapsed against him. "You're not alone, Christina," he told her breathlessly. "I'm with you every step of the way." Then he was on her again, shrieking at the demons, out of love for her and love for God doing his best, sacrificing himself to cast them out of her.

Her eye flared with light and pain. There was a certain awful beauty to it and, crying out, she thought this must be what it meant to see the Devil, or God.

# Chapter Thirteen

She knew she was dreaming. In the dream she knew that it would be a nightmare and that she could wake herself, but it was the first time she'd been aware of dreaming in this place, and she stayed with it. In fact, she started to awaken but dreamed she took herself back down into sleep in order to receive the dream.

*A medical waiting room, flat shadowless fluorescent lights, rust-colored chairs arranged in crisscross rows like hatch marks for keeping score. She is waiting. Across the room, which is both cavernous and claustrophobic, a distraught young man is being examined—head tipped very far back over the rust-colored chair so that his throat is exposed, but it isn't his throat they're interested in, hands gripping the open wooden squares of the chair arms, and she can see in detail, though from this distance she shouldn't be able to, his eyelid folded up and the intimate or-*

ange of the socket in which his eyeball with its wild brown iris bobs like a barely tethered balloon in the viscous sleet of his tears.

The man is Jesus. Her heart breaks because Jesus is weeping, not for the world but for himself, for his own pain and fear. Jesus is afraid. She could help him, soothe him. In the dream she means to go to him but goes somewhere else, and she understands that the young man is Satan looking like Jesus, looking like no one in particular.

It's the doctor who is Jesus, the doctor who will see her next. He straightens in his white coat and pats the shoulder of Satan-as-sobbing-young-man. Could Jesus-as-doctor be unaware that this is the Devil in disguise? Is it up to her to warn him? But then she sees—this is the right word, although it has nothing to do with vision—that it's the doctor who is the Devil, and she was right the first time; the young man is Our Lord and Savior Jesus Christ, not yet come into His own.

Satan-as-doctor tells Jesus-as-patient something she can't hear. The only way she knows it's bad news—knows the doctor has spoken at all—is by the young man's reaction. He screams. He wails and sobs, slides down in the socket-colored chair until his lanky legs reach across the flat gray carpet almost to Leila's own feet. He keens, covers his eyes; his pitiful peaked knuckles tear at her heart. She can't believe Jesus would act like this, but there's no question now about who this is.

*She thinks to comfort him, but now it's her turn. The doctor, whom she knows and has trusted and thinks now may be just a doctor with no underlying meaning, behaves as if they've long since agreed on the procedure he'll perform today, right now: He'll remove her eyeballs from their sockets, without anesthetic so she's awake and alert to give him feedback. (Unless she can do it herself? Take out her own eyes, lay them out for inspection on the metal tray? She'd have to be very careful, but other patients have done it with good results. No?) The reason for the operation isn't stated, and she has the sudden awful thought that she's misunderstood, been tricked, agreed to something she didn't mean to. Maybe she's the wrong patient, or he's the wrong doctor or not a doctor at all, Jesus or Satan instead. Then she remembers: This could give her full sight.*

*But the prospect of pulling out her eyes and laying them on a tray while still attached into their shiny red-orange sockets terrifies and sickens and, somehow, offends her. She tries to refuse. The doctor ignores her. She struggles to imagine what she might see with her eyeballs outside her head like that, and admits to a certain curiosity. Revulsion and fear are much stronger, however, and again she tries to refuse, but it's clear she no longer has a choice in the matter. The doctor, whoever he is, approaches her brandishing something sharp, gleaming, precise.* Already trembling from the dream, she woke to Russell stroking her hip.

She'd been asleep in the cellar. She ate in the cellar, too; he brought her meals he'd lovingly prepared—Dinty Moore stew because he remembered, although she didn't, that she'd adored it in high school, had scarfed it cold out of the can; Hostess cupcakes with the squiggles on top and the cream inside; bananas and grapes. He fed her, when he could have let her starve.

She prayed in the cellar. She wept in the cellar. She eliminated in the cellar, intensely relieved when he brought the two-pound coffee can he'd saved for this purpose, touched by his solicitousness when without complaint he took it away. She washed in the cellar—soapy washcloth he hurried to get to her while it was still warm, basin with warm water for rinsing, thin clean towel. He combed her hair. He helped her change her clothes.

The pain in her eye was constant now, as if a fine saw blade never stopped slicing across it, and pus drained out of it like slow, thick tears. There might also be blood; sometimes it felt like blood and there was a faint bloody odor, but she didn't quite have the nerve to taste it, which was the only way she'd know for sure. She could see nothing.

Constant, too, was her supplication to God, loud as a voice in her mind or whispered by her own lips: *Heal me, Lord, amen. Restore my sight, amen, and make me whole. Show me Thy will, oh Heavenly Father, and give me the strength to surrender to Thy will. Amen. Amen.*

She didn't know how long she'd been here. It didn't seem very long. It seemed forever. Sometimes the memory of who she'd been before Russell came into her life filled her with fiery longing, which she recognized as impure even as she wept and wrapped around her misery. Sometimes she really could not remember what that life had been like. She missed Cathy intensely, although Cathy was almost illusion, no more or less real than Leila Blackwell, whom she also missed. She was no longer Leila Blackwell, certainly, but she was also not yet Christina Luce, and so she was no one, and the cellar was the right place for her to be.

She'd become accustomed to Russell's hands on her, in much the way one can get used to unpleasant, even poisonous air there's no choice but to allow against the skin and deep into the lungs. He touched her whenever he felt like it—whenever, she'd thought bitterly, the spirit moved him. Not surprisingly, he was touching her even more since her aborted escape from the prayer service (three nights ago? It felt both longer ago and more recent than that, and light and darkness through curtained windows had been dislodged from what in theory she knew to be their cycle, and the watch with hands she could feel when she couldn't see them was, though remarkably still on her wrist, stopped). At any moment he'd be pressing the small of her back to guide her around the tiny house whose every pathway and obstacle she knew with awful certainty by now,

steadying her wrist when he handed her something—
a cup of water, a plate of food, a huge-lettered placard of Bible verses—as if without assistance she
wouldn't be able to locate objects in space, grabbing
her elbow to help her over the uneven floor that of
course hadn't changed since they'd been here. All
that had more to do with power and control than
with concern for her; she recognized it from its less
sinister permutations in what used to be everyday
life.

Given the circumstances, she could see why he
didn't dare let her out of his sight or his reach. When
they went out for groceries, he kept hold of her hand,
as if she were an untrustworthy toddler or a new
bride or what she in fact was: a captive. They slept
in the same dirty bed, wrists tied together, and more
than a few times during the fitful nights their flanks
or knees would rub against each other. She'd given
up trying to shrink away; sometimes, out of what
seemed autonomic or primal need, her body would
of its own accord curl toward him for solace, until,
remembering who he was and what he wanted and
why it was she needed solace, she'd cringe and vow
to stay awake and on guard the rest of the night.

But this time his touch was different, and her habitual vigilance, ratcheted up countless notches since
she'd been here, now spiked sky-high. Her body
went rigid. Her mind instantly cleared of dreams and
of any hypnogogic state. Pressing herself against the
scabrous wall, as far away from Russell as she could

get, which was only a matter of inches, she demanded loudly, "What do you think you're doing?"

"Hush." He spoke softly, but the imperative was unmistakable, as was his excitement. He was wearing only boxer shorts, and heat radiated from his mostly naked flesh. She didn't have to see or—disgusting thought—come into physical contact with his erection to know it was there.

His fingers slid just under her waistband, and furiously she imagined him imagining this scene while buying the pajamas for her. The flesh of her lower abdomen contracted and tingled, and she found herself wishing she were cleaner, shaved, had on fresh clothes, didn't smell unwashed.

Then, deliberately turning the thought around, she hoped she'd be out-and-out repulsive to him. She slapped at his hand. "Knock it off, Russell."

He eased closer to her and put his hand on her breast. She twisted and scratched his forearm. He pinned her to the bed long enough to wind the rope taut between his left wrist and her right one and bend her left arm back under her so that her own weight was used against her. "Don't fight me, Christina," he advised huskily. "Don't fight the Will of God."

She fought. She brought her knees up into his groin but was too close to get any force into it. She tried to bite the side of his head that was pressed against her mouth. Failing to do more than scrape her teeth through his dirty hair, she took as deep a breath as possible and screamed into his ear. The only effect was a fleetingly gratifying wince. She arched her back and bucked under him, heaved herself up in an attempt to roll them both off the bed.

He simply proceeded. At first he was tentative, and she wondered viciously how long it had been since he'd touched a woman sexually, so much of his ardor—and, from what he said, of his wife's—having been redirected toward Jesus and God.

But it didn't take him long to get into it. Gently he kneaded one breast and then, shifting his weight slightly, the other. He brushed her nipples with his palms. Cathy did that. Her nipples betrayed her now by rising, only slightly but doubtless enough to encourage him. He made a noise in his throat and raised up on his elbows to gaze at her in some sort of passion, obviously in preparation for a kiss. His breath smelled strongly of mouthwash; he'd prepared for this.

Taking advantage of the small, momentary space he'd unwisely allowed between them, she butted the top of her head hard up into his chin. His head and upper torso jerked back enough for her to push herself out from under him and scramble off the foot of the bed, arm outstretched numbingly as she made rapid circles to unwind the leash. The floor was gritty and splintery under her bare feet. "What are you doing, Russell?" Hearing herself on the edge of hysteria, she did her best to harden and deepen her voice. "So is rape a weapon in God's battle for my soul? How handy for you."

He rose like a spirit from the gray bedclothes, bent at an odd angle because of the tether, and all but vaulted to her. She felt the pressure on the rope give way; she saw his thin white knees. Then he had her in what might have passed for an embrace if her arms hadn't been pinned.

Though she snapped her head violently back and forth, he ground his mouth against hers in a parody of a lingering kiss. Chillingly, he reprised, "I won't hurt you." She tried to spit into his mouth, then bared her teeth under his hard lips.

He pulled back enough to proclaim, "The Lord has shown me how I am to bring you back to the normal and holy relations between men and women, as prescribed for us in The Word." This was a lot to say under these conditions, and he was nearly out of breath, a dangerous buffoon.

She kicked at his shins, stomped her heel down hard on his instep. He grunted but didn't release his grip. He was taller than she, but thinner, probably lighter. Surely she could fend him off. She jerked an arm free and grabbed a handful of his hair, pulling his head sharply down and sideways. "You think I've never done it with a man? You arrogant asshole, you think I need you to show me the light?" Thoughts of men she'd slept with flew through her mind, most not until this moment unpleasant, and of Cathy. *Cathy.*

"Yes," he hissed. "Yes, yes, that's exactly what you need." Flinging herself to one side, she lost her grip on his hair. "Homosexuality is an abomination in the eyes of the Lord," he thundered, and threw her onto the bed. His forearm slammed across her throat, while his other fist punched between her thighs to spread them. She was shrieking in fury, and he was chanting what could only be a battle prayer, "Oh Lord my God oh Lord my God oh Lord—"

Having never before been in a true physical struggle, she had no idea what maneuvers to try. But she gambled that Russell wouldn't know much more than she did; though he might have roughhoused with his brothers when he was growing up, she doubted he was a practiced street fighter or sexual assailant.

His full weight was on her, pressing down the full length of her body and then some. He was stroking her face and, incredibly, crooning. Stifling the instinct to flail and twist and spit, she instead forced calm and then the semblance of erotic response as she opened her lips under his.

Almost shyly, his tongue slid into her mouth. As if in a truncated caress, she lifted the hand tied to his, so that both their hands were in her hair and then, when he moaned and flexed his arm, in his.

She was aware in herself of an appalling instant of sexual arousal—electric pulsing through the mound of her pubis, ragged breath—before she clamped her teeth on his tongue as hard as she could.

He gave a strangled yelp and jerked back. She held on, this time putting his own motion to work against him, and when he did manage to free himself she was tasting blood. He rolled off her, wrenching her shoulder and, she could only hope, his own, before he got the rope unwound enough to create some slack.

They were both panting. Then they were both sobbing. He sank onto his knees at the side of the bed like a small child saying his prayers. Though she was hot and already covered by pajamas, she struggled to get the bedclothes over her, between her body and his. The rope had painfully abraded her wrist and was sawing at it again. Both eyes burned through the tears.

Forehead pressed against the disheveled sheets, Russell followed the cord and grasped her hand. Anything she did to get away from him would be temporary at best and wasn't worth the effort. He was far more upset than she was; he was distraught, and she, though shaken and angry, also pitied him. What must it be like to have one's consuming faith exposed like this as a fraud? Doubtless he'd really expected her to give in to him, had fantasized a sexual encounter impassioned and purified by holy love. Love of God. Love for her.

Their fingers had intertwined. Both of them were holding fast. "Help us, Jesus, give us strength, give us courage against this formidable foe."

# *Chapter Fourteen*

A calm set in. A routine developed. The cellar underneath the rundown, closed-up little house began to feel as much like shelter as prison, although it still was prison. She knew it was.

Even the crackling, oozing pain in her eye came to seem almost comforting in its familiarity. She was aware of having developed a ticlike squint and head jerk in response to the erratic slash of pain; this already seemed habitual, even basic to her personality, and therefore reassuring. If the pain went away she wouldn't know how to be in the world, like someone chronically depressed reacting with more trepidation than relief when the depression lifted, or a long-suffering partner leaving after the alcoholic sobered up because "she's not the same person anymore." Even the thickening visual blur and the eye damage of which it was doubtless symptomatic were only to be expected, her lot in life, her destiny.

She and Russell were getting to know each other. He was not someone she'd want to know in any other time and place, but under the circumstances it was a good thing, at least useful and sometimes an almost pleasant way to pass the time. Within their shared reality—profoundly solipsistic, at the same time bigger than either of them and beyond their control; absurd in any wider context but with a nice, clear, satisfying internal logic of its own—they had begun to understand each other.

Their attunement was, in fact, more subtle, intense and immediately rewarding than she'd ever experienced with anyone else. Even Cathy, who sometimes became preoccupied and didn't hear what she said; even Cathy, who sometimes misread or misinterpreted. Even Cathy.

By his posture and demeanor, by his voice, she'd come to know when Russell was especially missing his family. At those times she'd try to take advantage of his distraction to shift the balance of power between them or to better her situation by loosening the wrist tether, commandeering more of the grimy top sheet, changing stations from the talk radio he mostly listened to. She and Cathy had long derided these shows, but she had to admit there'd actually been a few interesting discussions since she'd been forced to listen. She'd never admit that to Cathy.

He dismissed the jazz she and Cathy liked as nothing more than strung-together discords, and, embarrassingly, the pieces she happened upon were in fact so jangly and discordant that they made her nervous, too. Cathy'd have pointed out how the sax and the keyboard complemented each other, how the bass wove it all together, but Cathy wasn't here. They compromised with Christian rock. Amy Grant and a band named Basket weren't half-bad.

By now, too, Russell had told her enough about his family that she almost missed them herself: Germaine's raspberry crepes, Stephanie's whispery insomniac flute in the middle of the night, the baby's adored balloons. Her yearning for Cathy, softer now, more wistful than frantic, blended more and more with his unhappiness at being kept away from those he'd loved most. There was a sense in which they were both victims, both hostages. There was, in fact, a sense in which this was all her fault.

For his part, Russell paid exquisite and virtually constant attention to her. His scrutiny, though still ominously obsessive, had acquired a solicitous, even tender quality, and he was clearly doing his best not only to please her but to anticipate her needs.

He'd come up behind her and start massaging her shoulders, and she'd realize then how tight her trapezius muscle and the ligaments in the back of her neck had been. He took to serving her ice cream before bed; for years as a kid, she'd had ice cream every night for a bedtime snack, and he confessed almost shyly to remembering that, although she couldn't imagine why she'd have mentioned such a thing to him. He drew her out about school, commiserated about the ridiculous reading program, asked intelligent and compassionate questions about her kids.

He did not ask about Cathy. At first, she longed to talk about Cathy, chafed at what seemed like betrayal every time it would have been natural to mention her and she didn't. Gradually, though, Cathy receded into the background of her thoughts; in this new reality, this life taking on shape and substance moment by moment around her like a bed being made up with her in it, starting out sprawled naked on a disheveled mattress, Cathy had no place.

Kindest of all, he began giving her eyedrops. Early on the morning after the attempted—what? rape? seduction? sexual conversion?—she'd awakened with pounding heart to find him squatting beside the mattress, her purse awkwardly on his upraised knees. Groaning and burying her face in the lumpy pillow, she'd thought probably she ought to object to or at least be aware of whatever he was doing with her purse—stealing something, searching for something, planting something incriminating. But it wasn't worth the effort. Her head ached. Her body felt bruised, both eyes seared. Her genitalia throbbed as if she actually had been violated.

"Good morning, Christina." He smoothed her hair back from her face. Since there was no point in trying to pull away, and he was going to do it whether she liked it or not, she allowed herself to like it a little. "How do you feel?"

"Oh, just great," she mumbled. "Peachy."

"How are your eyes?"

"Still mostly useless, if that's what you mean. Not a miracle in sight. So to speak."

"Do they hurt?"

"Yes." Doubtless it was a mistake to admit that. If nothing else, it would encourage him to keep the pressure on. But she didn't much care.

"Would this help?"

"Help?" She snorted. "Now *there's* a slippery concept."

He took her hand. She kept it limp. He pressed something into her palm. When she made no move to close her fingers around it, he closed them for her, carefully bending one after another, and she did her best neither to resist nor to cooperate.

The object he'd forced on her was a small, squat, plastic cylinder with a lid on the pointed end. Realizing what it must be, hardly daring to believe it, she lay very still. As if in anticipation, the burning in her eyes intensified, and she moaned.

"Christina," he murmured, and she didn't know what to read into the name the way he'd used it, imperative or entreaty, acknowledgment or utter disregard and fabrication. "It's your eyedrops," he told her, eager as a parent with a Christmas morning surprise.

Her right eye pulsed with physical longing. Rolling

the bottle into position between thumb and forefinger, but not yet lifting it to her eye, she demanded, "What do you want me to do with them?"

"Use them. Put them in your eyes." He sounded a bit nonplussed. "Isn't that what you need so your eyes won't get so dry?"

"I thought we were waiting for a sign from God."

"God made eyedrops, too," he pointed out, almost happily, as if she was the one who needed reminding. She heard his smile. "Go ahead."

She propped herself up at an angle, tilted her head back, unscrewed the squat lid and put the dull point of the bottle into the outside corner of her right eye. She could feel him watching her, avid as a voyeur. When she pressed the soft plastic and nothing came out, she thought she'd scream. Another squeeze produced a drop of moisturizer, warm from having been in her purse for so long, not nearly as soothing as if it had been cool but delicious nonetheless.

Into each corner of each eye she put two drops. Even if it was too late to prevent corneal damage, the relief was almost instantaneous and quite wonderful. Excess moisture dribbled down her cheeks, and she inclined her head sideways in an attempt to catch more of it. "Thank you," she breathed.

"You're welcome." Audibly pleased with her and with himself, he took the eyedrop bottle from her.

She reached to reclaim it, missed. "Can't I keep it? I need eyedrops every fifteen or twenty minutes. My ophthalmologist says he ought to design a drip system," this last with a nervous giggle.

He patted her arm. "You just let me know when you need it and I'll give it to you."

Since then he'd been keeping his word, and the ongoing dialogue between them about this highly personal matter was complicating their relationship. Maybe that was the point. After all, it was he who'd set things up so she'd be dependent on him. She knew that. She could see how it worked, but it still worked. Every time she asked him for eyedrops some part of her defense against him dissolved, and every time he supplied them she was, as much as anything, grateful.

She was also increasingly ashamed, as if she was repeatedly, not to say intrinsically, disappointing to someone whose opinion of her mattered. This was nothing new. All her life she'd felt much the same toward her mother, who'd loved her, wanted only the best for her, but whose maternal guilt over her disability couldn't be ameliorated by any action, accomplishment or attitude, because it was about something immutable in her very nature, at her very core. This had always been between them. It still was, though her mother had been dead for a decade.

Did Russell know about that? Since she'd told him about the ice cream, might she also have told him how, because of her eyes, she could never be good enough for her mother? Unlikely as it seemed that she'd have confided in him like that, his sorrowful solicitude—the way he shook his head over her, patted her, stared at her when he thought she wouldn't see him or wrenched his gaze away as if he couldn't bear to see her—stirred a familiar sense of fundamental unworthiness.

But, unlike her mother, Russell offered something she could and should do to fix herself, something she kept doing and then rescinding, doing and then rescinding, a lover not quite able to plunge into a wholehearted commitment, an addict unconvinced that abstinence wasn't the addiction. Russell knew what she must do: cast her lot with God. Eschew Satan. Change her name. Russell believed her visual impairment was her fault, the outward manifestation of sin, and that she could make it right. Astonishingly, she almost did, too; almost wanted to.

And he prayed. She could not imagine her mother praying over her; she didn't think she'd ever heard her mother mention anything like God. To God and to her, Russell said the same things again and again, so that by now she was, though silently and piecemeal, saying them, too. "Oh God, we ask that You help Your lost child Christina, amen. Lord Jesus, we pray for Your intervention and for Your grace, amen. Thy will be done, amen."

There were no more sexual incidents, and neither of them brought up what had happened between them. He was back to touching her a lot, as if he had a perfect right, but it didn't come across as erotic or violent, only proprietary. She began to wonder if she could have misinterpreted. Surely, if he'd really tried to have sex with her and she'd really fought him off, things couldn't have so thoroughly returned to what was now passing for normal.

She wasn't certain how long she'd been here, which surprised her. Had she ever pictured herself a prisoner, she'd have anticipated keeping compulsive track of the passage of time: scratching hatch marks on dungeon walls like those in the Tower of London she hadn't been able to see but had vividly, satisfactorily imagined as the blustery guard cum guide had recounted the tourist stories and Cathy had delightedly shuddered beside her *(oh, Cathy)*; notching a purloined bar of soap; listing days, dates, weather conditions, seasonal gradations in a notebook the guards would regularly check for escape plots and love letters; scoring her own flesh with her teeth as part of a twisted bedtime routine. Measuring the duration of captivity would have seemed, in theory, fundamental to surviving intact. Now, in real life, it seemed pointless, and too much trouble. Assuming Russell knew what day it was, she didn't have to.

How long, though, had she been gone? Would Cathy be home from her business trip? Would she have cut it short when she couldn't reach Leila by phone, afraid of what she'd find at home, afraid when she found nothing? Surely she'd have filed a missing persons report by now. Maybe school had started, and they'd had to find a sub at the last minute, and the principal had contacted Cathy, and everyone was searching. Or maybe she'd been with Russell such a short time that nobody but Cathy missed her, nobody but Cathy was trying to find her and bring her home.

Or maybe Cathy hadn't noticed she was gone, or didn't care. Or was relieved not to have to deal with such a high-maintenance partner anymore. Certainly it had been a long time since Cathy'd paid as much attention to her as Russell did.

"I'll be out for a while today," he told her over breakfast one hot morning.

Alarm buzzed through her. Her spoon clattered when she set it down. "Out?"

"There's something I have to do."

"You're leaving me here alone?"

"I'll have to tie and gag you, of course," he said reasonably.

"Oh," she said, "of course."

"I hate to, but we wouldn't want to leave you unprotected against the Devil's mischief while I'm gone, would we?"

"Why can't I go with you?" Pleading. Brittle so as not to seem pleading.

"You'd be in the way, I'm afraid." He patted her arm. "I'm sorry, Christina. Nothing personal."

In her life before Russell, being bound and gagged had never crossed her mind. Now she knew—intimately, viscerally—what it was like: rope chafing wrists, ankles, waist; rag pulled tight between her teeth and into the corners of her mouth like a dentist's tool, quickly soaked with spittle and continually triggering her gag reflex; being immobilized in the middle of a hot, noisy, lonely, edgeless room; at the mercy of everything—stray hallucinatory thoughts, alighting flies, itches and cramps, bodily functions.

Dread and panic made her reckless. "Why? What are you going to do?"

"Oh, now," he said archly, "you don't really expect me to tell you that, do you?" There was a pause, during which she could hardly think, and then he invited in the same coy tone, "Guess."

"What?"

"Where do you think I'm going? Guess."

"Oh, Jesus, Russell—" He made a threatening noise and she winced, but it was too late to correct herself. "How would I know?"

"I'll give you hints. Ask me questions. Yes or no questions." He settled back in his chair.

*This is stupid,* she wanted to shout. *I hate guessing games.* But the best available choice seemed to be playing along. "I don't know where to start," she managed to say. "It could be anything. I don't—"

"I'm going to bring something back," he prompted.

"Animal, vegetable or mineral?"

"No."

"What?"

He chuckled. "No."

"No what? None of the above?"

"Yes."

"Human, then? You don't think humans are animals, I bet. Is it a person?"

"Yes."

"Is it someone I know?"

"Yes."

"Ardith?"

"No."

"Stephanie?"

"No!" His indignation bordered on outrage. "Anyway, you don't know Stephanie. Play by the rules here, Christina."

*Cathy.* Afraid to say it, afraid not to, she whispered, "Cathy?"

"Ding ding ding ding ding! One point for Christina Luce, ladies and gentlemen!" His forefinger made a scorekeeping hatch mark in the air.

Her throat constricted. "You're bringing Cathy here? Why?"

"The Lord has shown me that she's the key to your heart." What she assumed was revulsion made his voice taut.

"You're planning to take her hostage, too?" Her voice climbed and broke.

"We need her. God has said to me, 'Bring the other one here.'"

*Oh, God, yes, I need her.* "What for?"

"I'm not sure yet," he said serenely. "The Lord has not yet revealed His plans to me. He will show me what to do at each step of the way. I don't need to understand His Plan, only to submit to it."

"You'll be guarding both of us? Trying to save both of us? One against two?"

"Ah, but Christina, I have the Lord on my team." Absolute seriousness; no trace of irony. Absolute confidence.

"You're going to kidnap her? At—at gunpoint?"

"Well, really, I don't expect her to come willingly, do you?" Amused. Nervous. Heavy metallic clicks, then the sounds of a zipper, a snap, adjustment of clothing. Did he just stick the gun in his waistband? That seemed awfully informal. And what if it accidentally went off in there? Like slapstick cartoon violence, the prospect made her want to guffaw.

Nauseated and dizzy, she was finding it hard to talk. "You—don't know where to find her."

"At your house. Or at her job. She works at Barnes and Noble downtown." His tone was smug, triumphant.

Chilled, she scrambled to put together a story sensible enough that he'd believe it, or at least be uncertain whether to believe it or not. "She's on vacation this week." As if she knew what week it was. "She went back East to visit her father."

There was a pause. Then, "Oh," he said, and "Oh" again, sounding so disappointed she almost pitied him, almost was ashamed of having foiled his plan.

But he must have decided she was lying, or he was convinced he had to do something and could come up with no better strategy, or heard the nagging of God, because after their morning Bible study and prayers, he left. First he brought her the coffee can, which still smelled of coffee more than of anything that came out of her body, and watched as she relieved herself. Then he gave her eyedrops. Then he bound and gagged her.

He didn't say anything while he was tying her, to a chair he'd lugged down the basement steps. She said, "At least take me upstairs. Don't leave me alone in the cellar," and he patted her knee as if to say this was something they both just had to get through. He took his time about it, adjusting, working the knots, not wanting to hurt her, or at least not wanting to be responsible for hurting her. They both knew that the ropes, having to be tight enough to hold her, before long would hurt, but he'd have done only what he had to do and he'd be gone by then and it wouldn't be his fault. After all, she'd brought this on herself.

She opened her jaws for the gag like a horse for the bit, bested, sulkily obedient. As it passed back over her tongue, the cloth tasted of cigarette smoke, and Russell didn't smoke. Someone else's breath, someone else's germs, must have contaminated it. She choked, thrashed.

He pulled her head against his belly in what pretended to be a soothing, tender gesture—she thought he might kiss her; she thought he might change his mind and take her with him—until he pinched her nose so she had to open her mouth. She hoped her nose was running onto his fingers. She hoped she had some disease. "I'll be back as soon as I can," he promised, carefully working the gag between her back teeth. "Wish me luck."

He kissed her good-bye like an affectionate husband leaving for work. She couldn't have responded or pushed him away if she'd wanted to. For safety, he blew out the candle; she could still perceive the difference between dimness and total darkness, and the burning odor sharpened when the flame went out. He went up the steps, his tread hurried. The floor above her creaked. The quality of the basement air changed as an outside door opened and closed.

# *Chapter Fifteen*

For a while she just waited.

For a while, then, she wasn't even waiting anymore. If time passed, it was without her. As if her lids were closed all the time, which she didn't think they were, she perceived light that didn't seem to be constant, but the shift could have been from her head drooping and then snapping upright, cobwebs swaying, or the vicious electric spritzing across her cornea. After a while she began to hear sounds, perhaps from outside the house, perhaps inside the house but outside her body; they changed in ways that suggested a cycle, but she had no template for them, and anyway it would be of no use to her to know whether the distant piping was the voices of children on their way to school in the morning, the voices of children on their way home from school in the afternoon or cats wailing in the middle of the night; whether the thrumming and rumbling she heard in the bones of her skull signaled heavy equipment in the street at the beginning of another workday or the gathering of explosive gases in the house or her own thundering, faltering heartbeat.

To no particular rhythm and in response to no discernible external or internal stimulus, her body cramped and released, itched, ached, subsided. She was hungry and then she was not. She was thirsty, until parched throat and caked lips became normal. Maybe she slept, woke.

For a while she felt obliged to call for help. Although she was intending to cry, "Help! Help me! Please help me! Somebody please help me!" the gag and the repetition almost immediately rendered the words mechanical, atonal and without inflection. To her own ears the noises she made sounded like a donkey braying, which sounded like the regular but random creaking of a rusty gate. Then they subsided altogether.

At some point she began hearing, feeling, smelling, tasting and especially *seeing* things she was almost certain were not, in any objective sense, there. Conducted or created by her swollen tongue and parched throat were the cruel tastes of chocolate, lemon, bratwurst, bile. She smelled an animal's wet fur. She saw a humanoid figure of vivid and indistinct beauty coming toward her, coming for her, passing through her, summoning her, filling her and leaving her. Jesus, who turned out to be Satan, who turned out to be God.

After a while, she became aware of a series of staccato cracks that she sensed had been repeated more than once. Fear, constant and free-floating by now, pulsed through her and attached itself to the sound. Certain it meant danger, she scrambled to name it: gunfire? hammering, maybe to board up windows and doors with her entombed here?

She made herself small and silent, without much hope of escaping notice. She envisioned herself as a single, contracting point without light, odor, body heat, heartbeat, breath, name. The pounding was muffled, distant, from above and ahead of her. Could Russell have kidnapped someone else? Was it conceivable that all this time she hadn't been alone with him? Could he have already seized Cathy? Could Cathy be close by?

Maybe Satan, knocking to be let in. Inviting himself in. Demanding. Maybe God.

Of course that was ludicrous. But no more ludicrous, surely, than the indisputable fact that she'd been bound and gagged in the basement of an abandoned house by a religious fanatic intent upon exorcizing her and saving both her soul and her sight.

Something heavy and hard scraped across some internal surface of the house, floor or ceiling or wall or hidden joist. Something opened—a door, a window, a hole, an abyss—and changed the air pressure in the house, so that things ticked and creaked, shifted, moved around her. Something approached: footsteps, clawing sounds, changes in the air, changes in the structure that confined and supported her. Searching for her. Hunting her.

Her first impulse was to hide, not to give herself away. She held her breath, tried to suppress even the slightest, most autonomic movement. A sudden itch between her shoulder blades instantly became very nearly intolerable. Needing to cough, she swallowed hard. Needing to cry, she bit her tongue hard under the gag.

Someone called, "Christina?"

Tears gushed and, in a similar sort of release, urine. Christina was not her name, but she would respond to it, joyously and with intense trepidation. "Yes," she meant to call. "I'm down here."

"Christina, it's Ardith. Are you in here?"

Ardith. Who if anything was on more intimate terms than Russell with both God and the Devil. Who spoke in tongues. Who did everything she could to lose herself in the Lord. Who believed in real, present, personal Evil, from whom one must escape, and literal, palpable, intimate, moment-by-moment salvation.

Whose voice, though, had become very careful and very firm when—maybe—she'd begun to realize what Russell might be up to. And who, if nothing else, could untie her from this chair, find water and food for her and get her to a doctor.

"Christina?"

Working to control her sobbing, which could choke her in the way that drunks choked on their own vomit, she struggled to breathe and to think. Under these rarefied circumstances, was Ardith friend or foe? Rescuer or torturer, guardian angel or Russell's accomplice? In which direction lay the greater risk, being discovered or being abandoned? Declaring herself or not? Summoning Ardith or hiding from her?

At the memory of how, against Russell's wishes, Ardith had supplied her with cool, wet eyedrops, her eye ached for lubrication and, daringly, not only for the thin liquid from the bottle but also for the viscous substance meant to be used when—as now, as always now—she was not wearing her contact. The bottle of eyedrops might be in her purse, which might be somewhere in this house. The tube of thicker lubricant she'd had no reason to take to the movie. For that if for no other reason *(forgive me, Cathy),* she had to get home.

She gathered all her strength and roared.

"Christina?" came the immediate alarmed response. Quick heavy footsteps crossed the ceiling, but away from the cellar door. "Christina, where are you?"

Ardith might have brought the police, and for a hallucinatory moment she was cast into another level of terror. Would they arrest her for being impaired?

She roared again, scraping her throat. She coughed, swallowed. Saliva clotted and rose into her ears, threatening to drown her from the inside out but doing nothing to relieve the terrible dryness.

An idea occurred to her. It might be foolish. It might cause her more harm. In some way she hadn't thought of, it might make things worse. The decision to let Ardith in might be exactly the wrong one, and the method she'd hit upon for doing so might turn out to be disastrous. Mercifully, there was no time to consider.

She tipped backward and to the right, just enough to lift the left front leg of the chair off the floor. Though she felt instantly on the verge of going over, she wrenched her body sideways. The chair leg banged down in what must surely be the exact spot it had been in before. With a huge grunt and groan, she twisted again, and this time the chair moved. Already she was panting and the ropes were cutting into her flesh.

Carefully she leaned back and to the left, raising the right front leg. Forcibly expelling breath and sound around the gag and the pooled spittle, she twisted against the ropes again. The chair moved.

"Tell me where you are. Hurry. I don't know how long he'll be gone."

She tipped too far and fell onto her left side, her shoulder hard into the ungiving concrete and concretelike packed dirt, the chair on top of her. She moaned.

"Christina? Christina?"

For a few seconds she lay trembling and dazed,

thinking maybe she'd just die here in the cellar and be done with it. Something skittered close to her cheek. Something light and sticky settled over her temple like a caul. The fall had jarred something loose in her eye, shattered something; white and red light exploded like fireworks, and her lid was nearly sealed shut with the drainage that matted and crusted before it had even left the socket.

Now she was hearing nothing from upstairs. Maybe Ardith had left, or was at this moment deciding to leave. Needing to shout, "No! Wait! Please!" she could do no more than whimper.

Despite the pain in her shoulder and hip, it was easier to inch across the dirty floor in this position. She must look ridiculous. It crossed her mind to wonder whether, if she'd realized the kinesthetic advantages, she'd have had the courage to deliberately make herself fall. Slight slack in the ropes allowed her to move arms, legs, torso, but only in truncated arcs with virtually no force behind them. Having no better choice, she kicked, struck out with her hands, flung her body from side to side, until she was breathless and surely bruised, and had made perhaps three inches of progress in the direction she'd settled on, for no really good reason, as being toward the steps.

Soaked with her own drool and even tighter in her mouth as if it had shrunk, the gag made it hard to catch her breath, and she thought she might pass out. Realizing that her head still moved more or less freely, she began jerking it hard up and down. After countless repetitions of the jarring motion, her temples throbbed and her neck spasmed and it seemed to her she might have worked herself a tiny bit closer to the steps and the upper, outside world.

Out of which no searching footsteps creaked anymore. From which Ardith no longer called for her. In which the only person she could trust to be taking an interest in her was Russell Gavin.

Because she could think of nothing else to do, she kept up the painful and painfully slow scrabbling, trying not to think about what she would do if she in fact reached the steps. The chair tied to her shifted a little from side to side, rubbing the ropes into her flesh but also giving her small hope that they might be loosening. Abrasions stung on her knee, flank, shoulder, cheek, and were surely filling with splinters and grime. Grit invaded her eyes.

The sounds of her own struggle filled her ears from inside: panting, racing heartbeat, straining and tearing muscles, bones thumping. When she heard thin wood splinter and collapse, it seemed, for a split second, to come from inside her body, and she was awed by the extremity of effort that would have been required to cause such dramatic damage.

Then, realizing she might really have hurt herself, she was weakened by a gushing self-pity. How unfair it was that she, who'd already suffered so much and had such a hard life, should be in this awful situation. It was too much to bear.

As if to remind her of how much more could go wrong, her already pitiable vision zapped bloody red, filled for a long moment with bursting kaleidoscopic patterns suggesting tortured souls and eternal flame and subsided into a dull orange fog through which nothing else was really visible but much that was horrible and horribly gorgeous was implied. Much more and much less, she thought, than was actually there, although of course she had no reliable idea what was actually there.

*Great,* she thought, lying there. *I don't even get to be blind when I'm blind. I'm condemned to see things when I'm not seeing anything. Blindness isn't an absence for me, which would be bad enough but I was more or less prepared for that, but a false presence.*

She determined she would surrender; there was a certain pleasure in the prospect. She made every attempt to surrender, to give herself up to some greater power or to some greater void. She thought, in fact, that she had given up, that it was over, every version of "it" for her, over and done with, settled.

But she couldn't yet escape the demonic niggles and stabs of the continuing requirement to *do* something, here and now. Should she indeed stop, lie still, even relax, and wait for whatever would or would not happen? Or should she push harder, put herself in greater immediate jeopardy for the chance of ultimately greater benefit? What *was* greater jeopardy? What was greater benefit? Immobilized now by indecision and exhaustion, she began again to sob, and immediately choked.

"Lord God in Heaven!"

Her throat closed. Her ears rang. Trapped, caught in an incomprehensibly sinful act, she gave up, closed her eyes and waited for whatever would happen to her next.

The gag was pulled harder back into the corners of her mouth, a new variant on the torture, until the hinges of her jaw could not open any wider and surely would snap, the corners of her mouth surely split. Then the knots at the back of her head came loose and the hard wet rag was removed, and she vomited, unable to turn her head fast enough to keep the thin emetic bile from spewing over her chin, cheeks, neck.

Ardith was praying. "My God, oh my God." With a handkerchief that reeked of roses the vomit was sponged off. "Are you all right? Christina, are you all right?"

She could not answer. Her head shook up and down and sideways with no regard for meaning, and her mouth, reveling in the absence of the gag, contorted and drooled but refused to form words.

"Where's Russell? He came by the church and said he was going to be gone for a while and would I look in on you. Did he tell you where he was going?"

*Cathy,* she thought desperately, and forced herself to croak, "Cathy."

"What?" Ardith was working on the bonds around her chest. A ropelike scarf dangled, and it came to Leila how easy it would be for Ardith to tie her with that. Unable to find the end of the rope, Ardith knelt cumbersomely and dug with those thick scarlet fingernails into a knot underneath the chair.

"He went to get Cathy."

"What?" Huffing from behind and below her, the usually full-bodied voice strained thin. Frustrated, upset; she'd done something wrong; Ardith was angry with her; Ardith would hurt her or walk away. "Who's Cathy?"

"My—friend."

"What do you mean, *get?*"

"Kidnap."

"He's going to kidnap somebody else? Why?"

Explaining it with any subtlety or complexity was beyond her, as was judging whether she should tell Ardith any of the truth. She took a deep, ragged breath. "He says we're living in sin."

"Who's living in sin?" Pause. "You and Cathy?" Pause. "Oh."

There was a discernible change in the quality of the other woman's touch, a hesitation, a stiffening. The hands left her abruptly, as if to avoid something dreadful, contamination or temptation. She steeled herself for what would come next.

Then the work on the ropes resumed, and Ardith declared evenly, "The Word tells us to hate the sin but love the sinner."

She ought not to have been grateful for that. "He does," she found herself insisting. "He'd say he does love me and that's why he's doing this." Ardith snorted.

Leila's arms came free. Intense visceral relief made her shudder, then painful tingling from shoulders to fingertips. She badly needed to rub her arms but couldn't control her fingers to do it. Her legs came free, and creakily she stretched one and then the other. From the stiffness of her body and the reeling of her mind, she might have been bound and gagged for days.

"He says I have to change my name," she told Ardith, her voice wavering indignantly.

"What's wrong with Christina? I've always liked the name Christina—"

"My name is Leila Blackwell. Leila means dark or black. It really does. But what's wrong with that? And Blackwell—black well. Russell says it's a satanic name."

"And you should change it to Christina, because that means Christ-worshipper."

Leila stiffened. "Right."

"Christina what?"

"Luce."

"Loose?"

"L-u-c-e, as in light."

"As in Lucifer."

"I thought of that. Lucifer is the devil, right?"

"He started out as an angel, the most beautiful

thing God ever created, second in command of Heaven. But his was the sin of envy. He wanted the worship that belonged to God for himself. So he and one-third of the heavenly host were cast down out of heaven to live among us on this earth."

"Really? Literally? Among us?" Leila tried not to sound as incredulous as she was, but bitter, hysterical laughter made her throat ache.

"They're right here," Ardith explained matter-of-factly. "Most of us can't see them, most of the time, but the spirit world is intermingled with ours like this." Probably she was lacing her fingers.

During this discourse, Ardith had begun unwinding rope from around Leila's torso. The heat and sweet-sweat fragrance of her stout body fluctuated as she leaned close, reached over, swung her arm around to dislodge a loop, leaned back again. Soon, though, that method became too clumsy, and she gathered the rope to her and carried it in almost comical circles around and around the chair. Her heels thumped. Panting, she declared, "We'll call the police."

"I have to go to the bathroom. I've—I've made a mess. I'm sorry."

"We'll get you cleaned up."

She dared to go on. "And I haven't had anything to eat or drink for a long time." She could not quite declare herself hungry or thirsty; for one thing, she was no longer sure that was true.

"He's been withholding food and water?"

"From himself, too. He said fasting would bring us closer to God, or something like that."

"Fasting works against the flesh, which is where sin resides. We often fast and pray. But nowhere in the Word does it say we're supposed to make ourselves sick." Ardith was emphatic.

"And I need a doctor."

"Are you hurt? Are you sick? Did he do something to you—"

"He pushed me down. He hit me. 'Slain in the Spirit,' he called it."

"We are Slain in the Spirit when *God* does it unto us, not man. We are overcome by the Spirit, and we fall. It happens. It has happened to me. I don't like it much. I don't like losing consciousness. I don't like falling on the floor. But it happens. Russell has no right to make a hoax of it—"

"What I really need a doctor for is my eye."

She felt Ardith straighten, though at only kneeling level. Breath tinged with coffee and wintergreen puffed into her face as she was peered at. "Did he actually do something to your eyes?"

"The lubricants I need to keep them from drying out are at home. He won't let me go home." Her voice cracked on the profound word. "Prolonged dryness causes damage to the cornea. Probably I've permanently lost more of my vision. I could go blind. I could already be going blind. It's oozing. I think it's bleeding. And it hurts."

"I'll take you to a doctor. I'll take you home."

215

"Why? Don't you think I'm a sinner, too?"

"We all sin, honey. That's why Jesus had to die."

"You and Russell are both born again, aren't you?" Afraid she might be using the wrong terms, she stammered on, while Ardith gently rubbed her arms and hands where the ropes had been. "You believe the same things."

"Russell is a fanatic."

She nearly laughed in amazement. "No shit."

"People like Russell take the Word and twist it. They are the instruments of Satan in one of his more clever disguises."

Circulation was returning to her hands and feet; the relief was excruciating. "Are you going to stop him? He needs to be stopped. He's after Cathy—"

"First let's get you out of this basement. Can you stand? Can you climb the stairs?"

She intended to stand up. Her image of herself standing up was clear and visceral. But, as if unwilling to chance that it was no longer tethered, her body didn't respond. Struggling to focus on what had always been an autonomic action, she leaned forward, groped for the edges of the chair seat, contracted the thigh muscles that ought to have pushed her up onto her feet. Beyond a random and ineffectual twitching, nothing happened.

Could she somehow have been paralyzed—a sign from God or the Devil; her body finding yet another way to betray her? Terror intensified her clumsiness as she tried again, slid sideways, grabbed for support in what as far as she knew was thin air and collided with Ardith's thick forearm, which steadied and then lifted her.

Mumbling, apologizing: "I don't know what's wrong with me. He hasn't been gone *that* long."

Ardith's other arm came around her waist, and the woman's sturdy bulk was a bulwark for her to lean against. "Give yourself a minute."

But already she was being asked—forced—to take action, to move up into the house, out of the prison and den of the cellar. She balked. Wordlessly, Ardith insisted. They went up the first step.

"Eyedrops. Please. I need eyedrops."

The body against hers tensed, but there was no interruption in their careful, urgent, tandem progress. Up two more steps. "Where would they be?"

"In my purse. Unless he took them out."

Up another three steps. She didn't know how many steps there were; usually she was careful to count. "Where's your purse?"

She despaired. "I have no idea."

Sound narrowed, then opened. "We made it," Ardith gasped. "We're out of the basement."

They must be in the short hallway. Half a dozen more shuffling steps, and then from the dull excremental odor she knew they were at the bathroom. With a hand on the small of her back, Ardith was urging her forward. "The toilet's right in front of you. Shall I—do you need help?"

She wanted to say yes. She wanted to succumb

altogether to helplessness and let herself be undressed, lifted, sat down and afterward cleaned. "No," she said. "I'm okay."

"I'll go look for your purse. And clean clothes. Do you have clean clothes?"

"I was going to a movie."

"Pardon?"

"These are the only clothes I have here." Talking about them, fumbling to get them off, she was newly aware of how filthy they were, and underneath how repulsive her body. She could hardly bring herself to touch the waistband and zipper of her skirt, the elastic of her underwear, the dirty, hairy flesh of her thighs, and her hands themselves were disgusting, coated like a feverish tongue, smelly, badly coordinated, neither knowing what the other was doing. The acute discomfort of being watched made her even clumsier, but when she felt Ardith turn away the feeling of abandonment nearly caused her to give up entirely.

"There's that dress he got for me—" she started to say, but it seemed to her that Ardith was no longer within earshot.

She relieved herself; there was not much to be excreted, but the feeling of desperately needing to void subsided only slightly. She turned on the lefthand faucet, hoping for hot water. A sliver of soap had adhered to the rim of the sink; when she pried it loose it all but pulverized in her palm. Tepid was the best the water could do, and she winced when she splashed it onto her face, under her arms, between her legs.

Sometimes she and Cathy bathed each other. That was one of the ways she knew Cathy was beautiful, and that she was beautiful in Cathy's eyes, under Cathy's hands. The association was tenuous between that warm, sudsy, loving, erotic, fragrant activity and this barren one. This was real. The other was so utterly imaginary that its passing didn't even sadden her.

She felt for a towel and found none. Shivering, she started to reassemble the dirty clothes. "I had some clothes in my car," Ardith said breathlessly from behind her. She hadn't heard her go out of the house or come back in. Hazily she wondered who else had come and gone. "I don't know if they'll fit, but they're clean. And here's your purse."

As if in anticipation, her eye flared. The purse was nudged against the back of her hand. She took it, rummaged, did not find the bottle of lubricant, felt faint with disappointment, then wrapped her fingers around it in the side pocket where she always kept it so she could get to it easily when she needed it. Russell had put it back where it belonged. Absurdly touched, she got the bottle out of the purse and the lid off the bottle, then squirted liquid into her eye without tipping her head back, luxuriously letting it trickle down her cheek. For a few minutes her eye would feel better, as if it were not being harmed.

"Here," said Ardith. "We have to hurry. Try this."

"What? Try what?"

"This shirt. Hurry."

Obediently she struggled out of the shirt she'd been wearing every day since she'd left home, however long ago that was. Not knowing what to do with it and in danger of falling apart under the fear of doing something wrong, she just held it out and it was taken away. She extended a stiff arm and a sleeve was tugged up over it, the garment stretched across her shoulders, the other arm put into the other sleeve.

When she couldn't manage the buttons, Ardith said again, "Here," and did it for her, first down the front and then the cuffs, one after the other, bracing Leila's trembling knuckles against a firm belly, long nails brushing her wrists. "It's a little big," she pronounced, "but it'll do. Here are some pants."

"What, no underwear?" Partly she was trying for sarcasm, but she hated the idea of putting on clean clothes over such soiled undergarments.

"Sorry. We don't accept donations of used underwear. You never know where they've been." They both chuckled.

The pants were stiff, scratchy, too big around the waist and too long. Ardith rolled them up. "Let's get you out of here."

"Wait." One more squirt of eyedrops. Depositing the bottle with extreme care in the front right pocket of the pants, then panicking and checking, checking again to make sure there were no holes. A curious and disturbing reluctance to go out of the house. Clutching Ardith's arm.

Ardith patted her hand. "It's okay, honey. First let's ask God for strength," Ardith decided, and sank to her broad knees on the grimy bathroom floor. "Let's pray," and launched immediately into that intense, oddly inflected chant: "Heavenly Father, amen, be with us in this time of trial and temptation, amen, and help us to do Thy will, amen—" The exhortation dropped in pitch and volume as its intensity rose, quickly becoming a passionate murmur. "Buoy us with Thy love and Thy strength, amen, and lead us in the path of righteousness, amen, for Thy name's sake, amen—"

The language of Ardith's prayer transmogrified into something unknown. Because its overall configuration—rhythm, arrangement of vowel and consonant sounds—stayed the same, the transition from English was seamless, and it came as a shock to realize that now Ardith was speaking in tongues.

Leila's skin crawled. Panic and then fury propelled her out of Ardith's passionate grasp, out of the stinking bathroom, along the corridor whose walls she tapped with both fists to stay her course, through the living room where only a few objects rose in her path, through the crowded garbage-smelling kitchen and out the back door into the shadowy, glaring night.

Behind her Ardith bellowed, "Christina!" but she did not answer to that name.

# *Chapter Sixteen*

There was no wind, but the air felt harsh and aimed, as if puffed from a gun. Her eye spasmed.

Without stopping, she fished the bottle of eye-drops out of her pocket, which inside the pant leg descended to the middle of her thigh. Though the relief was enormous every time, the drops were too thin to help for long, and her lid kept reflexively closing.

*The police. Call the police. Where's the phone? What's the address? Where was I? Where am I?*

Again and again she forced her eyelid open and squirted the lubricant in. She marveled at the strength and stubbornness of the tiny muscles, protecting the delicate eyeball even from a helpful intrusion, doing their job no matter what.

*Call Cathy. Get home to Cathy. Warn Cathy, protect her, if it's not already too late.*

A sudden throbbing sprang like a fierce little animal into the dull red ache of her eye, followed by a sensation like silent hissing. Even when she could get the lid to stay open, narrowly and for brief painful moments, she could see almost nothing past the red flares and white slashes and yellow-green multiplying starbursts that, horrifyingly, were coming from inside her eye, inside her head.

*Get to a doctor.*

*Would I risk going blind for Cathy?*

Not knowing how to do any of the urgent things she had to do, she just kept moving, in awkward haste, in no specified direction. The frantic mantra beat an erratic, nearly meaningless rhythm in her mind—*call the police, find a doctor, get home.* She was flailing through murky, cacophonous, gelatinous time and space.

She kept tripping over obstacles that were insulting as well as injurious because they wouldn't be obstacles to any normal person. Or, excessive and misplaced caution created obstacles where there were none, so she was tripping over thin air.

She struggled to think. How would she find help? Try to follow sirens in the hope of latching on to someone else's emergency? Grope randomly for a public phone? Throw herself on the mercy of the first passerby she met? As far as she knew, there'd been nobody walking at all, and only two passing cars; fear of anyone she could think of who'd be out at this time of night—except Cathy or maybe the

223

police, looking for her—was offset by fear that by morning, when respectable people were out and about, it would be too late. Too late to save Cathy. Too late to protect whatever might be left of her vision. Too late to defend against Russell, against run-of-the-mill thugs meaning her a simpler sort of harm. Too late to escape from either God or the Devil, whichever was gaining on her. Too late, somehow, for her ever to go home.

She fell.

Even as she believed herself to be badly injured and unable to get up, she knew she was not. Hands and knees abraded, tongue bitten, shoulder and hip jarred and aching, yet she could move, wasn't bleeding much, hadn't broken anything. She didn't want to move, didn't see the point.

She forced herself to her feet. Or meant to: for long, vertiginous moments, she didn't know where she was in space, standing or kneeling or falling, how far from something to hold on to, how close to a barrier or trap. The image recurred of all those blind people rocking back and forth, so she started rocking, and in some strange way did in fact feel herself more kinesthetically anchored, calmer. Sternly she stopped herself. Or meant to: whether she was in motion was not clear.

Her eye burned. She couldn't tell whether it was still oozing or even bleeding, but the eyedrops Ardith had retrieved from her purse would do no more than alleviate the surface symptoms. For long moments she couldn't even find the eyedrops.

But the red miasma and the fireworks display in her eye had cleared, and she was fairly sure the visual cues she was receiving were again from outside herself. Ahead was light, a bluer white than streetlights and a more elongated shape. Blurry, haloed, it might be a block away or a few steps. She did her best to head toward it. She couldn't actually hurry, but her heart pounded and her breath came short, as if she were rushing full speed ahead, all the unpleasant effects of haste with none of the practical benefit.

Caroming, veering, not even trying to identify what she was stumbling over or running into, she made her agonizingly slow way in what seemed to be the direction of the lights. She wished she could run. She wished she could tell for sure what the lights were, what she was going toward. A car sped past, too close, sinister. She must be in the middle of a street. If she jumped back or even took a hasty sideways step, she might fall. If she looked away from the light, she might not be able to find it again, but focusing on it caused disorientation and pain. Her heartbeat nearly closed her throat. Only when the car was gone, not having hurt her, did it occur to her that she could have flagged it down, begged for help, if nothing else asked for directions. Sickened by the missed opportunity, she pressed on.

Raised voices, from slightly clockwise of the direction she was going, might be partying or fighting, either of which she ought to avoid. A curious humming, almost subliminal, made her wonder about power lines and machinery, although it did seem to have qualities of the human voice. She couldn't tell where it was coming from. Somehow, she kept going.

An eerie forest of lampposts rose around her as she started to descend a slope, perhaps a wheelchair ramp into a building. This must be the light she'd been homing in on, confusingly broken up now into individual globes like blue-white lollipops but arranged, apparently, in an overall rectangular pattern.

Underfoot the pavement altered. She hesitated, moved one foot carefully back and forth to ascertain the lay of the land. Something thrummed nearby, probably a generator, for some reason a little unnerving. What was this place?

This did not have the feel of a hospital or a police station. On the theory that it was a store, she tried to decipher the red neon sign, but the number of words, the shapes of the letters and logo, the overall configuration shifted continuously and didn't match any store name she could think of.

She needed medical care and police protection, not a shopping opportunity. Cursing, she started to retrace her steps back up to the street. Then several things occurred to her and made her turn around again: There'd be people in there whom she could ask for help. There'd be phones, and maybe ophthalmological supplies.

She couldn't tell whether the store was open or the glaring blue-white stripes of illumination were just night security lights. Somewhere in the wall of tall windows was the door. It was no more likely to be one way than the other, so she chose randomly and took a few cautious steps to the left. Then voices sprang from the opposite direction, coming out, crossing the parking lot, and she pivoted, called out, "Excuse me! Excuse me, I need help!" There was no discernible response. Maybe she hadn't called loudly enough. Maybe they'd discounted her as a panhandler. Maybe, somehow, she'd been wrong and there hadn't been people at all.

She made her way along the wall until she came to a railing, guessed correctly that it marked the automatic door, and stepped in, ducking as if she could avoid the assaultive sensory jumble. After a moment she located the rattle of the cash register and pointed herself toward it. Boxes cluttered the aisle; somebody stocking shelves, she supposed, but apparently not there at the moment. Maneuvering around the boxes and a cart, she bumped into a display and something fell and rolled. She didn't stop to pick it up. Her eye was searing.

As she rounded what seemed to be the last corner on the way to the cash register, where surely there'd be an employee and eventually customers, she caught a blur of familiar shape and color directly at eye level, prominently displayed on the end of the shelf. The orange-slash-on-green of the rectangular boxes housing bottles of the rewetting drops she used dozens of times a day. The thick, square blue boxes, shiny shrink-wrapped, containing nested ampules of the viscous lubricant for when she was not wearing her contact. The darker green cardboard with thinner white letters encasing ointment tubes. She'd know them anywhere.

She stopped. Her hands were shaking. Her eye burned eagerly, the way a mouth might salivate in anticipation of food. Trying not to knock anything off, but hardly able to restrain herself, she edged her hand along the shelf until it found the right place and reverently took down one of each type of daytime lubricant, then two of each.

Then she realized she'd left her purse behind and had no money. She couldn't buy the things she so desperately needed. They were within her reach; they were in her hands. But she couldn't have them.

She put them in her pockets.

It was easy. Somewhat wryly, she'd always imagined shoplifting to be one of the things she couldn't see well enough to do. But now she had in her possession the things she wanted, just like that, and if she didn't take them out of the store to use them she wouldn't have to contend with the security system. One way or another she'd find a place to put the medicine in. She'd go to the corner farthest away from the cash register, with her back turned and her shoulders hunched as if she were peering at something on the shelf. Or she'd beg to use the employee restroom; claiming an emergency would not be a lie.

Made giddy by purpose, she went back and grabbed a tube of nighttime ointment. She couldn't use it now because it gummed up her vision, but it would be heavenly when she slept tonight, whenever and wherever that was, and if she could take the tube off the card before she left the store, there was a chance it wouldn't set off an alarm.

A hand dropped over hers, and a familiar scent struck her. She couldn't place it, but she knew to pull away.

"Christina, you scared me to death."

Bulk in the aisle on her right, a mellifluous contralto voice.

"I've been driving all over looking for you. The Lord led me here. Praise the Lord, amen."

*Ardith.* She backed away.

"Wait, Christina, I'm your friend. I won't hurt you."

Wresting her forearm out of the other woman's grasp, she whirled, stumbled into and around the boxes she'd avoided before. Senses sharp again, she headed for the outside doors, judging the angle by the swish and the change in air quality as they opened and closed, the long dark rectangle on the floor that was probably a mat, the smell of people coming inside from outside. On the way she managed to dig the containers of eye medicine out of the long pants' pockets and stash them on a shelf; she couldn't risk being delayed by security.

Behind her Ardith boomed, "Christina!"

She must have gone out the entrance door, because she bumped into people hurrying in. Breathlessly, she apologized. A teenage girl snarled, "Ex*cuse* me!" and an older man barked, somewhat mystifyingly, "This is a goddamn *store*, lady!"

Only after she'd rushed on into the dimmer out side courtyard did it occur to her that they might have been entering an exit, so the collision might have been their fault, not hers. And that she might have stopped them and appealed for help.

Shimmering gray pools of light. Headlights and taillights approaching and receding without rhyme or reason, so she could neither stay out of their paths nor flag them down. Hard surfaces under her feet, cracks, curbs, rough and pliant surfaces, shrubs, a post against her cheekbone in a glancing blow that hurt disproportionately and brought tears.

"Christina! Please, wait!"

Scraping the knuckles of her right hand along a wall to keep from veering leftward into the street. Longing to run full out but needing to be careful, sliding her feet, moving as fast as she could, which was pitiably slow. Pain in her eye matched by pumping heart, ragged breath, coursing adrenaline.

Imagining hands on her shoulders, feet in front of hers to trip her, hair pulled, clothes torn. Then imagining ropes, tape, the gag, and for a split second less afraid of those things than of fleeing alone into the night, of finding help, finding Cathy, living the rest of her life blind. For a split second, she slowed, stopped, waited. Then revulsion propelled her around a corner she could barely see or hear.

"Christina! Christina, stop! I'll take you home!"

Hesitation a beat or two longer, temptation, but then the near certainty that this was a ruse.

She wasn't likely to be able to outrun anyone, even the ponderous Ardith. Could she hide? Because she couldn't reliably guess what other people could and could not see, hide-and-seek had never been her game as a kid, and the concepts of concealment, optical illusion, invisibility were largely theoretical. But there was no time to think of anything better.

Flattening herself face-first against the wall, she crept along it to an edge, turned the corner, forced herself to go faster, turned again. This ought to put her on the back side of whatever building this was—unless she'd been at the back in the first place and this was the front, more public, more visible and vulnerable.

Still pressed against the rough wall, she tried to increase her crablike sideways pace. She came upon a few indentations, none useful. She found a door—locked, of course, and flush with the wall. It wasn't hard to imagine herself just circling this building again and again and again, a rat in an inverse cage.

"Christina?"

Ardith. But where?

"Russell!"

Terror paralyzed Leila, then sent her off the wall into open space.

"Russell, no!"

A single dull pop.

Brief silence, and then three screamed syllables in a language beyond language. Another truncated report, another instant's pause, a fleshy thud.

"Oh God my God I am Thy vessel amen I am Thy servant amen—" Russell. And Ardith. And, she realized, gunshots. Russell had shot Ardith.

She heard him crouch, then fall to his knees—"I am Thy instrument Thy sword Thy bullet amen I am Thy murderer amen I am a murderer in Thy name amen oh my God what have I done what hast Thou had me do—"

She heard the sweep of his hands across what must be cloth and bloody flesh. Heard him gasp and retch. Imagined him recoiling from the terrible wound he'd made in the name of God; then, in the name of God, allowing himself to finger the edges of it, to take the measure of its width and breadth and especially its depth, to let the blood he had spilled flow over his hands. Heard him whisper something that did not seem to be addressed to his jealous God—an apology, a prayer.

*Talk about slain in the Spirit,* she thought wildly, and had to press her knuckles against her teeth to keep from shrieking with horrified laughter.

She heard him stand up. "Christina?" he crooned, as if he knew she was nearby, as if she would come when called, and in fact she had to resist a bizarre impulse to answer to the name. "Christina? Christina, I love you. I'm sorry." He was backing away. "I have failed you, and I have failed my Lord." He had turned. "I'll pray for you. I'll pray for us all." He was gone.

Then she heard no more foreground sounds, only the ambient city noise and the frantic white amalgam, internal but pervasive, of her own ragged breathing, heartbeat, rushing adrenaline, swirling thoughts, wheeling and diving senses. Her eye crackled.

Russell had shot Ardith.

She tried not to know what had happened. Since she couldn't see it, she was not expected to know. No one would take her as an eyewitness.

But she knew what had happened. Russell had shot Ardith, because Ardith had gone against the Will of his God. Russell had shot Ardith for setting her free.

An overpowering, primitive instinct, the organism protecting itself without regard for context or consequence, made her flesh shrink, her skin contract, her body leave the wall to curl around its soft parts. She made herself very still. She would stay here until someone rescued her. *Cathy, Cathy, please, I need you, Cathy, please come, here I am, help me.* She was blind. She'd been traumatized. A madman was gunning for her. She would hide here. She would wait to be found. Nobody could expect anything more of her.

Except Ardith. Who, if she was not dead, needed help and, if she was dead, needed witness.

She was utterly unsheltered. The space she was in had no shape. Undifferentiated sound swarmed over her. No direction held any less danger than any other.

Leila forced her head up out of the burrow of her arms. Never convinced that other senses compensated for one missing, now she willed superacuity from not only hearing and touch but also smell and taste and clairvoyance and mind-reading, hoping to catch the tang of Russell's breath mints or the stench of Ardith's blood or some hint of what to do and what would happen next. But the mélange of sensory and extrasensory input was all but useless. Everything she thought to do had terrible risks. Anything might happen.

Quaking, she got to her hands and knees. In case of low-hanging obstacles, she stayed down and kept her head bowed. In case of holes in the ground or unsafe rubble or dangerous creatures in her path, she barely crept along. But she had to find Ardith.

She got to her feet. Holding her hands out like a cartoon blind person, she took several teetering steps, then slightly increased her pace.

Someone was nearby, crouching, lying in wait. She sensed body heat and mass, low to the ground. "Who's there?" as though the enemy would give a name. Her shin hit something and she lost her balance, bent double, braced herself on the warm, motionless, solid but pliant obstacle, and found herself holding a soft ringed hand, which, for a split second, seemed to return her grasp.

# Chapter Seventeen

A body. Ardith. Ardith's body, redolent with the fragrance of perfume and what must be the scent of blood. Leila wondered wildly how copper smelled and tasted anyway, and how the cliché had originated. Had someone sucked on a penny? She did not smell or taste anything she'd have called coppery. But she smelled blood.

Sinking to her knees, she forced her hands out until they located what she was searching for and dreading to find: not an arm's length from her, Ardith's body. A shoulder, a large hoop earring, the base of the throat framed by an open collar. No pulse.

Leila shouted, "Help! I need help!"

With no protective mask or gloves, next to no knowledge of CPR or first aid, she bent close and skimmed a hand over the topography of the cloth-covered flesh before her until she located the belly, chest, lips. No breath. She laid her palm and then her ear on Ardith's bosom. No heartbeat.

"Help! Somebody! Help!"

The person most likely to hear and respond was Russell. She jammed a fist against her teeth.

The fight-or-flight instinct competed with the drive to help. Exploding adrenaline made her thoughts preternaturally—and probably deceptively—clear. *Fight* was not at the moment called for, though she would stay vigilant. *Flight* could wait.

She was readying herself for a clumsy attempt at mouth-to-mouth resuscitation, patently useless but the only measure she could think to take, when her trembling right hand strayed to Ardith's left flank and into a viscous swamp. "Oh, Jesus!" Jerking away, ashamed of her cowardice, berating herself for not gathering as much information as possible about the dimensions and nature of Ardith's wound, she wiped her hand hard on the ground as though the dirt of unknown composition would cleanse her of Ardith's blood, obsessively scraping and clawing well past any possible efficacy. With an effort she stopped herself; the blood left on her knuckles was probably her own.

Now the urge to flee was all but irresistable. She stopped, though, long enough to find the scarf she'd guessed Ardith would be wearing, unknot it and pull it loose. For a confused moment she thought maybe she could fashion a tourniquet around Ardith's torso. All she could do, though, was to press it against the wound in a gesture no more than symbolic since it might staunch the blood for a minute or two but certainly wouldn't stop the bleeding at the source. Then she scrambled to her feet and ran, hobbled, lurched away. Anywhere away.

Something hard and sharp slammed into her temple and reverberated. Reeling, she caught herself on what was apparently a signpost, though she had no hope of reading what it said. Her head throbbed and she felt sick. This clumsy, groping movement could hardly be called a headlong rush, but it had the same panicky quality, the same delusion of fleeing to somewhere safer. Already she had disoriented herself enough that she didn't know exactly where Ardith's body lay, would have to search in order to find it again, and this made the fact of it, its ubiquitous presence, all the more horrifying.

There must be something she could use to identify the location for the police, some landmark or directional indicator. Her eye blazed when she peered upward and tried hopelessly to focus, and for all that she couldn't even tell that there was a sign at the top of the pole, let alone what was written on it. There were long unlit stretches between streetlights, which were simultaneously glaring and too dim. There might be buildings.

Suddenly outrage seized her. Why was she trying to use vision? The straining of her eyes was both ludicrous and a betrayal of her own basic nature, as insulting as it was ineffective. When she squeezed shut the offending organs, she was further infuriated by the deepening of her terror. Vision had never served her well; why did she persist in acting as if it would?

With great sustained effort, she managed to calm herself enough to take in data from her surroundings. To her left, the feel of the air and the ambient sounds seemed less dense, less solid, and she thought she could isolate the trickle of shallow running water. Was she near the river? Was there a faint moist odor? But the river went all the way through town. There must be some way to tell where she was, where Ardith was, along its course.

Suddenly, close by but far above her, bells began to peal. The melodious chiming startled her badly, but she forced herself to pay attention, and after a few bars she recognized a hymn. A church, then. She was near the river and a church with a carillon.

Blindly she cut across the street and through what seemed to be an opening, knowing she might be getting herself into an even more dangerous place. It was some sort of open space, a lot with no buildings in this densely built-up part of town, but not vacant, for there were rows of swaying objects taller than she was, spongy material underfoot, mounds. She smelled growing things. A garden, she thought incredulously, and these were cornstalks; she grabbed one and it broke, emitting a sappy green odor and revealing to her touch cornsilk and long, slightly abrasive frondlike leaves, still concealing the delicate little cobs that must be there.

A garden. She'd blundered into a garden, probably a community garden from its size and location. A garden should be a benign, nurturing place, and there was a strong temptation to relax, as if she were home safe, but she knew better. She was lost and going blind in an alien part of the city in the middle of the night. The threat posed by Russell had taken a new and very specific form. And somebody or something else was in the garden with her. She stopped short, tried to hold her breath.

Some other living thing, with an energy different from that of the plants, but whether human or not she couldn't tell. More than one; several; many. Breathing. Swaying.

"Hello?" she called timorously. No answer, but a change in the quality of the presence, as if positions had shifted because she was there. "Hello? Who's there? I need help. Can you help me?"

Behind her was Ardith, and Russell. Ahead were these unknown creatures, breathing, edging toward her in an odd configuration. She might elude them all by going sideways, if a route was available, and almost involuntarily she turned to the left, reconsidered, for no good reason turned to the right.

"Please help me. Who's there?" Her near-whisper sounded brazen.

"Who's *there?*" came the strident, mocking response, and the laughter that followed told her there were ten or twelve people in a loose, milling cluster.

She chilled, but ventured again, "I need help."

"We all need help, sweetie. It's the human condition." More appreciative laughter, a few hoots as if at a pleasing performance, and still the sense of rocking motion, individually and en masse.

"Somebody's been shot back there. I'm in danger. I'm being chased. Somebody's already been shot, maybe killed."

"Bummer."

Desperately then, "I'm going blind."

There was a pause, a happy murmur, the sound of strangely gaited rapid footsteps coming close. She was loomed over—assaultive body heat prickling her skin, depleted oxygen crimping her lungs. She held her breath, held her ground. Her wrists were roughly grasped. She jerked her forearms in toward herself, flung them out, made fists and punched, but her hands were forced outward and upward to someone's face.

Unsure what she was resisting, she tried to scratch and poke, against her will feeling and knowing that she was feeling the curve of a woman's jawbone, the hollow under a ringed ear, a bristle of bangs. Her fingertips were forcibly pressed against the cheeks, as if to leave prints. Then the woman let go and put her own fingers lightly onto Leila's face, thumbs under jawbone, pinkies imprinting temples, the other fingertips like brads along cheeks and nose.

Reading her, Leila realized with a shudder of both

horror and pleasure. Taking her measure. Collecting tactile information about her in lieu of visual. With considerable distaste she'd read about Helen Keller doing that, but she'd never known anyone who did, and certainly would never have done so herself by her own volition. But here they stood, hands traveling each other's faces, entering what should have been each other's personal space in a way decidedly impersonal and yet intimate, almost pornographic.

She thought to back away. Instead she found herself closing her eyes, holding her breath, running the tip of her tongue along the fleshy horizontal inner cleavage between her lips, following with her attention the careful but by no means gentle progress of the fingers across the planes of her face, and moving her own fingers until they came to the other woman's eye sockets, which were empty.

She gasped and jerked her hands away, then brought them back without being instructed. The eyelids gave like paper.

Smiling, the woman kept feeling her. The insinuating hands were at her hairline now, around her ears, down along her collarbone. Touching more than necessary at a first meeting, surely; taking liberties.

"What's your name?"

"Christina." She'd intended it to be a disguise, but giving that name shamed her.

Under her fingers, the woman nodded, an odd and oddly thrilling sensation. The hands had been removed from her now, leaving her exposed. She hadn't noted any diminution of discomfort when her eyes had been under that presumptuous touch, but now, without it, the pain was much worse. She needed lubricant but didn't dare move to get it.

Then her face was cupped and held in the strong, cool hands, and the woman declared, "Well, sweetie, *Christina,* you have definitely come to the right place for going blind."

Voices rose like a Greek chorus. The others must have surrounded them without her realizing it. She was afraid.

"We're all blind here."

"You've come to the right place."

"Pleased to meet you, sister."

"We're all blind."

"Welcome to the Country of the Blind."

# Chapter Eighteen

*In the country of the blind, the one-eyed man is king.*
Although the adage rang in her ears like a recovered memory of ritual abuse, she'd actually come across it only once in her life, at about ten years old. In print, she thought, since the memory included the smell of the page held very close to her nose, the heat of the reading light at an exact angle from over her right shoulder, and nothing auditory. She did have a vivid image—remembered or imposed after the fact—of the way the words had looked on the page: italicized, centered. There had been a vertiginous sensation of leaping forward, of flying through time and space without a net, as she'd comprehended for the first time how words could be made to say more than they said by not quite saying what they meant.

With that terrible, beautiful sentence—illustrated: foreground reds and blues, dull inchoate brown in the background—had come a new, primary understanding about herself, and also about language: words were a kind of germ warfare, sneaky, poison seeping into you right along with stuff you needed to survive in this world.

Since then, of course, she'd discovered countless such idioms embedded in the language like mines, dangling like asps amid the protective coloration of everyday syntax, striking out of deceptively cloudless speech: *The blind leading the blind. Seeing is believing. What you see is what you get.*

But it was *In the country of the blind, the one-eyed man is king* to which she kept returning, spellbound. As in the best fairy tales, beloved for their very grotesquerie, its meanings were nested each inside the other, and metamorphosed over time as she was ready to put them to use in understanding the world and her place in it:

Blind was bad. Normal was good. The closer to normal you were, or could pretend to be, the better.

The less vision you had, the more of a peasant you were, the more under other people's control. She didn't have much.

Normal sight was to be treasured like royal blood. Without it, you'd never amount to much.

Woefully inadequate masses would revere and obey a personage only slightly less deformed than they were, whom any normal person would pity.

And—horrifyingly; alluringly—there could be a whole *country* of the blind, metaphorical or even literal. For a while she'd been preoccupied with anthropological speculation about how this country would be organized with blindness as the standard. No written language, maybe; no Braille or its equivalent as a translation of print; oral tradition intricately developed. No colors—would colors exist if nobody had use for them? More texture; more sound and odor. No light. For that matter, no darkness.

Now here she was, if not precisely in a country of the blind then in a village, at least; a clan, a band. It wasn't clear to her yet who these people were or where exactly they lived, but they claimed, proudly, all to be blind, which was unnerving enough. And the leader, the revered personage, had not only no vision at all but *no eyes*.

Her name was Seph. Leila heard the word in numerous voices and contexts before she realized it was a name, and then she thought it might be *Steph*, for Stephanie, like Russell's daughter (surely this couldn't *be* his daughter, could it?), or *Seth*.

The syllable was further obscured by the peculiar acoustics of the garden. Within the amalgam of city noise—the white-water rush of the encircling interstate, closer and more defined horns and tire squeals, sound waves pounding from a passing car-radio bass, voices in the middle distance and nearer, the chittering of locusts against a concrete backdrop—the surfaces of the garden absorbed sound much like plants absorbing carbon dioxide, and emitted a quiet that offered nourishment whether she could take it in or not. Individual sounds were muffled, wrapped, woven, softly distorted. But, finally, she decided it was *Seph*.

"I'm Seph."

Was that an adjective, like "I'm sick" or "I'm lost"?

"My name is Seph."

Although she could see virtually nothing but the red and white and black shapes of her eye's own making, she still strained to see, quite as though vision actually was the most credible of the senses, or in yet another self-deprecating attempt to pass. Nevertheless, she tried to see.

There were lights, but they illuminated nothing useful to her. There were patches of shadow denser than others, but she couldn't identify or even reliably locate any of them. There were undulation and ululation, visual and auditory haloes.

She was half-sprawled on the ground, propped sideways against something large, sturdy, constructed of heavy metal (Dumpster? compost bin? storage shed?). Seph was standing over her, speaking downward.

"You blind, Christina?"

"No!" She was *not* blind. She had some vision. Unsteadily she got to her knees, then to her feet.

Seph pronounced, "Oh, too bad," the curling of her lip clearly audible. Leila's eye was dry and painful, but she was afraid the bottle of eyedrops in her pocket would be taken away again if Seph and the others knew it was there. Since presumably they couldn't see what she was doing, could she extract it without them knowing, squirt the lubricant into her arid eye with not even the slightest sound to give her away? She was afraid to risk it.

As if on cue, a mutter rose—disapproving; threatening. From body heat and body odor and the pillowing of sound, she estimated there might be a dozen people in addition to her and Seph. All of them blind, all of them apparently hostile to her. *"Sighted,"* they hissed, an epithet. *"Normal."*

"I—I don't see very well," she found herself protesting. "I am visually impaired—"

"Not enough."

"Not good enough."

"Impaired?"

"Who you calling impaired?"

"If I don't get to a doctor I could lose what sight I have." Imploring and, at the same time, defending herself.

"Cool."

"Stay, then."

"Stay with us. Stay with your own kind."

"Somebody's been shot back there. I have to call the police."

"No cops."

Laughter. "I don't think so."

"No cops."

"I have to get to a doctor. Help me—" They couldn't help her; they were *blind.*

"We'll let you stay the night. In the morning you have to leave," Seph decreed, and turned away. The others milled and dispersed without any further acknowledgment of her. They'd been encircling her; now, on all sides, they were gone.

She hadn't thought about staying here and certainly didn't want to—*Cathy, I want to come home, Cathy, are you all right?*—but the rejection stung. Tears brought false and dangerous short-term comfort to her searing eye; they would actually further dry the tissues, worsening the pain and eventual corneal damage. But she couldn't stop crying. *Not good enough? Not blind enough?*

Hugging herself, trying to decide where to go and what to do now, she found she was swaying, found that the swaying made her feel better. Many blind people did that, and it always offended her. She'd often had to resist the urge to push down on the shoulder of the blind man on the bus bench so he'd stop leaning back and forth like a grotesque windup toy, to walk out of the classroom where the blind teacher's metronomic swaying made it almost impossible to concentrate on anything else, to tell the mother on the playground not to let her blind child *do* that. "It makes us look stupid!" she'd want to yell. "It makes us look handicapped!"

Now she swayed, and all around her at a distance was swaying, and it felt good. Somehow it helped her feel steadier, better organized in space, and gave her an unexpected sense of where she was in relation to other objects. She shifted her weight from side to side a few times, tried forward and backward and settled on that, toes to heels, toes to heels, toes to heels. Quickly, the motion was comforting. Before long it had become her ambient kinesthetic field, and her awareness of the swaying diminished, so that she'd notice her own continuing motion again only after what must have been a full minute of rocking. Once or twice she tried to stop, but not very hard. The swaying made fishing the eyedrops out of her pocket a bit harder, but she managed.

She was tilting her head back to receive the cool moisture when someone approached her. Slow footsteps, heavy breath, sudden faint body heat and odor, a tamping of ambient sound. Someone was very close to her, ahead and to the right, at about the two o'clock position. Someone was only inches away.

*Russell,* she thought, with a disturbing mixture of fear and eagerness, and gave a strangled cry, and took an off-balance step backward, colliding with a barrier—from the loose metal clatter of it, probably a dilapidated chicken-wire fence. Frantic to make sense of something, anything, she speculated that the fence could indicate the edge of the garden as a whole or a boundary between plots. That didn't tell her much, and might well not even be correct, but she stored the impression away as better than nothing if she had to tell the police or Cathy where she was.

Of course, it made little sense that this would be Russell. "Who's there?" she forced herself to demand, as if whatever name the stranger offered would mean anything to her. The absence of a reply didn't tell her anything either. She dropped the bottle back into her pocket, instantly checked that it was still there. The person had gone away.

Unmistakable sounds of lovemaking suddenly wafted from somewhere between her and the hazily brighter place where she thought there must be a parking lot or some other illuminated area. Panting, moaning, wet hot noises. Two women, by the sound of it, though desperation to identify things in this crazy new environment probably reduced the reliability of her perceptions. Aching for Cathy pulsed in her chest and belly, bending her over.

Someone was playing a harmonica, the same maudlin song fragment over and over. Not recognizing it, she thought she might be hearing the result of composer's block, or lack of technical skill, or short attention span, or obsessive-compulsive disorder. For a while she wanted nothing more than one more phrase, one more note, a tying off of the musical strands; when in desperation she composed it herself in her mind, sang it softly, there was in fact a certain relief, even though nothing was finished.

Someone was snoring. The lovers had been satisfied, or given up. Two women, maybe the same ones, were engaged in a rancorous pseudodebate over whether cats or dogs made better pets: Dogs were loyal. Cats were independent. Dogs were smarter because they learned better. Cats were smarter because they wouldn't be taught.

The harmonica tune stalled out again at the same spot, and again started over. The snoring spiked loud and ragged; now it sounded like choking.

Abdominal cramps, which now that she'd noticed them seemed to have been getting worse for some time, set her to worrying about food poisoning. Her eye hurt, and rummaging again in the long pocket for the eyedrops was too much trouble. She had the need to both urinate and defecate. There was no one to ask where to go. Her belly ached. The first overflow drops of pee had already unpleasantly moistened her crotch. She was going to be sick. She was going blind. She was lost among blind strangers with nobody to hold her head. She could not do what she had to do.

Misery flooded her. The harmonica player had stopped; had the song found an ending while she hadn't been paying attention?

Surely there were facilities around here somewhere; surely these people didn't just fertilize the garden with their waste. On the slim chance that a port-a-potty might be near enough and bright-colored enough for her to see, she squinted and peered; nothing. Maybe there was a public rest room nearby. "Excuse me?" she ventured, but she didn't say it very loud and nobody responded.

Though tempted just to soil her clothes and be

done with it, she finally roused herself enough to crawl away from the most concentrated crowd noise. Trying for privacy was probably pointless; if all these people really were blind, they wouldn't see her anyway, and since she couldn't tell where she was moving from or to, she might well be making herself more rather than less conspicuous. By the time she finally chose a spot, adjusted her clothes, spread her feet, squatted and relieved herself, the physical urgency and then release were enormous, but she was acutely embarrassed, by the noise and stench she made among all the other noises and smells, and by the primal pleasure.

Cleaning herself with a scrap of tissue from her pocket, she was repulsed by her own intimate odor, rancid despite her sponge bath at Ardith's hands. She needed a long hot soak, with soap and shampoo and bath powder, deodorant and lotion. She needed clean clothes; these Ardith had given her—in an act of what might have been kindness or personal fastidiousness or dogma—were badly soiled and ill-fitting. She needed to brush her teeth. Physical yearning for these things, and the knowledge that she wasn't likely to get them any time soon, made her squat with her head on her knees for a long moment, unable and unwilling to move.

Ardith. Had been shot. Was bleeding on the ground somewhere. Was dead or dying. Leila could think of no possible way to help.

Finally, chilled, she tugged her clothes back on.

Then there was nothing to do but lie down on the ground and will unconsciousness.

Perversely, she instead grew hyperalert. Sensory data crowded in, and she began to perceive certain patterns. Plants rustled heavily in a breeze she wouldn't have felt if the plants hadn't warned her. The fragrance of ripe tomatoes made her salivate. Three or four people were talking quietly a little distance to her left, and the harmonica had started up again, a different tune fragment this time. She gritted her teeth, but when the half-dozen notes were not repeated even once, she found herself doing it, playing the phrase over and over and over in her mind, humming it.

Noticing that traffic noise was most pronounced ahead and to the left, in the eleven o'clock position, a steady rumble that suggested a major arterial street, she reasoned that the garden gate would likely not be on that side, although she couldn't have defended that conclusion. It came to her that here she was not imprisoned. No one would stop her from leaving.

Crouching, staying low, she edged to her right. After the first few sidling movements, she could no longer tell which way she was going in relation to where she'd just been, let alone where she wanted to go, as if she knew. With the flats of her hands she patted and stroked the ground as far as she could reach, encountering both packed and tilled earth, mulch and gravel. Plants flattened and snapped under her hands and knees; she recognized bell and jalapeño peppers by the smell when they broke. Every time she put a hand down in a new place, she half-expected it to sink into Ardith's flesh and blood.

Here was a wooden edge to something, some sort of raised bed. Leaning against it, she used it as a guide until it ran out. Here was a flagstone path. Kneeling on one stone until she'd positioned her hands on the next, she kept herself on it until it dead-ended at a bench, and then she had to get turned around and follow the flagstones back the other way. The path seemed to have lengthened, and at one point she thought it angled where it hadn't before.

When she could no longer ignore the protesting of her knees and back, she got shakily to her feet. Extending her hands, she took one step after another after another, bumped into some tall growing thing, tripped, walked some more, found a chain-link fence.

A fence. She took a deep breath. The fence ought to lead to the gate. Even if she was starting at the wrong spot, following the fence long enough ought to bring her to the gate. Premature triumph stopped her for a moment: She'd almost done it. She was almost free.

After a brief, agonizing debate over which way to turn, she turned left, and immediately kicked something firm and ankle-high on the ground. A pumpkin, maybe; she didn't stop to identify it, but when she stepped over it, thick vines and big flypapery leaves whipped up under her pant leg. Following the fence would probably mean she'd be treading right through garden plots rather than staying on a path, and she felt remotely guilty, but when her shoe collided with what must be another, larger pumpkin, she kicked it savagely out of the way. It bounced back on its sturdy vine, and she took time to kick it again, to bring her heel down on it. Not yet ripe and hollow, it didn't break, but she thought she made a dent in it and was inordinately pleased.

She smelled strawberries. Wasn't it too late in the season for strawberries? Wasn't it October?

She came to a corner and turned left. Then, just like that, she came to the gate.

Easily she found the latch, flipped it up and pushed the gate open. It creaked and rattled, and she had to remind herself that nobody cared if she escaped. She stepped through, conscientiously shut and latched the gate, turned to face the outside world. And had no idea what to do next.

Behind her was the gate, through the links of which she'd laced her fingers. Everywhere else was murk. Visual murk, of course: haloed lights here and there in an otherwise undifferentiated darkness. Auditory murk: hums, rumbles, swishes, taps impossible to locate or interpret. Tactile murk: nothing to touch except the ground—apparently a broken sidewalk, although it might be nothing more than random chunks of concrete. Olfactory murk.

She could not bring herself to move into the murk.

She could not, in fact, bring herself to let go of the gate. Her eye stung. With great effort she managed to loosen the grip of one hand to get the bottle of eyedrops. It was gone. Frantically, she fumbled all the way down to the bottom of the long pocket, poked into the linty corners, pulled it up and inside out. It was empty. Her eye seared.

Very cautiously, she turned herself around hand-over-hand until she was facing the gate and her fingers were once again clawed through the links. Knowing better, she tugged at it, and was sharply disappointed when it wouldn't open, even though she herself had latched it when she'd come out.

It took courage to work a hand loose and slide it sideways toward where she knew the latch to be. At first she didn't find it, and under fingers made nearly useless by panic, the seam where the gate fit into the fence felt unbroken.

But then the back of her flailing hand came up under the latch and knocked it off. Startled by the collision and the noise, she cried out and trembled, but she pushed on the gate. It opened inward an inch or two, then stuck. She shoved it, butted her shoulder into it, leaned against it with all her weight, and then, on the brink of hysteria, somehow remembered it opened outward. She pulled it open and walked in.

And had no idea where she was inside the garden, either, and sank to the ground among rows of fat round things—cabbages? cauliflower?—which she did her best not to crush but supposed she was anyway. It was cold. She curled up. Her eye hurt. Tears soothed it for the moment and would only make it worse. She wept. Ardith was bleeding to death somewhere, Cathy was in terrible jeopardy and there was nothing she could do except wait to go blind.

In the night Seph came to her. Even at first contact—the first inkling that someone was close by, the first fragrance, the first light touch—she did not mistake Seph for either Russell or Cathy, although she'd been dreaming of them both: Russell stalking Cathy. Cathy capturing Russell. Both of them on top of her, and her struggle to get out from under them. In Russell's arms she could see perfectly; she had no dream images for full sight, but in the dream she understood that was what it was, a blessing, a reward and a renunciation. In Cathy's arms, she saw in the dream the way she saw in waking life when her contact was in, her glasses on, eyedrops lubricating, light neither too bright nor too dim; she was, in fact, reading, letters and words wonderfully clear although the content was not.

"It's Seph," Seph whispered.

For a split second the dream continued. She had no eyes. Her eye sockets were seeping, not blood but vision itself dribbling away like blood: There should have been more blood, there should have been none.

"Don't be afraid," Seph whispered, catching her shoulders to roll her back, catching her hands and kissing them, touching tongue and teeth to her eyes. "I won't hurt you."

# *Chapter Nineteen*

Day broke. The quilt of ambient sound, already ragged, raveled into separate, harsher noises that she was working to identify before she was fully conscious. The quality of the air changed, not warmer yet but lighter, less dense. She smelled coffee and car exhaust. Dawn pierced her matted eyelids. Under them, her eyeballs recoiled; she buried her face in her arms, but the savage brilliance still got in.

From the ache in her chest and the residual happy, painful images slowly breaking up in her mind, she surmised she'd been dreaming about school, which was going on without her, which she could not imagine going back to now. If she'd ever known how to teach anybody anything, she never would again. Still, she was smelling the heady aroma of new crayons, hearing the sudden wonder in the voice of a six-year-old at the moment when squiggles on a page

259

revealed themselves to be the letters of the very first word in the world. Once she'd had a role in that sweet drama.

Seph was gone. Seph had stayed with her for a long time last night. Seph had—not loved her, but not raped her, either; in no way assaulted her. She touched her eyes. She touched her clitoris, tender and still slightly engorged. Gingerly she allowed herself tiny, quick memories of Seph's nipples, navel, knee.

*Cathy.*

"Christina."

Not Seph. Male, but not Russell. Gravelly, phlegmy; longtime smoker and drinker, probably younger than he sounded. Black Midwestern accent, broad vowels, high and low inflections widely separated on the scale and slightly flattened.

"Christina? You there, girl?"

"Leave me alone."

She felt him crouch. Something with something else stacked on it was placed on the ground, rattles of varying timbres and durations. She was cold. In the night she hadn't been cold, but now that Seph had left her and it was morning, chills sped through her. "Here's breakfast."

"Oh. Thanks." She pulled herself into a semi-sitting position. Her eye hurt and was crusted at the corners. Her joints ached. The dull need to empty her bladder made itself known. She was ravenous. "What is it?"

"Bread. Light rye, I think. And mushmelon. Coffee."

"*Mush*melon?"

"Yeah. What's your problem?" Instantly defensive, but for the wrong reason. "What's the matter, you don't like mushmelon?"

She couldn't bring herself to ingest any of it yet but knew she wouldn't be able to resist much longer. "Where'd this stuff come from?"

"Yo, girl," he warned. "You don't want it, fine. There's plenty that do."

"No, I—" She reached out, swept her hand back and forth, nearly knocked over a paper cup, nonthermal, full of something hot. There was the odor of very weak coffee.

He took it away. "Seph said feed you before you go. But, hey, if it ain't good enough for you—"

"Just asking," she told him testily. "What's *your* problem?"

"You're a guest here. Didn't your mama teach you manners?"

"What I am," she said, "is in trouble. I was kidnapped. I escaped. Another person didn't. I have to get to a doctor for myself, and I have to get help for her, and I have to get home."

"No shit! Kidnapped?"

"Does anybody here have a cell phone?"

"Uh," he said dryly, "no."

Steam drizzled across her cold face as he held the cup out toward her again. They both fumbled until

261

she had it in two hands. The coffee was so weak she doubted she'd have known it was coffee if he hadn't told her so, and as it was she thought he might be wrong, or deliberately poisoning her, or playing her for a fool. She knew she was making a face, but if he was blind, as he claimed to be, it wouldn't matter; she stuck out her tongue as if gagging and he didn't react.

"Where are we, anyway? Is this some kind of garden?"

"Used to be a community garden. Pretty much abandoned now, except for us."

"Things are growing," she shot back, not to be tricked, proud to display her perceptiveness. "Tomatoes and green peppers."

"And corn."

She pressed, unclear what it was she wanted to know. "You *live* here? Out in the open? In plain sight?" She snorted. "So to speak."

"Hey, there's shelter. Cute little gazebo in the northeast corner. Big storage shed over there." Hearing him gesture, she was incensed that even he, even here, would point. "And we're kind of hidden away, you know? Not a lot of folks just happen by."

"Where exactly are we?"

She meant the query to be cagey, but he answered readily with street names she recognized as being in the warehouse district, a section of town she'd never been in before. "Nobody's tried to make you move? The cops? Social Services? The Urban Garden people? The Coalition for the Homeless or the Federation for the Blind?"

"We don't stay here days. We're out and about."

"Doing what?"

The tone of his voice denoted a shrug. "Making a living. Having a life. You know. Doing what everybody else does, girl."

Hunger won out over distaste and unease about contamination. The bread didn't smell moldy and the melon slices were mushy only where they'd been cut. There were fig bars, too, an exorbitantly delightful treat, stale only along one end. "Thank you," she mumbled with her mouth full.

"So," he asked, in a voice too friendly and too loud, "how'd you find us?"

The best she could come up with was, "Serendipity."

"Come again?"

"Chance. Accident. The random nature of the universe." Russell would have called it God's Will, or Satan's.

"You got lost, right?"

That was as good a summary as any. "Right."

"Yeah, well, join the club, girlfriend. One way or another, that's how all of us got here. We once were lost and now we're found." He gave a hooting laugh.

She couldn't resist. "Were blind but now you see?"

"Not hardly."

"Sorry."

He missed or ignored the sarcasm. "We found Seph or Seph found us."

"Are you all really blind?" The temerity of the question shocked her. Just saying the word *blind* shocked her. She'd never really known anyone with vision like hers or worse, and blindness was not something to be mentioned between strangers.

"Yep." Proudly.

With a brashness born of equal parts trepidation and curiosity, she ventured, "Seph doesn't have any eyes at all."

"You noticed. Cool." The hoot again.

"I didn't have much choice. She held my fingers on her eyes—her eye sockets—until I got it." The shiver that passed through her was unadulterated revulsion, she was sure, but it crossed her mind that it could easily be taken for admiration, attraction, even awe.

"She does that. Freaks some folks out." A fond chuckle. "But, you know, she was the first. Kind of pioneer. An inventor. Everybody tries to be like her, and can't nobody quite do it. I guess she's got a right to be proud. I mean, she pretty much changed the world."

Leila scoffed, "The world?"

"Yeah. This world. Mine. Changed everything."

"What do you mean, everybody tries to be like her?"

"Well, for starters, we none of us got any eyes."

She gasped. "Shit. Really?"

He took her hands in his. Guessing his intention, she tried to pull away but was neither quick nor firm enough. Turning the flats of her fingertips toward him, he laid them on either side of the bridge of his nose, under his eyebrows, where eyes should be. They sank in slightly. She felt the circles of bone, the ridge of brow, the lids and lashes, the globular cavities.

Now her fingers were moving without direction from his, exploring, probing, caressing. One of his eyelids twitched as if about to open, and the desire to feel *inside* the empty socket (would there be raw flesh? scabs? bare bone?) was only slightly overpowered by the desire not to. She lowered her hands, and he didn't stop her.

"You were all born without eyes?" she marveled. "How is that possible—"

"No, no, not *born* this way. This is the new, improved model."

"I don't understand," she insisted, although she feared she was beginning to.

"That's the dues," he explained smugly. "How you get to stay here. You keep trying to make yourself like Seph, in Seph's image. You do as much as you can to meet her, what would you call it, standards."

"Her blindness standards? Her eyeless standards?"

"You got it, girlfriend."

"So the blinder you are the better, and having no eyes is as blind as it's possible to get."

"Yep." She heard his grin, imagined his nod. "To be who you are all the way. Who you are and then some. To go as far as you can go. Extreme identity."

"How did you lose your eyes?" Afraid to hear the answer, she listened intently and refused to be distracted by the hot slash of pain across her own eyeball.

"Seph took them."

"*Took* them?"

"*If thine eye offend thee, pluck it out.*"

"You did something she didn't like?"

"I could see light and shadow. That's not cool. It confuses you. Dilutes you. Seph says you gotta be one thing or the other."

"And she plucked out your eyes?" She was incredulous, but there was a mad internal logic to this that had her ready to believe almost anything.

"Well, she cut them out." Proudly.

"My God."

His hand came clumsily to her eyes, thumb and forefinger measuring. Snapping her head sideways to get away from him, she banged her temple against some protrusion; the pain seemed out of all proportion to the small impact. Tears sprang to her eyes again. He felt and misinterpreted them. "Hey, girl, it's okay. It's great, actually. It's like faith."

Rubbing the new sore spot on her skull, she hissed furiously, "It's crazy, is what it is. What is this, some kind of masochistic cult?"

"May be. But we got each other, and we got Seph. Who you got? Hmm?"

"Cathy," she said.

"Ooo. Cathy. She your main woman, huh? Waiting for you at home, is she?"

"Yes."

"She blind?"

"No."

"Full-sighted?"

"Yes."

His tongue clicked against his teeth in disapproving sympathy. *"That's too bad."*

She'd come upon an orange, peeled and eaten it, spat out the seeds, thought about orange trees sprouting in this aversive climate. Now her hands were sticky, and wiping them on her filthy shirt didn't help. "You just sat there and let her cut out your eyes?"

"Something like that."

"Didn't it hurt?"

"Sure."

"Don't you miss your light perception? Wasn't it a huge loss?"

"Sure, at first. But you gotta know who you are. You gotta be proud. Now I'm *blind.*"

*"You're nuts. You're sick."* On her feet now, she tried to scan the garden space for the gate where she'd lost her nerve last night, or for any other exit. The fence she'd been leaning against was not a border after all but seemed entirely haphazard, demar-

cating nothing, leading nowhere in particular.

"You could stay, too," he invited, "if you gave her your eyes."

"Get away from me."

"Hey. Your choice. But you oughta at least think about it."

For a split second the idea did have a certain sick appeal. Horrified, she pushed away from him and away from the group crouched together eating. He didn't try to stop her. Wherever Seph was, she didn't make her presence known.

Leila's right eye pulsed, protesting, asserting itself. Gasping at the bright pain, she backed up against the fence, which swayed in sections like blankets stiff on a line and clattered as she slid down it to the rubbled ground.

Crosslegged, elbows on inner thighs, she cradled the hurt part of herself as if it were a child in distress. Both hands cupped over her eye, she rocked, crooned. Pity engulfed her, and the yearning to make things better, a charitable impulse as if her organ of sight were not quite part of herself. Soothed just by her intention, the eye began to calm.

Then her left eye, which had never had vision and had not been hurting, suddenly buzzed like a shorting-out electric wire. She cried out and flattened her fingers, pressing both round, firm eyeballs in place.

No one approached her for a long time then. As much as anything, she felt self-conscious, the way she often did in groups. She'd always thought that was because she couldn't pick up non-verbal cues, smiles and nods from any distance away, body language inviting or rebuffing conversation; or because it took so much repetition for her to recognize someone; or because people with full, easy sight didn't know what to say to people without it. Now, feeling the same discomfort under these conditions raised suspicions that the awkwardness and alienation were more basic to her nature than that. Even here, she didn't fit in. Even here, she was different, not good enough and alone.

*If you really loved me, Cathy, you'd have found me by now.*

The instant she was aware of the fully formed thought, she had no doubt of its validity. It had been weeks, maybe months. She hadn't been spirited away to Iran or Lebanon, for Chrissake, or even another city. And Cathy could *see*.

And not just Cathy: all of them. All of the sighted fuckers. The cops. The school administration. The other teachers. Her supposed friends. They could all *see*. If they missed her, if she mattered to them, if they wanted her back in their lives, they'd have found her by now. Russell had found her, hadn't he?

Ardith had found her.

And Seph would, too, if she decided to. For whatever perverse purposes, Russell and Seph paid attention. Russell and Seph wanted her. She was valuable to them in a real, immediate way she patently was not to Cathy or anybody else.

Hurt and humiliated by this new, sharp realization, she was also energized by it. The resurgent feeling of purpose and direction had nothing to attach to yet; she would *do* something, dammit; she'd show Cathy and the rest of them, but she didn't know what or how.

The black male smoker/drinker from the Midwest was with her again. This time she hadn't heard him coming. He set a large soft bundle on the ground. "We picked out some clothes for you. Seph says they'll suit you."

She found herself smiling as if at a sweet little secret. Seph's sense of touch was well-developed. Seph's hands knew what they were doing. It was not hard to imagine that, having stroked and straddled and traced so many parts of her body, Seph would be able to extrapolate her clothing sizes and flattering styles along with much else. "The shirt's red and the pants are brown," he told her. "In case you care."

"I suppose that comes from Seph, too."

"It all comes from Seph," he assured her.

"And how would she know colors?"

"By feel."

"Oh, please. And does she read minds, too? Walk on water, maybe? Heal the halt and the blind?" But she could make out enough of the shirt's color to tell that it was, indeed, red or burgundy or deep orange. She shivered.

"Whatever," he dismissed her, and she heard him turn away.

"Wait!" He paused, and she fought to control the desperation in her voice. "Where can I—is there someplace to change?"

"What, for privacy?" He gave his hooting laugh. "Girlfriend, we're all *blind*, remember? Trust me, nobody'll notice."

As if she'd said something truly moronic, she blushed and sputtered. "But this is a public place. Out in the open in the middle of the city. There are other people—" He'd gone.

Hurriedly she changed into the new clothes, trying to ignore both the cold and her unclean underwear. The shirt sleeves and pant legs were slightly too long, and she was perversely gratified that Seph hadn't judged the sizes perfectly. Rolling up the cuffs, she reminded herself to be even more careful than usual about tripping. Before she bundled the dirty clothes Ardith had given her and left them on the ground, not knowing what else to do with them, she checked the pockets once more for the eyedrops, still unwilling to believe the bottle wasn't there.

Her eye would hardly open at all now, and even through its twitching lid, glare seared. Everything glared—the sun itself, the sky, windows and walls of buildings, leaves and stalks, the shirt she struggled to button with one hand while shielding her eyes with the other. Her cheek muscles ached from squinting. She couldn't raise her head. Many a winter recess in elementary school she'd spent like this, head down, eyes squeezed shut, unable to pry herself away from the brick wall of the school because of ubiquitous glare.

People were moving purposefully around her now, and she caught pieces of conversations about the day ahead. "Time to go," someone declared at her shoulder.

"Go where?" She knew at least the category of where she herself must go—a doctor or hospital, to get attention for her eye, and a place with a phone to call Cathy and the police. "Where is there a phone?"

"The closest pay phones are by the main library."

"Where's that?"

"Four blocks that way." Someone lifted her free hand and stuck it out at an angle, then dropped it.

"I don't have any money."

"Here." Two coins were pressed into her palm. Awkwardly, she determined them to be a quarter and a dime.

"Thanks."

Her reluctance surprised and worried her. Why should she be even slightly tempted to stay here? Why should the prospect of starting a new life as a member of a group of blind street people have any appeal to it at all? "Do you like living here?" she demanded.

This guy smelled of coffee, cigarettes, unwashed clothes and Polo cologne. "Ain't a bad place to be."

"What's good about it?"

"You got homies, you know? Everybody needs homies."

"I have—somebody."

"He blind?"

"She's fully sighted. What's that got to do with it?"

"Everything. Got everything to do with it. Blind is who you are."

"It's one thing I am. And I'm not blind."

"That's the problem. You ain't one thing or the other."

"This is who I am."

He bent close, laid a hand on her knee. "Thing is, Christina, you could stay here if you wanted to."

"I have to get help. I have to get home. I'm a teacher. Somebody's waiting for me at home—"

"You don't belong there."

"I sure as hell don't belong here."

"You could, though. You could be one of us."

"She said I had to leave this morning."

"She'd let you stay if you showed her you want to."

In a swift, smooth motion, he moved his hand from her knee to her face, rough thumb and pinky braced against her cheeks, middle finger on her forehead at the rumored location of the third eye (which in her case, she thought grimly, was surely no more useful than the other two), index and ring fingers caressing her eyes. "Fuck you," she breathed, not moving.

His voice had become husky, seductive. "I mean, it ain't like it's a high price."

"I'm not blind."

"You ain't sighted, either. Neither fish nor fowl, neither this nor that. Make a choice here, Christina. Take a stand. You'll feel better."

"Get away from me! You're nuts! You're all nuts! What makes you think I'd want to stay here, anyway? Why would I let some crazy blind woman mutilate me? Get the hell away from me!"

"Suit yourself. But just remember, you are *lost.*"

When he left her, the space around her emptied, lightened, cooled. Still famished, she gnawed a little on the melon rind, hoping to find a shred of edible pulp. The tepid coffee filming the bottom of the cup was gritty and acidic. Her eyes hurt.

She could not summon a clear image of Cathy; her voice, her fragrance, her touch, the web of their lives together seemed as much fantasy as memory, and quite unreachable from here. Russell, however, was real, and the ropes and gag, and the Devil, and the ragged burning of her eye. Seph was real.

*Maybe I should stay here.* She wouldn't, of course; she knew she wouldn't. But there was a strange, dangerous pleasure in playing with the possibility. How would her life change if, once and for all, she eliminated any chance of ever having any vision? Would losing her eyes be a different sort of loss than losing her sight? Would she know then who she was?

A commotion some distance away, at what might

be the far end of the garden, made her reflexively look up, as if she might be able to see what it was about. People were moving in that direction, giving every appearance of hurrying although they didn't actually move very fast, and she went, too. Everybody stumbled; everybody held on to everybody else. Someone grabbed her elbow; she hooked two fingers under someone else's belt. She was no more and no less helped than helping.

Here was the gate. She banged into it, along with her companions on both sides.

Russell's voice soared above all other sounds, wordlessly chanting. She recoiled. Then, still connected to the others, she strode directly toward him until, through blurring and painful glare, she could just make out his watery silhouette.

He stood alone just on the other side of the fence. Although his features were indistinguishable, she saw that his head was unbowed, his stance proud, and she knew he'd be fancying himself a holy warrior, more than ready to be martyred for his God. His white shirt gleamed; she was surprised he wasn't wearing a tie. He was praying, and as she listened the prayers changed from, "Oh Lord my God, amen, be with me in this time of travail, amen, be with me in the presence of mine enemies, amen, Thy Will be done, amen," to tongues. Nonsense syllables or meta-language or scam, depending on your point of view, inflection and syllable construction the same as the chanted English, so it took her a few moments to realize she was not directly understanding what he was saying anymore. But on some other level—meta-level or self-delusion—she thought she did understand.

The citizens of the Country of the Blind streamed out the gate and surrounded him. Their swaying was sinister now, and they were closing in, no doubt guided by his signifying voice and the heat and odor of his fervor. Among them, Leila swayed closer and closer, propelled by his passion and theirs and, increasingly, by her own. This was the self-righteous lunatic who'd kidnapped her at gunpoint, tied her to a chair and gagged her, tried to rape her, deliberately put her at risk of going blind. This was the wacko who'd shot Ardith, who'd put Cathy in danger, might actually have harmed her. This was the fanatic who'd taken it as his crusade to strip her of the most basic and intimate parts of herself, even to her very name. This was The Enemy.

The idea of ejecting him from the garden had enormous appeal; the idea of imprisoning him here, bound and gagged and pissing himself, had even more. Her eye needed attention, the police needed to be called, Cathy warned or rescued, Ardith saved or avenged, Russell imprisoned or committed. But she allowed herself a few moments of self-indulgence and moved with the crowd, heard herself chanting with them, "Nor-*mal*. Nor-*mal*."

Seph was beside her, leading the chant, "Nor-*mal*, nor-*mal*, nor-*mal*." Seph had a knife. It glinted, clinked, tinged the already charged air with a faint metallic odor and taste.

"Nor-*mal*, nor-*mal*, nor-*mal*, nor-*mal*." The chant was rapidly becoming meta-language, nearly meaningless or with meaning profoundly heightened and deepened.

Russell had increased both his volume and his tempo, a challenge. But the mob's chanting stayed low and rhythmic. Leila could no longer tell whether she was vocalizing or not, whether vibration was spewing from the back of her throat or into her from the others. "Nor-*mal*. Nor-*mal*. Nor-*mal*."

Out of the miasma of Russell's holy babbling erupted his name for her, "Christina! Christina Luce!" It was not her name.

"What did you do to Cathy?"

"Nothing."

"Where is she? Is she all right? Did you do something to her?"

"She wasn't home. I waited. I went back a few times. She never came home. It wasn't God's will for me to take her."

Giddy with relief, Leila barked an incredulous laugh at how easily a Master Plan could be thwarted. But then worry tightened her throat again: Where was Cathy? Had something happened to her completely unrelated to Russell Gavin? Had she been in a car accident? Had she given up waiting for Leila and simply left?

"Instead he led me to Ardith. Satan is clever, but

he is no match for the Lord. Praise the Lord! Amen!"

"Ardith is a Christian, like you—"

"The worst heathen is he—she—who twists the Word. Ardith twisted the Word. God commanded me to stop her and entrusted me with the power to do so. Praise the Lord!"

"What did you do, Russell?" She knew. She wanted him to say it.

"I stopped her."

"You shot her. I was there."

"Praise the Lord."

"You killed her. Did you kill her?"

"Praise the Lord!"

Fury exploded. She would kill him. But she controlled herself enough to coax, "Where is she, Russell?"

"She is in Hell."

"Where is her body?"

"Her body lies in the shadow of the house of God."

"Which church?" But he was off again, outside language, and wouldn't or couldn't tell her more.

Seph thrust the knife into her grasp. She would stab it into the hollow of his throat. She was almost to him. Extending one hand to push people aside and to find her way, she raised the knife in the other. There was no doubt now that she was shrieking. She would stop him, here and now. She would avenge Ardith, and Cathy, and herself.

But Seph got to him first. Leila almost didn't see her, had to retract the blade hastily so as not to cut her by mistake. "Nor-*mal,* nor-*mal,*" thundered through her, around her, behind and under her, and now she was not saying it at all, was standing there alone and voiceless between Seph and the rest of the Country of the Blind, barely able to see but intently watching.

Seph placed her hands on Russell's face. He stopped chanting and froze, facial expression concealed and no doubt altered by her lightly arched fingers and pressing thumbs, but the attitude of his body was ecstatic, shoulders thrown back, palms open to heaven. He was panting, maybe crying.

Still holding the knife in her right hand, Leila took a breath and laid her left hand over Seph's. A stab of pleasure through the lowest reaches of her abdomen, close to pornographic, sickened and then emboldened her. Seph's knuckles indented her palm. The pads of her fingers fit into the flat depressions of Seph's nails. Through Seph she felt Russell trembling.

"You take him, girlfriend," Seph crowed, and slid her hand out from under Leila's.

She caught her breath at the sudden direct contact with the flesh and bone of Russell's face. His mouth was open; she felt his teeth. His cheeks were pocked and stubbled. A pulse throbbed in his temple. There was something tender and intimate about the silky arches of his eyebrows. His eyes closed when she brushed the damp lids, and in both eyeballs were pulses, too. His Adam's apple plunged, leaped again.

Under his jaw on each side was another rapid pulse; knowing those spots would be sensitive, she pressed and he winced. She pressed again. He made a small sound but did not pull away.

Finding his eyebrow ridge and cheekbone, her left forefinger and thumb formed a *C* around the eye socket, and she brought the knife up to it. She expected him to fight her off, cover or close his eyes, at least shut up. Instead, he thrust his face forward, as if in offering, actually widening the exposed eye, and his babble intensified in volume, pace, incomprehensibility, beyond language into mantra.

The crowd kept hooting and muttering without reference to what was now going on, as solipsistic and self-stimulating as Russell himself. But Seph knew what she was doing. "You go, girl," she breathed into Leila's ear, and Leila shivered. Seph drew away then, and the tip of the blade pierced Russell's skin. He flinched almost imperceptibly, and moisture formed between her flesh and his, blood or tears. She hoped it was both.

Inside the curve of her thumb and forefinger, his eyeball quivered. She moved her thumb to rest on it, wishing for a way to keep the lid open so she could explore its slimy surface. Through the thin film of protective skin, she pressed hard. The little globe resisted, slid around slightly like a baby's spring toy.

Carefully, concentrating to control the violent quivering of her hands, she traced with the knife point the eyeball in the socket. After two or three passes across pulpy flesh and encircling bone, she could feel, through the knife blade and handle, how the eyeball sat in the socket and how it would come out.

The tip and then the shaft of the blade would sink in. Blood would spurt. Russell would scream. The eyeball would pop out, attached to its tendons until she sliced through those, too, and the slippery little sphere bounced into her palm like a jacks ball. Somehow, she'd been good at jacks.

Russell's resolve broke, or his Lord changed his assignment. He knocked the knife out of Leila's hand and punched her, a blow that glanced off the side of her chin and sent her reeling. "Get away from me, Satan!" he roared, and advanced on her.

She stood to meet him. He reached for her. She lifted her knee into his groin. He cried out, bent double. She went for the back of his neck, missed, and he sprang up under her and took her in his arms. She struggled, loosened his grip, bit his shoulder, but he had her now and was dragging her backward with him. Somehow, he had the knife. She felt its cool blade under her ear. "Stay back!" he was screaming at the crowd. "Come any closer and I'll kill her!"

*As if they care. As if I'm one of them.* "Hold him! Call the police!" But she had no reason to think they would.

An eerie quiet had fallen upon the garden. Pigeons cooed. A lone dog barked in a steady three-two-three-two staccato rhythm. A siren scalloped a shrill border. Weeds rustled. Leila's footsteps and Russell's, their rapid breaths, made a trail of soft, purposeful sounds. They were, she thought, almost to the gate.

Someone hit Russell from behind, jolting his embrace loose so she could fling herself out of his grasp. The crowd fell on him, howling. She heard metal clank against something hard, saw sunlight glint. Russell screamed and went down.

"Take his eyes! Take his eyes! Take his eyes!"

"No!" They paid no more attention to her shout than to Russell's. "Stop!"

"Take his eyes!"

Leila threw herself into the melee, kicking and punching randomly, landing more than a few clean, hard blows. Bodies wrenched themselves out of her way and she burrowed through the mass until she got to Seph, who was straddling Russell with one hand pressed over the lower half of his face and the other wielding the knife toward his eyes. He was bellowing incoherently and twisting his head, but Seph bore down and held him still enough for her purpose.

Leila grabbed the knife. Aim slightly off, it was the blade she grasped; the pad of her palm sliced open. Her eye flared, and Russell bucked Seph off and scrambled out of reach.

Seph spun toward her, and the two of them faced each other, no need to see. Seph crouched and hissed, "Fucking sighted! Fucking traitor!"

Leila hefted the knife in a position she hoped was threatening, though Seph's outline was bleary and what she could hear and smell of her seemed to be coming from everywhere at once. Seph was nearly chanting, nearly beyond coherent speech. "He hates us because we're *blind*. He hates you because you're blind. The core of what makes us who we are, he thinks is the mark of the devil."

Leila could imagine Seph flinging her head back and spreading her arms. Would a blind preacher use visuals with a blind audience?

"Let's show him the truth! Let's convert him!"

"All right!"

"Yeah, sister!"

Quietly, straight to Leila, Seph added wryly, "Let him see what it's like. So to speak."

"Take his eyes!" someone called, and others picked it up.

"Christina," she felt and heard him intone. "Christina, join with me. Join with the Lord. Together and with the Lord's help we are invincible. Christina—"

She punched him. Her knuckles crunched into his jaw. His head snapped back. Wildly thrilled, she hit him again. Her fist sank into his belly. He grunted and doubled over, the top of his head grazing her chest.

A recurring dream motif had her trying to hit someone—*needing* to hit someone; her life or her soul depending on hitting someone—and being unable to connect. She'd misjudge distance, so the blow would be glancing, or would miss altogether; the air would turn viscous or her muscles would jelly, gentling the motion of her hand; her target would move, or vanish. In the dreams and when she first awoke, there'd be a sensation of impotence almost sexual.

In real life, she'd never until this instant hit anybody but Russell, never tried, although certainly she'd been tempted, indulging in detailed fantasies about swatting the obstreperous child, knocking out the hijacker with one punch he wouldn't be expecting from her, flattening the mugger on the street, sobering the hysterical stranger with a perfectly placed smack, knocking the wind out of the supercilious pseudo-helper. But such satisfying violence had always seemed quite beyond the reach of someone without depth perception or peripheral vision.

An appreciative, slightly sardonic "Oooo" rippled from the crowd, and Seph pronounced, "Nice move."

Belatedly realizing that Russell was backing away, Leila grabbed for him, missed and yelled, "He's getting away! Don't let him get away! He killed somebody! Call the police!"

There was movement in the throng, but she couldn't tell whether they'd closed around him or whether anybody had set off for the phones four blocks away.

"Amen! Amen! Amen! Thy Will be done!" He had turned. He was getting away.

"Stop him!" Leila took several long quick strides, collided with other people, pushed past. Reaching for him, she found other clothes and hair and limbs, thrust them out of her way. "Stop him!" She heard the gate.

"Oh Lord my God fill Thy child Christina with the Holy Spirit, amen, so her ears might hear and her eyes might see the Truth I'll pray for you, Christina, God's Will be done." Then, as far as she could tell, he was gone.

She went after him.

# *Chapter Twenty*

The temptation was strong to collapse or wrap herself around a lamppost or otherwise immobilize herself until a guide came along. Any guide.

But she ran. Her gait was stiff. She slammed into something, tripped over something else. She might well blunder into traffic, fall down steps, knock something over, hurt or make a fool of herself. But, for a few flat-out strides, she was running. Out of fear and horror, certainly, and the slapdash intention of catching Russell, but propelled also by an upsurge of new kinesthetic vigor. She had never run before.

A shape loomed in her path, very close by the time she was aware of it. Too late, she swerved. The man stopped her, hand glancing off her breast before finding her upper arm. "Seph wants me to take you to our doctor."

"What? Why?"

"For your eye. So you don't go *blind.*" His sneer was plainly audible. He jerked her arm. "Come on. You don't have to wait so long if you get there early."

"A phone first."

"The doctor first."

"I have to call the police. Russell is dangerous. He killed somebody—"

"The doctor first."

"What's it to you?"

"Seph says."

She bit back sarcastic mimicry. There was no need to choose, either to prove a point or for practical reasons. The doctor's office would have a phone; she could call the cops, and Cathy, from there. Although this person presumably had less sight than she did, he knew the way and she manifestly did not.

They were already moving, not running but walking much faster than she ordinarily would. "To a doctor?" she repeated breathlessly. "You're taking me to a doctor?"

"You don't want to be blind, right?" Serious this time. "You don't want to stay with us?"

"Right," she declared, wondering what vulnerability she was exposing, what sin confessing.

"Well, Seph told me to take you to a clinic we know and leave you there. So I guess you win. Congratulations, Christina."

"Leila," she corrected. Nobody here had ever heard her real name. He didn't ask what she meant, and she didn't elaborate.

Visions of Nazi doctors performing grotesque ophthalmological experiments were not enough to stop her from scrambling to keep up. The guide was tugging her in only a slight exaggeration of the way sighted people often did; when she tried to extricate her hand from his in order to grasp his elbow in the traveling technique he surely must know from the other side, he would have none of it. If anything, his grip tightened and his pace quickened. The muscles of her thighs and lower back clenched in the sustained effort to keep her balance. She stumbled, cried out. The guide ignored her and kept going. For perhaps fifteen minutes they seemed to be traveling through uninhabited space; she had no impression of any other pedestrians, and they passed only one vehicle, some sort of delivery truck whose back-up signal beeped shrill as a siren.

Then they were careening now, dizzily maneuvering through what must be morning pedestrian rush hour on the downtown mall. Leila loved the mall. She'd never been here without Cathy. "Misty" from the saxophone in front of McDonald's had long delighted her as a legitimate way for the legless horn-player to earn money because in exchange he was adding a dollop of beauty to the world; now it struck her as eerie, ominous, the background score for a scene in which something frightening was about to happen. The quick, gliding shuttle buses jingling their incongruously merry bells were passing too often and too close.

"Spare change, spare change," sang a sweet, trained soprano, very soft and clear. Leila banged her shin on the foot rest of the wheelchair backed against a department store window through which she could not see. "Spare change, spare change," gently cascading inflection with no urgency at all, certainly not demanding or begging, scarcely even a request. "Spare change, spare change." Coins clattering into her plastic bowl did not alter the dreamy rhythm. "Spare change, spare change."

Veering away from the insinuating voice, Leila slipped off the curb, its edge obscured by the attractive crisscross patterns of the mall's paving and by the aesthetically pleasing low slant of the sidewalk. Her ankle turned, and she exclaimed and grabbed for her escort's arm. A passerby inquired, with disproportionate alarm, "Are you all right, ma'am?"

There was no interruption in their headlong pace; in the midst of the precarious motion she managed to right herself. She smelled hot dogs and was hungry, chilled as they passed through a deep canyonlike building shadow and then was propelled down a sudden flight of uneven cement steps, through a thin door, into a room that tasted of coffee and hydrogen peroxide, stale cigarette smoke and reefer and disinfectant, booze and vanilla air freshener.

The hand left her arm. Other people were in the room, some coughing. A television nattered. A young woman spoke from her right. "Hi, can I help you?"

Leila reached out, then looked around, didn't find the man who'd brought her here. The outside door up at street level opened and closed.

"Ma'am? What can I do for you?" *Come on, lady, declare yourself. Why are you here?*

Taking a step toward the voice, she collided with someone sitting there, who grunted when she mumbled, "Oh, sorry." Too inhibited even now to feel her way around the knees and hip and shoulder of this person, which was what she really needed to do, overcompensating in the other direction, she ran into an empty metal folding chair, which clanged and slid across tiled floor. "I have keratitis," she announced breathlessly, pivoting her head back and forth in hopes of picking up some clue about where the receptionist was. "I need to see an ophthalmologist right away. I have very little vision and I can't risk losing—"

"Over here."

"What?"

"I'm over here." Apparently she was looking in the wrong direction, and that was distracting the receptionist from what she was asking for.

"I need help," she insisted and took another hesitant step. Her eye flared, hot white light obscuring almost everything else, pain crackling. "Where? I can't see—"

"Oh, wow." The young woman was close in front of her now, leaning in.

"What?" Leila raised a protective palm to her throbbing eye.

"Your eye's really red. And it looks like it's oozing." *Gross,* Leila knew she wanted to say. *Yuck.* "Does it hurt?"

"I need to see a doctor. An eye doctor."

"Hold on. I'll get somebody. Here, sit down." She all but pushed Leila into a chair, which skidded backwards under her weight.

"But first I need a phone." But the woman had disappeared.

Gingerly, almost surreptitiously, Leila touched her cheek. Viscous drainage was, indeed, starting to seep from her eye. She tried to remember whether Dr. Dale had warned her about this symptom: "If you're ever abducted by a religious maniac who won't let you take care of your dry eye condition, you might develop a red, oozing sore on the surface of the eyeball." The pain, now that her attention had been drawn back to it, was of a different quality, more localized, deeper. The overhead lights burned. She lowered her head and covered her eyes.

The phone at the desk rang, the twittering of a multiline office system. She rose and followed the sound, which bifurcated now as a second line began to ring. She leaned over the counter, got the receiver in her hand, lightly swept the phone set with her fingertips to learn the configuration of buttons, then punched one after another of the vertical column until she got a dial tone. The ringing had stopped; no doubt she'd cut off both callers. After a moment's hesitation while she considered what time it most likely was and what day, she dialed Cathy's work extension. Voice mail picked up. Cathy's recorded voice brought her nearly to the point of collapse. The beep sounded. "Cathy," she whispered, cleared her throat and repeated more strongly, "Cathy. It's me. I'm—"

"Uh, ma'am? Excuse me? That's a business phone."

Waving a hand and nodding, Leila said hastily, "I'm okay. I'm at some kind of medical clinic downtown, but I don't know where." She started to ask the receptionist for the name and address, then reminded herself that Russell had found her in the Country of the Blind and might well have followed her here; she couldn't risk being the bait that would lure Cathy into his grasp. "I love you, Cathy. I'm okay. I'll be home soon."

The thought of breaking off even this ephemeral contact was unbearable, and she'd have continued like that if the young woman hadn't said sternly, "The doctor will see you now. This way. What's your name?"

"Leila. Blackwell." Bereft, she fumbled the receiver into the cradle.

"This way, Ms. Blackwell."

Leila had again covered her eye. "Where? I can't—" An arm circled her waist and she was pushed and pulled among chairs and feet, across a short open space and through a flimsy swinging door.

"Hey," protested someone in the waiting room. "I was here first."

"Just chill, Fred," the young woman told him, as if she'd said it countless times before. "This is an emergency."

"Well, fuck, *this* is an emergency, too, you know. Just look at this. My foot's all swole up and blue—" He was still talking as the door swung shut.

"Here's a chair." She was positioned and then shoved down. "And here's Dr. Gill."

Dr. Gill (his last name? or Gil, a first name? Why should that matter?) turned out to be kind and attentive enough, but not very knowledgeable about ophthalmic matters. He asked a few general questions, persuaded her to take her hands away and with gloved fingers carefully forced the lid open, but when she winced he didn't persist. There were a lot of things it could be, he told her. She needed to see a specialist. Judith would take her to the emergency room.

He didn't ask how she'd let her eye get into this state. He didn't ask what hospital she preferred or if she had her own doctor or what insurance she carried. He assumed she'd need Judith—presumably, the young receptionist—to get her to the county hospital, that there'd be no one else she could call for help. Clearly he thought she was one of his homeless clientele.

"I have to call the police."

"The police?"

She took a breath. "I was kidnapped. He killed someone. I have to call the police."

He had been writing in a chart open on his lap. Now his glasses glinted as his head came up, and the faint scratching paused. "Did he hurt you?"

"He wouldn't let me take care of my eye."

"We'll get you help for that. Are there other injuries? Were you assaulted in any way?"

"Not really."

He put his hand gently on her arm. "Ms. Blackwell, I know this is hard to talk about, but I hope you'll let me help you."

"He hit me a few times. He tried to rape me. He withheld food and water. But I'm okay except for my eye. But I know he killed somebody, and I think he's after someone I love." Her voice broke then. "Please, show me where there's a phone."

"Right here." She didn't see it. He put it in her hand.

It took a while to make the 911 operator understand, and then a while to make a plan; no, she couldn't come to the station because she had to go to the hospital. Yes, it was an emergency. So was this, yes: dueling emergencies. Her need for medical care was urgent. Her need to stop this maniac was urgent. Could an officer meet her at the ER? In the meantime, could they send someone to check on Cathy? She gave both work and home addresses. Please, make sure Cathy's all right. And could they try to find Ardith's body? Ardith Ewing. Near the railroad tracks, under a church with a carillon.

Although the dispatcher agreed to all requests, Leila wasn't at all confident that any of it would happen. She hung up with the sinking feeling that this was the best she could do and it was nowhere near enough.

Dr. Gill had exited the room and she heard his quick footsteps and rapid-fire instructions. Judith came quickly, hustled her out a back door and into a car. The ride was short and nearly wordless. For the brisk walk into the hospital, Judith took Leila's arm and hustled her across the parking lot, up a ramp, through an automatic door, into the hospital. "Good luck, Ms. Blackburn," Judith said, and dropped her arm.

Alarmed, Leila exclaimed, "Wait!" but apparently the other woman was gone.

Her first reaction was a sort of moral indignation: This person worked with blind people all the time. She knew Seph and the others. How could she just leave her here? Didn't she know this was a crisis? Couldn't she see that Leila needed more help than this? What if the cops came and she wasn't there to meet them? What if the time she wasted wandering around trying to find the emergency room was enough to make the damage to her eye irreparable?

But almost immediately she was taking stock of her situation, gathering data, deciphering and strategizing. This must be a lobby. The ambient echoes suggested muted activity.

Surrounding her were thinly upholstered chairs; she rested her hands on them one after another to wend her way through, knowing there must be an aisle somewhere but not wanting to take the time to find it. If this was a hospital lobby, there should be an information desk somewhere nearby. She listened for phones and pages, for the interrogatory and declaratory tones of questions being asked and answered. Someone hurried past her weeping. Several other people walked off tiled floor onto muffling carpet. Elevator bells pinged. Automatic doors behind her hissed open and shut, letting in fresh air and then cutting it off.

Now she was in an open space, with few usable landmarks. Under ordinary circumstances it embarrassed her if somebody called, "May I help you?" or, worse, came to her; now she wished fervently for such intervention, but none came. There was nothing for it but to keep walking, sliding her feet so she'd locate any steps before she fell down them, holding out her hands to encounter railing or wall or furniture.

Ahead and to the left was what looked to be a staircase or an escalator. She imagined herself wandering around forbidden areas, blundering into sickrooms, inserting herself without meaning to into the most intimate conversations, cluelessly loitering beside a deathbed. She shuddered. Her eye blazed and she cupped both hands over it, bending as if the pain were in her gut, groaning.

"Are you all right, miss? Can I help you?"

Habit almost made her reject the offer, and she did hastily rearrange herself to look not quite so pitiful. But she gasped, "Is this the emergency room?"

He hesitated, as if not quite understanding the question. "No," he said finally, carefully. "This is the main lobby of County Hospital."

"I need the emergency room. My eye—" It was too much to explain.

"Right through those doors," the man said helpfully. Probably he was pointing.

"I can't see." For practical purposes at the moment, that was true enough.

After the slightest of pauses, conveying that he didn't exactly know what to do or was reluctant to do it, the man took her arm. She stiffened. Was he a hospital employee and this was part of his job? Or was he on his way to or from visiting someone, and she was outrageously imposing? Or was he a mugger in ridiculous disguise, a pickpocket, a fanatic of one sort or another who'd "help" her according to his own image?

She let him lead her. They crossed a cavernous space, away from both elevators and escalator. Overhead light changed from glaring to too dim. They went through sliding glass doors she might well have crashed into if she'd been alone, then along a short shiny corridor that turned, she thought, twice. The guide was going too fast. Her free hand flopped and twitched, trying to trail along the wall. She kept stumbling, sometimes into him, and he kept muttering, "Oh, sorry! Careful! Oops! Sorry! Are you all right?" until she didn't want to take another step but had no choice.

She recognized the emergency room the instant they entered it: unpleasant fluorescent illumination from overhead and reflected from white floor; unpleasant chattering from a high mounted television, fussy children, stressed-out parents; unpleasant odors of vending-machine potato chips and candy, breath made vile by cigarettes, beer, unbrushed teeth, disease. She'd fit right in.

The man propelled her to a cubicle along one wall, presumably Admissions. They waited. Holding on to her elbow as if she'd escape or collapse or get lost if he let go, he leaned to one side and then the other, apparently looking for someone to whom he could hand her over. The police would do, she thought, but there was no sign of them.

Finally he picked up a clipboard with a dangling pen. "I guess you just sign in here and they'll call you."

"I can't see—Could you—"

He was getting impatient, trying to hide it. This was more hassle than he'd volunteered for. "What's your name?"

"Leila Blackwell."

He entered the name on the list, probably writing,

*Lila,* as most people did; maybe she ought to correct the spelling. "Reason for visit?"

She hesitated, then decided on, "Eye injury."

He wrote it down, replaced the clipboard on the counter and took her to a chair, where he left her with an apology and a hasty "Good luck." His retreating footsteps were obscured when a loudly laughing woman rushed in. Belly laughter in an emergency room was bizarre, repugnant.

Her eye burned. Her field of vision, narrow and filmy as it had already been, was now washed translucent orange-red; a few calligraphic black marks appeared and disappeared, and painful starbursts. Realizing the throbbing in her hands and wrists was from clutching the arms of the chair, she concentrated on forcing her grip to loosen, one finger after another and then the palms. Her hands fell into her lap, and for long moments her arms shook.

Yearning for Cathy thundered through her, fulminating misery that could be ascribed to any of countless things. In fact, she could not think of any aspect of her life that was not miserable, and she sat there stunned.

Other names were called. She began to feel invisible, as though not being able to see made other people unable to see her. Some small, distant part of her mind produced the information that she could get up and search for the Admissions cubicle again, or hail the person who was calling other patients' names, or even wander back into the labyrinthine hospital until somebody noticed her. But between the idea and the actions necessary to carry it out—standing up, taking steps, locating objects and people and pathways, forming words—was a morass. She'd just sit here.

"Ms. Blackwell? Leila Blackwell?"

She jumped. "Yes!" she cried, too loudly. "Yes, yes, I'm here!"

While she was getting to her feet the clerk disappeared. Leila knew she was supposed to follow her but had no way of telling where she'd gone. She stood there. "Over here." Leila edged toward the voice, found the counter and then the cubicle without running into anything, sank into a chair, exhaled.

She started to explain, but the Admissions clerk was already asking questions. Name, address, phone numbers, employer, person to contact in case of emergency. All this information no longer really identified her, but the clerk entered it into the data base as if it did. "Cathy Blackwell," Leila said with a distant sort of pride. "Cathy with a *C.*" Social security number. Health insurance. No, she didn't have her membership card. Doctor's name; she started to say Gill, then Dale, then kept that information a secret, too, and just shook her head. The fluorescent lights were nearly unbearable; she struggled to keep her eyes slitted open. Reason for visit. "I have a serious eye condition. I haven't been able to treat it properly for the past few weeks. It might be corneal dystrophy or a corneal ulcer—"

"Take a seat back in the waiting area," the clerk told her blandly, keyboard still clicking. "A doctor will see you shortly."

"How long do you think it will be?"

"I don't know, ma'am."

"But this is an *emergency*—"

"Yes, ma'am," the clerk snapped, the first sign of vitality she'd shown. "This is an *emergency room*. You'll have to wait your turn. Just take a seat."

Leila did not do as she was told. She moved a few steps away from the Admissions cubicle and stopped, placed her feet shoulder-width apart, crossed her arms, settled in. Expecting the clerk to object, perhaps actually to come out and try to move her, she readied verbal and physical resistance. But nothing of the sort happened. The clerk called other names. The TV chattered. People sighed and coughed and sat there heavily waiting. People came in. Her eye was hot and sticky, and the few things she could see—ceiling lights, white walls—all hurt.

She began listening for the location of pay phones. She would call the cops again, and Cathy. She thought she heard the clink of coins and then ten tiny beeps as someone dialed, and she took a deep breath and started in that direction.

"Leila Blackwell."

She stopped. "Yes."

"Leila Blackwell."

"Yes! Here!"

"Follow me, please." Apparently she managed to

do so, since nobody stopped or corrected her, and she found herself in a terribly bright examining room struggling to provide for a harried woman in a white smock a succinct explanation of what was wrong with her eyes and how she'd come to be in this predicament. She didn't get into being kidnapped by a religious nut. She didn't mention the Country of the Blind. Given the exigencies of the moment, those were tangents, and she doubted she'd be able to muster the words to make any of it make sense and hold this woman's attention. Just the facts, ma'am, and the fewest possible.

She did say, "The police are supposed to be meeting me here. I need to give them some information. A statement. If they come while I'm in here, will somebody tell them where I am?" The woman said yes, but not very convincingly. This was probably not the first time a patient coming in off the street had claimed to have a story to report to the police. Leila sighed.

Although she kept her eyes shut while she waited for the doctor, the tiny room pulsed painfully around her. When she shielded her eyes, her hand came away slimy, and she tried not to think about what infection she was spreading. Probably she didn't wait very long, but by the time the door opened again her sense of self had contracted to the little globule throbbing, burning, oozing, critically endangered.

The doctor was young and chatty. Leila did not want to chat. The doctor's hands were soft and cool, and her breath smelled of seaweed: a vegetarian, Leila guessed; a health nut. The light she used to peer into Leila's eyes was not nearly strong enough, but it stabbed. The questions she asked—what had caused the left eye not to develop normally? how much could she usually see?—were beside the point.

"My ophthalmologist is Michael Dale."

"I don't know him."

"Is there a phone I can use to call him?"

"You need to be admitted. I'll make the arrangements."

"I need to see Dr. Dale. He's been treating me for years—"

The doctor gave her hand a cursory pat. "There'll be plenty of time for that, hon. You can discuss it with your attending. Let's just get you admitted and go from there, okay?"

"Listen to me. I know what I need. I need to consult Dr. Dale. I need eyedrops and ointment. And I need to talk to the police."

The doctor was already on her way out. Over her shoulder she said, "I think it's too late for that," and almost immediately someone came in with a wheelchair to transport Leila up to the ward.

# Chapter Twenty-one

Both her eyes were patched. Thick medicated fluid seeped in under the patches, creating a heavenly dankness. Her eyes, face, scalp, body, her soul were profoundly soothed.

A dangerous illusion, for Russell was still at large. Cathy was still in danger. The police had not come, and now she was even more helpless to do anything herself.

Dim viscosity swaddled her, muting all her senses, as if she were suspended in a tank filled with lubricant for the dual purposes of depriving and healing her senses. Conversations, the fuzzy featureless din of televisions erratically spiked by the insinuating blat of the public address system, assorted beeps and rattles and cries, all flowed together into a sea of warm sound. The sheets under and over her seemed held away from her flesh by a protective film.

For the first time since Russell had appeared in the rest-room mirror, tension eased. It was too soon; she knew it was too soon. But the urge was strong to relax as she hadn't since very early childhood, abandon reasonable vigilance along with the habitual hypervigilance, relinquish any need to affect or even to know what was going on.

"Not yet," she kept telling herself. But the admonition seemed out of context and nearly nonsensical.

Most of the time she was not asleep, but she was not awake, either. She drifted in and out of a pleasant, murky half-consciousness. Every now and then a straw would be nudged against her lips, and obediently she'd suck and swallow tepid liquid until she was told to stop and the straw was taken away. The semisolid foods she was fed were comfortingly tasteless, and she had no interest in identifying them. When she was assisted onto the bedpan, elimination was another profound relief, but she didn't think of it herself, had no independent urge. Most immediate, most clear, was painlessness. Blissfully she sank into the absence of pain.

"Ms. Blackwell?"

The absence of pain was viscous and buoyant as a presence. It surrounded her, held her up, held her down.

"Leila Blackwell?"

Reluctantly, she turned her head toward the voice. "Yes."

"I'm Officer Bucher and this is my partner, Officer

Maestas. You want to report a crime, is that right?"

"Yes." She struggled to sit up, couldn't be sure whether she was or not, gave up. The movement had reactivated the discomfort in her eye, slight but dreadful because of what it might portend. Her head was slowly spinning. It seemed a long time ago that she'd had a story to tell; she had the hazy impression that she'd already told it, already discharged it, was done with it, and now she couldn't quite get started. "Yes," she said again, hoping to buy time for her thoughts to clear. "I—I'm glad you're here."

Officer Bucher had a nasal tenor voice made more strident by a strong Pittsburgh accent. "We had some trouble finding you," he groused. "There was some confusion about your name."

"I was kidnapped. By a man named Russell Gavin. I saw him kill somebody. I heard it. A woman named Ardith Ewing. I heard him shoot her. He confessed that he killed her. In God's name." Could all this be true? "And he's after my partner, Cathy. Cathy Blackwell." She had begun to tremble. "I—I told all this to somebody on the phone—"

One of them pulled up a chair. Bucher, apparently, because Maestas was still standing when she said crisply, "Why don't you just begin at the beginning, ma'am?"

Whether or not it was the beginning, she began with Russell forcing her at gunpoint from the theater rest room. It was obvious Bucher would have liked more information about her disability, her relationship with Russell, her relationship with Cathy; she heard him taking notes, and he kept muttering, "We'll get back to that later. We'll talk more about that later." Both his air of disorganization and his slightly threatening tone made Leila want to be careful of what she said, and she tried hard not to be.

Maestas, though, was a skillful interviewer. Her queries were to the point, her grasp of the situation quick and, if not subtle, sufficient for the purpose. Feeling herself in good hands, Leila talked. Maestas interrupted now and then with questions. "Where were you held?"

"In an empty house owned by Russell's brother." She'd already told them that.

"Where?"

"I—don't know."

"You don't know?" That was Bucher.

"We were going south on the interstate for a while, but after we turned off onto side streets I lost track of where we were."

"Well, ma'am, that sort of makes it hard—"

Maestas cut in. "What do you remember? Tell us everything you remember."

Leila quieted herself to allow details to surface. She mentioned the amusement park they'd passed, the convenience store. Then, excitedly: "And the house number was Two-five-six-four."

"I thought you couldn't see." Bucher was almost triumphant.

307

"I felt it. And anyway, I have some vision. Or I did."

"Two-five-six-four what?" Maestas pressed. "What street?"

"I don't know."

"Ma'am—"

"What's the brother's name? That owns the house?"

"Gavin." She spelled it.

"First name?"

"Carl."

"*C* or *K*?"

"*C*," she guessed helplessly.

There was a pause. Were they taking notes? Formulating a strategy? Exchanging skeptical or frustrated or bored glances? Had she made her case convincingly enough that they would do something?

Then they both got to their feet, making noise more complex than most people made when they moved: heavy metal objects thumped, lighter metal jangled, leather squeaked and the basic displacement of air by their bodies was different, more sure-footed and purposeful, wider-stanced.

Bucher said, "That's all for now, ma'am. We'll get back to you if we need more."

Maestas touched her shoulder. "We'll find him, Ms. Blackwell. You just concentrate on getting well."

"Please," Leila whispered, but they were gone.

Time lost shape then, melted like crayons in sun.

She had a vague impression of time passing, and also of time pooling, and also of time as a thick, infinite bath.

She was a child, holding things close, touching things because she couldn't see them, just beginning to realize all that she would miss but reveling in the form of the tree rather than the form of the leaf, weeping creamy tears of sorrow and gratitude.

She was swimming in children, all of them touching her, touching her eyes, touching their own.

She was bound and gagged. She struggled, ought to be struggling, was not, was sinking into the space defined for her and then flowing out of it.

She was in the arms of someone she loved, whose body trembled under her lips and hands, who caressed and informed her with fingertips and the tip of a tongue.

She was fleeing, but not afraid. She was gliding, sure-footed, both away from something and toward something, running full out.

At some point, the tubes dripping moisture into her eyes were disconnected and the patches removed. The abrupt exposure and the cessation of the sweet, steady stream panicked her. When the intense blue examination light was shined into her eyes, she protested and writhed but realized it didn't hurt. Both eyes were flooded again and fresh patches pressed snug to hold the moisture in place.

Again she drifted into semiconsciousness. It didn't seem a wise thing to do, but the agitated, suspended state had a powerful pull, like a vast anxiety dream in which the dreamer dreams she must awaken, dreams the house is on fire or her lover needs her or an intruder looms by her bed, dreams she must awaken, it's urgent, she has to wake up, *wake up,* dreams then that she is awake and handling the crisis, so that the persistence and deceptiveness of her own dream state work against her. She was aware of people coming and going and of her fear of them; she dreamed it was Russell, Cathy with her eyes bulging above a gag, a first-grader with a gun in her hand, Ardith bleeding and barely alive and speaking what should have been her last words over and over and over in a language only God would understand, Seph with a knife. And maybe it was. Or maybe it was only someone bringing her food she didn't eat but could taste in her dream, water that dribbled sweetly from a straw that invaded her mouth with harsh solidity, a thermometer, a blood pressure cuff, medication into the hidden eyes, questions to which she dreamed answers. Sounds cycled, or merely changed, or randomly repeated. The fading and brightening of ambient light had some kind of dream meaning that simultaneously eluded and satisfied her. Oranges, marigolds, blood: aromas wafted through her consciousness and unconsciousness like ribbons tying them lightly together.

The bandages were removed again. Again, her eye flinched from the light, protective muscles contracting and lid shutting hard, as if to reject the notion that this was an organ of sight. Something like a tiny wooden tongue depressor on the underside of her lashes forcibly propped the lid open. In the halo of the intense blue light she caught a glimpse of a face. Then a piercing white light made her bite her lower lip and moan. The examiner murmured, "Sorry," but didn't stop.

At last the light went out and her eyelid was allowed to drop. Hands pressed over shuddering eyes, she heard no sign of anyone near her and assumed the doctor had gone, leaving her exposed. It came to her that she had seen, not just perceived, the blue and white lights, and the suggestion of the looming face; if those were not purely dream images, then she must not have lost all her sight.

She lowered her hands. Without warning, lubricant was squeezed into both eyes. The relief was instant and enormous. She squinted, blinked, let her eyelids gently fall. "How much can you see?"

Evidently this doctor or nurse was still in the room, asking the ubiquitous question that was, as usual, impossible to answer, even if Leila had been willing to open her eyes and attempt a description. Helplessly she shook her head.

"Can you see light?"

"Yes." Even through her eyelids, she could see light.

"Can you see me?"

Her eyes opened as if of their own accord, responding to the suggestion of seeing. She did see

311

him, indistinctly but undeniably. "Yes. Sort of."

"How does what you see now compare with your normal vision?"

"I—don't know."

"Better? Worse? Clearer? Fuzzier? Greater or less field of vision?" He was getting impatient.

So was she. "I can't tell."

She saw and heard him sigh and sit back, then get to his feet. "Do you have a regular eye doctor? You'll need to have him look at you as soon as possible. The keratitis is under control now; there's no drainage or bleeding. We'll leave the bandages off, and if nothing else develops you'll be able to go home. But your ophthalmologist will need to evaluate any change in your vision."

"When?"

"Right away."

"When can I leave the hospital?"

"Oh. I'll write the discharge order and the nurses will take care of the paperwork and we'll get you out of here before six o'clock. You'll be home for dinner."

"Thank you," she said, but this time he really was gone.

If she thought ahead very far—to questions like how she would get home, whether Cathy would have returned from wherever she'd gone, what Dr. Dale would find when he examined her eyes, what would happen to Russell, how this whole experience would or would not turn out to have changed her life—

she'd be unable to attend to the tasks at hand. Carefully she sat up on the edge of the bed. Mild vertigo didn't last long. She stood up. She had no idea where the bathroom was, but in the wall to her right was a likely looking door. It seemed to her that she could see as well as she usually could without contact or glasses. Catching herself staring rigidly ahead, like a blind person, she smiled and deliberately loosened her posture, stopped shuffling, eased into a more relaxed gait and started the process of retraining herself to look around.

She closed the bathroom door and felt for the light switch, immediately turned the glaring fluorescence off and washed and dressed in the dark. The soap had a light clean fragrance. The washcloth was warm and pleasantly rough, the towel nicely absorbent. Finding the tiny mirror, she took a deep breath and flicked the light on again. Her eye, though still not painful, instantly throbbed and struggled to close, but she managed to catch a glimpse of herself. Hazy and brief as it was, the image pleased her.

When she stepped back out into the larger room, beauty accosted her, visual beauty, flooding her narrow field of vision, actually sending her swaying back against the wall. A thin exquisite streak of rose and violet along the edge of thick gray-indigo. A sunset, she realized, as astonished by the circumstances that had linked to allow this to happen—open window shades, open privacy curtain, tilt of the earth, composition of the atmosphere, her own timing—as by the beauty itself.

A person fully sighted would have seen it sooner and in different detail, would not have been taken by surprise. A blind person would not have seen it at all. But Leila was utterly ambushed.

The earth turned. The vision changed. What she was doing could not be called watching; she took it in and let it go.

Someone entered the room, a woman in a blue or black uniform. "Ms. Blackwell, it's Consuelo Maestas." Did she know anybody named Consuelo? "Ms. Blackwell. Leila. It's Officer Maestas from the Police Department. I have some more questions."

"All right." Carefully she sat down on the edge of the bed.

The other patient in the room, of whom Leila had no impression whatsoever, now turned the TV volume all the way down. The sudden absence of the noise was startling, and the intent listening created a sort of auditory vacuum that at first made it hard for Leila to focus on what the cop was saying. Something about recording the conversation.

The distraction didn't last long. "Who is Ardith Ewing?"

Adrenaline exploded through Leila's body. Past the thudding of her heart, terrifyingly mirrored by a tiny flickering in her right eye, she did her best to answer. "She's a friend of Russell, the guy who kidnapped me. Well, not exactly a friend, although they share some of the same religious beliefs. Well, not exactly the same—she thinks he's nuts, and dangerous, not to mention in the thrall of Satan. She helped me escape. Did you find her?"

"We found her body. Shot once in the abdomen and once through the temple."

She'd missed the head wound. Her skin crawled with the realization of how close she must have been to it without knowing.

"She was in the parking lot of St. Mary's Cathedral. Near the tracks and the river. Just like you said."

"It has a carillon."

"Just like you said. What can you tell me about this, Leila?"

Acutely alert now, Leila repeated the account she'd already told Maestas and the other cop, from the point at which Ardith entered it. Although she had no intention of changing anything, she was anxious about the consistency between the versions of the tale, worrying that she'd overlooked something important the first time through or was conveying a suspiciously different impression now.

Over the scratch of pen on paper and the whir of the tape recorder, Maestas said almost nothing. Leila finished, and subsided into troubled silence. The cop turned off the machine with a definitive click. "Any idea where we might find Russell Gavin?"

"I know his home address in Florida," she realized, and recited it. "The last place I saw him, I think a few days ago, was downtown somewhere, not far from the mall. There's a group of blind street people who live in some sort of urban garden—"

"Oh, Seph. The Country of the Blind. Gavin was with them?"

"I was with them, sort of. Briefly. He followed me there."

"I bet Seph had a field day with him. She's somethin' else, that lady."

"You know Seph?"

"Oh, we know Seph."

"How much do you know about her and her followers?"

"They're blind. They hang out in the community garden nobody uses anymore, sleep in the gazebo and the shed. During the day some of them panhandle on the mall and some of them work or go to school."

"You guys just let them be?"

"They'd be in a lot more danger in the shelters. They're not hurting anybody."

"They don't have eyes."

"Seph doesn't. I guess she was born that way. The others do. Some of them have some sight, I think."

"I was told Seph actually cuts out their eyes as the price for staying with her."

"Yeah, well, Seph has a flair for the dramatic. I've never seen anything like that."

Fooled by people who claimed to be her own kind. Leila seethed.

"We'll find Seph and see what she knows about Russell Gavin."

Maestas stood. Leila stopped her. "Ardith was killed because of me."

"No. Ardith was killed because of Russell Gavin. Listen." The cop took her hand. Leila turned it so that they were sharing a firm handshake. "We'll get this guy. We'll stop him. You've been very helpful. Where will you be if we need to talk to you again?"

"Home," Leila said. "I'll be home."

# THE TIDES

## MELANIE TEM

Many residents of the Tides nursing home see the past more clearly than the present. So when Marshall, an elderly patient with Alzheimer's disease, begins to see a mysterious woman named Faye, no one pays all that much attention. Even Marshall's daughter, Rebecca, the Tides' young administrator, writes it off as simply another sign of Marshall's deteriorating condition. But when Rebecca delves into her father's past, she learns that he was once married to a disturbed and dangerous woman—a woman who he now believes, even in his lucid moments, has returned. As sinister and fatal accidents begin to plague the Tides, Rebecca fights desperately to survive a madwoman's dream. A dream that's stronger than death.

___4574-5                                    $4.99 US/$5.99 CAN

**Dorchester Publishing Co., Inc.**
**P.O. Box 6640**
**Wayne, PA 19087-8640**

Please add $1.75 for shipping and handling for the first book and $.50 for each book thereafter. NY, NYC, and PA residents, please add appropriate sales tax. No cash, stamps, or C.O.D.s. All orders shipped within 6 weeks via postal service book rate. Canadian orders require $2.00 extra postage and must be paid in U.S. dollars through a U.S. banking facility.

Name_____
Address_____
City_____State_____Zip_____
I have enclosed $_____in payment for the checked book(s).
Payment must accompany all orders. ❏ Please send a free catalog.
      CHECK OUT OUR WEBSITE! www.dorchesterpub.com

The Horror Writers Association presents:
# THE MUSEUM OF HORRORS
edited by Dennis Etchison

A special hardcover edition featuring all new stories by:

## PETER STRAUB
## JOYCE CAROL OATES
## RICHARD LAYMON
## RAMSEY CAMPBELL

*And: Peter Atkins, Melanie Tem, Tom Piccirilli, Darren O. Godfrey, Joel Lane, Gordon Linzer, Conrad Williams, Th. Metzger, Susan Fry, Charles L. Grant, Lisa Morton, William F. Nolan, Robert Devereaux, and S. P. Somtow.*

"The connoisseur of the macabre will find a feast on this table."
—Tapestry Magazine

---

# MARY ANN MITCHELL

# Ambrosial Flesh

Jonathan's favorite sacrament was always Communion, the eating of the body of Christ. Since he was taught that we are all made in the image of God, it seemed natural to him to take it one step further—to eat actual flesh from a living body, starting with small bits of his own. . . .

But now Jonathan's an adult. His religious belief may have faded, but his taste for flesh remains as strong as ever. He's long since moved on, from eating his own flesh to eating that of others. But when his wife discovers his secret, Jonathan is faced with a problem. And his solution leads him not only to new extremes, but also to a meeting with a mysterious stranger—a stranger who holds the key to an evil force far greater than any Jonathan ever dared imagine.

___4902-3                                    $5.99 US/$6.99 CAN

# Elizabeth Massie

# Sineater

According to legend, the sineater is a dark and mysterious figure of the night, condemned to live alone in the woods, who devours food from the chests of the dead to absorb their sins into his own soul. To look upon the face of the sineater is to see the face of all the evil he has eaten. But in a small Virginia town, the order is broken. With the violated taboo comes a rash of horrifying events. But does the evil emanate from the sineater...or from an even darker force?

___4407-2                                           $5.99 US/$6.99 CAN

# Welcome Back to the Night
# Elizabeth Massie

A family reunion should be a happy event, a time to see familiar faces, meet new relatives, and reconnect with people you haven't seen in a while. But the Lynch family reunion isn't a happy event at all. It is the beginning of a terrifying connection between three cousins and a deranged woman who, for a brief time, had been a part of the family. When these four people are reunited, a bond is formed, a bond that fuses their souls and reveals dark, chilling visions of a tortured past, a tormented present, and a deadly future—not only for them, but for their entire hometown. But will these warnings be enough to enable them to change the horrible fate they have glimpsed?

___4626-1                                    $5.99 US/$6.99 CAN

# Elizabeth Massie
# Wire Mesh Mothers

It all starts with the best of intentions. Kate McDolen, an elementary school teacher, knows she has to protect little eight-year-old Mistie from parents who are making her life a living hell. So Kate packs her bags, quietly picks up Mistie after school one day and sets off with her toward what she thinks will be a new life. How can she know she is driving headlong into a nightmare?

The nightmare begins when Tony jumps into the passenger seat of Kate's car, waving a gun. Tony is a dangerous girl, more dangerous than anyone could dream. She doesn't admire anything except violence and cruelty, and she has very different plans in mind for Kate and little Mistie. The cross-country trip that follows will turn into a one-way journey to fear, desperation . . . and madness.

___4869-8                                    $5.99 US/$6.99 CAN

**Dorchester Publishing Co., Inc.**
**P.O. Box 6640**
**Wayne, PA 19087-8640**

Please add $1.75 for shipping and handling for the first book and $.50 for each book thereafter. NY, NYC, and PA residents, please add appropriate sales tax. No cash, stamps, or C.O.D.s. All orders shipped within 6 weeks via postal service book rate. Canadian orders require $2.00 extra postage and must be paid in U.S. dollars through a U.S. banking facility.

Name_____
Address_____
City_____State_____Zip_____
I have enclosed $ _____ in payment for the checked book(s).
Payment <u>must</u> accompany all orders. ❑ Please send a free catalog.
     CHECK OUT OUR WEBSITE! www.dorchesterpub.com